ANNE OF MANHATTAN

Anne of Manhattan

a novel

BRINA STARLER

WM

WILLIAM MORROW

An Imprint of HarperCollinsPublishers

ANNE OF MANHATTAN. Copyright © 2021 by Dana Starler. All rights reserved. Printed in the United States of America. No part of this book may be used or reproduced in any manner whatsoever without written permission except in the case of brief quotations embodied in critical articles and reviews. For information, address HarperCollins Publishers, 195 Broadway, New York, NY 10007.

HarperCollins books may be purchased for educational, business, or sales promotional use. For information, please email the Special Markets Department at SPsales@harpercollins.com.

FIRST EDITION

Designed by Diahann Sturge

Title page skyline image © Takeshi Ishikawa/Vecteezy.com
Emoji on page 104 © FOS_ICON/Shutterstock, Inc.

Library of Congress Cataloging-in-Publication Data has been applied for.

ISBN 978-0-06-302074-0

21 22 23 24 25 LSC 10 9 8 7 6 5 4 3 2 1

For Rebecca,
this dream is dedicated to you.
Forever and always,
love, your big sister from another mister,
Brina

ANNE OF MANHATTAN

May 3
Dear Diary,

Today the middle set of Hammond twins threw up on me. Yes, both of them. Their mom was out at the store, so I had to figure out how to get two preschoolers into the same bath and actually wash them. It was like wrestling a tub full of eels, if eels screamed when water touched them and liked to pull my hair. As terrible as it is for me, I do get why Mrs. Hammond needs to "run out to the store for just a sec" all the time.

   This isn't, by far, the worst foster home I've lived in, but grocery shopping sounds like heaven—if I could do it alone.

Forever tired,
Anne

June 15
Dear Diary,

Welp. I'm back at Poplar Grove group home. Mr. Hammond died of a heart attack, very unexpectedly according to Mrs. Hammond, but not very unexpectedly if you ask me. Which no one ever does. But the doctor also didn't seem to think it was much of a surprise, seeing as Mr. Hammond hadn't changed his "lifestyle" a bit since last year's *nearly* deadly episode and most of his medicine was still sitting in the kitchen cabinet. Anyway, I'm back here because Mrs. Hammond took the kids, all six of them, and moved in with her sister. Which is fine, honestly. I didn't really want to move to Cincinnati anyway.

　　Off to wrestle that TV hog Jimmy Saltzer for the remote.

Anne

June 30
Dear Diary,

My new caseworker says she's found a foster home for me and I'll be moving next week! (Between you and me, I'll be quite relieved to live somewhere else again. Lillie is being awful again, she's <u>such</u> a bully.)

　　Anyway! My new home is all the way up to the north side of the island, on a farm or something. The people who live there are a brother and sister, both single and pretty old. At least forty, I think. My roommate here, Dani, thinks it's weird that they still live together, but I think it's kind of cool. At least they always have each other, if nothing else. I wouldn't mind moving around so much if I had someone to do it with, like a brother or sister. It must be nice to know exactly where your family is, because they live in the same place you do.

I hope I like it there.

Fingers crossed,
Anne

July 6
DEAR DIARY,

I'M AT THE BOTTOM OF A WELL OF AGONY AND DESPAIR.

THERE WAS A MISTAKE AND THEY DON'T WANT ME.

TODAY HAS BEEN THE ABSOLUTE WORST DAY. EVER.

TRAGICALLY WEEPING,
ANNE

July 7
Dear Diary,

I might have overreacted a bit when I wrote you before. The thing is, everything always seems worse at night. When it's dark and the shadows are creeping around my bed, it's hard to remember the good stuff. But when I woke up this morning, it was all good stuff. For a while, I just sat in the window seat of the most amazing room I've ever slept in and listened to the birds talking to each other. I wonder what they were saying. Well, I guess I should go down for breakfast now. Maybe I can get an hour or two of exploring in before I get picked up to head back to Poplar Grove.

Gotta run!
Anne

July 7
Dear Diary,

I can stay at Green Gables! Marilla and Matthew said they'd like me to stay, just to try it out, they said don't get too overexcited, but I'm hopeful, so hopeful. There are no more words left in me to write, because I'm filled all the way up to the top of my head with joy!!!

Blissfully floating on clouds,
Anne

August 5
Dear Diary,

I met a girl today, Diana Barry. Her family lives next door, if you can call four acres away with a horse pasture between Green Gables and their house "next door." It was instant friendship! She made me laugh so hard, I snorted Capri Sun out of my nose. I knew we would be best friends when she started laughing too, but not in a mean way. So happy I made at least one friend before school starts, less than three weeks away. Ugh. New girl again. It's supposed to be a really nice school, though, and Diana goes there. She said it's not so bad, wearing a uniform. At least I won't have to worry about trying to hide how little clothing I actually have, like I used to all the time at my old schools. Sometimes it was a real strain on my creativity, if I'm honest.

Hoping for the best,
Anne

August 25
Dear Diary,

TODAY I MET THE MOST HORRIBLE BOY ON THE FACE OF THIS PLANET. HE IS NOW MY MORTAL ENEMY AND I WILL BRING HIM DOWN IF IT'S THE LAST THING I DO.

Yours furiously forever,
Anne

Chapter 1

I f there was one thing Anne Shirley would stand firm against all arguments, it was that a person could never have too many books. That being said, it *was* possible she'd taken more than was strictly practical when she packed up her childhood room for her final year in grad school at Redmond College. Her adoptive mother, Marilla Cuthbert, had tried to persuade her to leave most of the collection in the attic of Green Gables, her home for the last twelve years. But picking which books to leave and which ones to take was a Sisyphean task. Every time she thought she'd managed it, a book in the "stay" pile would catch her eye, and then another, and another, and yet another.

The result was having to navigate a maze of cardboard boxes squeezed into every available space whenever she needed something across her new bedroom. The mess was making her eye twitch; disorganized spaces just added unnecessary stress to her life. Everything in its place and all that. One of the downsides to the tiny Hell's Kitchen apartment she was renting with her best friends Diana Barry and Philippa Gordon was that it didn't have much storage. Or any, to be exact. The only solution was to try and convince their landlord to let her build bookshelves that would cover one of the bedroom's walls. And maybe some in the living room. Perhaps a lone shelf above the toilet. There were a *lot* of books. But that was a problem for another day, because tonight the roommates were abandoning the never-ending chore of unpacking and going out instead.

It was nice to be back in the city with two of the three girls she loved best in the world.

Philippa's family was from Connecticut and she'd been gone for the entire summer, but Diana and Anne were both from Avonlea, a small tourist town in the Hamptons. They'd seen plenty of each other over the last few months, barring the Barry family's annual two-week vacation spent in the south of France. Most of Anne's time had been split between working in the Green Gables Winery, helping inspect the vines with Marilla's brother, Matthew, and bartending in the tasting room. Perpetually single and not in the least disturbed by it, Matthew had lived up at the family home that shared the property with the winery since well before Anne came to foster there at twelve years old. Walking the fields with the elderly man had been one of her favorite summer activities for years; he'd become a wonderful father figure for her over time, and she wouldn't give up those afternoons for a hundred trips to Europe.

Although Anne always missed Diana *desperately* when she

was gone. The stories her friend told when she came home again helped make up for it, since Anne herself had never actually been off the island before college.

Although she'd had a great summer at Green Gables, Anne did appreciate having a wider variety of choices again for an evening out. The sum of Avonlea's nightspots were either pricey restaurants with white tablecloths and a dress code or dive bars that smelled like the fishing docks. The town was a perfect example of the odd mixture of old and new, unimaginable wealth and those struggling to just get by, untouched preservation beaches and the gentrified boutique tourist towns that made up the Hamptons.

Shoving aside a stack of boxes with a grunt, Anne finally managed to get to her closet, clothes being the one thing she had unpacked fully. She pulled out a dress she'd been saving since last spring that she'd found for a steal in a vintage shop not far from her old dorms. Loving the feel of the thin cotton, she dropped it over her head, twisting to slide the metal zipper up one side. It was a pretty thing, blue polka dots with white, capped sleeves and a scoop-neck collar. Closely fitted down to her waist, the material flared out in soft folds until it just brushed the tops of her knees. It was shockingly comfortable, and the deep blue complemented her pale, freckled skin nicely. But best of all . . . it had *pockets*.

Even after four years at NYU and two years at Redmond College, a small private university located on the edge of Greenwich Village where she was enrolled in the graduate program, the endless wonders and surprises the city held never failed to delight her.

Rubbing her lips together one last time in front of the mirror hanging on the wall opposite her bed, Anne pressed one fingertip against the corner of her mouth to erase a smudge of muted rose lipstick. Then she slipped into a pair of flats, because "beauty is pain" was bullshit and she didn't subscribe to that idea at all. In the postage-sized living room, Philippa was fiddling with the strap of her own shoes, a pair of three-inch heels, because the tall brunette never seemed to get blisters. Or acne. Or bad hair days. Anne had to remind herself that she *really, truly liked* Phil—she could make even the tragedy of pairing socks and sandals look good.

As she entered the living room, the other girl glanced up and broke out in a delighted smile. Oh, right, that was why. Because Phil was the sweetest, most generous person, always ready to boost a friend's confidence and genuinely happy to do it. She was easy to love. Anne knew she'd lucked out when they'd been assigned roommates during freshman year of college.

Phil gave Anne a once-over. "You look so cute! Like a sexy Donna Reed, but without the pearls."

A laugh came from the other end of the couch, where Diana sat. "Yeah, but a lot more likely to burn down the house while cooking."

"Really nice. Don't lie, you had two helpings of the chicken and dumplings I made last week." Anne narrowed her eyes at her best friend, outfitted in orange shorts and a brilliant pink tank top that showed her dark brown skin to its best advantage. She'd always had a natural talent for finding the colors that suited perfectly. Except that one unfortunate incident with the puce tank dress when they were fifteen. But really, hardly anyone looked good in puce.

Her other best friend raised one brow, eyes sparkling with mischief, and elegantly crossed one long, smooth leg over the other. "Is that what that was? I thought it was potato soup. My grandma would have chased you out of the kitchen with a wooden spoon if you'd told her those lumps were supposed to be dumplings."

"*Wow.*" Anne pressed a hand to her chest with a mock gasp. "First of all, how dare you. I spent at least twenty minutes making that. See if I ever cook you dinner again."

"I'm crushed."

"I'm so very serious."

"My life will never be the same," Diana said sweetly, as she got up from the couch to herd Anne and Philippa out the door, being the only one who ever managed to keep track of the time. Diana and Anne had been inseparable since the seventh grade when Anne moved to Avonlea, and she knew Diana was only teasing. Probably. She did have an unfortunate history of feeding her best friend dubious food, like the rum cake Marilla made when the girls were fourteen that Anne had thought was just a pineapple Bundt. They'd only stolen a few slices, but the older woman had a heavy hand with the liquor and the two girls were pretty tipsy by the time they'd polished their pieces off. Mrs. Barry had been *so* angry. Anne still inwardly winced whenever she thought of how Diana had thrown up all over her mother's new Gucci boots.

Oops.

"Tell me again why we're going all the way out to Brooklyn to drink beer we could probably get at the corner store and play board games, of all things?" Philippa asked as she navigated her way down the sidewalk during their two-block trip to the subway. Anne envied the grace in which she avoided the cracks and grates, as smooth as if she were walking across a polished wood floor.

Then what her friend had said sunk in. "Wait, we're taking the subway to *play board games*?"

"Anne!" Diana exclaimed, giving her a flat look. "Didn't you open the link to the bar's website I texted you? It's not just board games. They supposedly have everything, all sorts of board and trivia games, even a small vintage video game arcade."

"You said *bar*! You said bar, and the potential for sexy guys in low-slung jeans, with beards. What else did I need to know?"

"Oh my God, you dork."

Phil giggled at the flabbergasted expression on Diana's face. The three girls chatted about their class schedules the rest of the way to the subway. School started up again in just a few days, and Philippa and Anne were headed back to Redmond College. Philippa was, fingers crossed, graduating from the School of Medicine by winter break, so she could start her doctorate studies early. Diana was a dozen blocks or so south, at Parsons, in her final year studying design at the School of Fashion. The desk in her bedroom was already crowded with piles of couture sketches and heaps of scrap material that seemed to multiple with alarming frequency.

Two years for Redmond's Master of Education program was standard, but Anne had stretched it to three in the interest of not creating too much pressure and stress while working full-time as well. Monday would be the first day of her last year, *finally*. There had been a brief dream in high school of being a Serious Author, but it began to morph into something else when she started to help her fellow writing club members put a shine on their own work. That was when she discovered there was nothing she loved better than watching a story made from half-formed ideas and nuggets of creativity take shape. It gave her a sense of deep satisfaction to guide others as they found their voices and discovered how to write the story only *they* could tell. She was surprised and pleased to realize she seemed to have a natural talent for it.

So, Anne adjusted her dreams and shifted her focus to becoming a teacher, with the encouragement of her English instructor Ms. Stacey. She especially liked the idea of working at a university, or *maybe* a high school. As much as she loved babysitting, she recognized that working on a lesson plan that included learning the ABCs would drive her bonkers within a year.

She had her eye on a few opportunities this year, to get a job at a university in the city after graduation. Her mentor, Dr. Lintford, was known to have an in with several deans, including the one who headed Priorly College, where Anne desperately wanted to end up. She'd almost gone there instead of

Redmond—it had been a close choice—and the small, private college was a perfect place to start her career.

But tonight, she was going to put it all out of her mind, and just enjoy her last evening of summer with Diana and Phil.

After what seemed like an endless trip out to Brooklyn, the girls trooped up the subway exit stairs and followed the GPS on Diana's phone. They ended up in front of a bar that had an eighties video arcade mixed with a traditional pub vibe, snuggled between a tattoo parlor and a Korean grocery store. The two themes shouldn't have worked together, but weirdly, they did.

The noisy bar was just as interesting inside, beams of bright light scattered throughout the room, cutting through the dim atmosphere. Old, battered arcade game booths mixed with pinball machines, Skee-Ball, and large flat-screen TVs set up with every gaming system imaginable ran along the back wall. Another side of the room was crowded with shelf after shelf of boxed games. She didn't even know there were that many board games in existence, and it seemed like Archie's Amusement Arcade had them all. Between the front door and the pinball machines was a crowded bar and an open area filled back to back with round tables, nearly every seat taken. It seemed like 1980s nostalgia was having a serious comeback.

As a Run DMC song slid into Guns N' Roses, Diana led them through a sea of patrons, using her sharp elbows twice to get to a clear spot at the long, wooden bar when necessary. As she struck up a conversation with a bartender blessed with a disturbingly sexy, bushy beard who had made a beeline to her and Phil, Anne idly turned and scanned the room. Being the shortest of the three of them, and most likely to get crushed by people who didn't seem to notice she was standing there, she was used to hanging back and letting the other girls order drinks. Her eyes skipped over the noisy crowd, noting with a shudder the karaoke setup in one corner. Absolutely not. There wasn't enough vodka in the world. The vintage arcade games looked fun, though. It had been years since she'd seen Galaga, much less tried her hand at it.

At the dartboards set up next to Ms. Pac-Man, movement caught Anne's eye, as a man with his back to the rest of the bar threw a perfect bull's-eye. The burly guy with two full-sleeve tattoos playing against him let out a loud whoop, as the first guy turned around for a fist bump. Anne's stomach dropped like she'd started the downhill on the world's tallest roller coaster. She would recognize that lazy, confident stance and lopsided grin of self-satisfaction anywhere. It'd been over six years since the summer night she last saw him, the night she'd vowed to never, *ever* think about again, but suddenly it felt like yesterday.

Without conscious thought, Anne pressed her fingertips against her mouth as if she could banish the unwanted memories of a long-ago kiss.

Gilbert Blythe, bane of her teenage years, longtime academic rival, golden boy of Avonlea, and the only one who'd even come close to wounding her heart, was supposed to be three thousand miles away in California. He'd left for UC in Berkley at the end of the summer after they graduated high school, to study journalism or something, she couldn't quite remember. None of their mutual friends knew what he'd been up to since, it was like he'd dropped off the map completely. Apparently, he didn't even come home for the holidays anymore, his parents flying out to celebrate on the West Coast instead. Not that she asked. But Avonlea was very small in a lot of ways; it was impossible to spend more than a weekend there and not be updated on every piece of gossip that happened since her last visit.

So what in God's name was he doing in Brooklyn?

As if he could hear her thoughts across the rowdy bar, Gil turned his head from where he'd been talking with his friend, deep brown eyes locking on hers with uncanny accuracy. Even at this distance, she could see he'd gone still, straightening from where he'd leaned one shoulder against the wall while waiting for his friend to take his turn. Then he was moving, weaving between two tall tables crowded with people, oblivious to his friend's confusion at his abrupt exit. Refusing to acknowledge the traitorous stutter of her pulse, Anne steeled herself with a determination not to show her nerves at his shocking reappearance. He strode through the spotlights breaking up the dim bar, trademark tousled curls shining an envy-evoking burnished mahogany, a sharp contrast to the bright orange she'd been cursed with since birth. Muscled shoulders flexed in a way that had her mouth going dry, under a tight T-shirt Diana would laughingly call "smedium"-sized, as he closed the distance between them with a singular focus that was annoyingly familiar.

Gil halted in front of her much too close for comfort, one lone dimple popping out as the intensity in his eyes morphed into a mischievous glint. She struggled to ignore the phantom pressure on her lips again, lifting her chin in an attempt to channel calm dignity. She would be the mature, smart adult she'd grown into, not the teenage girl who'd been lost in silly romantic fantasies of kisses under the moon.

"Anne," he said, sliding his hands into the front pockets of his jeans with a casualness she wished she could emulate. The dimple deepened as his smile grew into a grin she knew all too well, one that had never failed to make her wary. That smile was trouble. More specifically, trouble for *her*.

This was bad. This was very, very bad.

Chapter 2

Then

"The point is practically all you do is sit in the house reading and it won't kill you to get outside for a weekend." Diana's hands were on her hips, that familiar determined expression on her face telling Anne she wasn't going to take no for an answer. "Sunshine? Fresh air? All our other friends, who you're going to miss when we leave for the city next week?"

A pinch of guilt wormed its way through Anne's exasperation. She still had so much to do before they headed off to college. Packing her room at Green Gables was overwhelming, knowing now that she'd graduated high school, it was time to put away her childish keepsakes. Pull down those tattered posters of various bands and sort through the stacks of books that had spilled over from the bookcase into piles that leaned against every wall. Not to mention removing the sprawling collage of photos she'd taken with her friends over the years from over her bed, where she'd thumbtacked them, much to Marilla's horror. Matthew was going to paint the room while she was at school; she didn't want to make the job harder than it had to be, since the arthritis in his knees had gotten worse over the last few years.

Things like that would suddenly remind her that both siblings were in their late sixties now, a fact that made her stomach flip over when she thought about it.

At least Marilla had taken mercy on Anne after watching her agonize over what to keep and what to put in bags for donation or the dump. She agreed most of the childhood mementos that neither of them was eager to part with, such as Anne's numerous academic decathlon medals and the collection of journals she'd filled with angst-ridden teenage poetry, could be stored in the attic. But sorting through the things she wanted to take with her, for what was sure to be a very tiny dorm room at New York University, was a time-consuming task she'd been putting off for very obvious reasons.

It was *hard* to accept that she'd be leaving Green Gables for an entire year, missing the first turning of the leaves in the fall and the way daffodils poked up around the porch in the spring. Sure, she'd visit often, but it wouldn't be the same.

"Look at this mess," she replied finally, waving one hand at her room. Diana had hopped her way through just to get to where Anne sat on the floor by the window seat, sorting clothes she'd had tucked away in the closet with the idea that someday she might want to wear them again. Obviously, her friend understood it wasn't possible for Anne to just drop everything and run off for a weekend camping trip to the beach, even if half the graduating class was going to be there. Three days and two nights of sand, sun, burned food over a firepit, and probably a lot of dubious hookup choices made in the spirit of most likely never having to see the other person again.

Okay, that *did* sort of sound like fun, even if that last item wasn't something she was interested in. Dates in high school had been few and far between, barring her first real relationship in junior year with Roy Gardner. He was tall and slim, with thick black hair and smooth brown skin that never seemed to be marked by the curse of teenage acne the rest of them suffered. His slow smile and the measured, thoughtful way he spoke had drawn her in; Roy was just the sort of boy she'd pictured when dreaming of her first boyfriend. For almost four months they were happy. But then she began to feel restless, and all the things that had seemed charming and sweet before just irritated her now, though she couldn't ever pin down exactly why. When she'd told him that it wasn't him, it was her, she'd *meant* it. That didn't seem to make him feel any better, unfortunately. Somehow, they'd managed to stay friends, which Anne appreciated. Owing to the fact that she'd never really had any before coming to Avonlea, every loss was a blow.

"The mess will be here when you get back, and you have plenty of time to figure it out."

"I want to spend more time with Marilla and Matthew before I go."

"Marilla was the one who sent me up here to try to get you

to come with us! Apparently, you're driving her crazy; she says she's practically stepping on you every time she turns around."

Wow, okay. But . . . fair. She'd been feeling really emotional lately, the end of summer just barreling toward her, and maybe she'd been a tiny bit of a pest.

"I don't know, D. I'm not much of a camper."

"Pleeeeeease. With a cherry on top?"

Throwing her hands up, Anne caved to the inevitable. "Fine. I'll go."

"Don't sound so excited about it," Diana teased, extending a hand to pull Anne to her feet, then turned to the clothing piles that covered the bed. Digging through, she found what she was looking for, holding up in triumph a never worn, royal-blue bikini Anne had purchased in a moment of insanity.

"This comes with us."

"No."

"Absolutely. You *kill* in it. I don't know why you refuse to wear it."

Anne made a grab for it, but her best friend held it out of her grasp, using the extra inches of reach she had to her best advantage.

"Jane made me buy it. It was on clearance! I don't wear it because no one wants to see that much pasty skin on display."

"Noooope," the other girl sang, still holding the swimsuit their mutual friend had badgered Anne into buying aloft with a grin. "Just because you aren't blessed with the beauty of melanin like *moi*—seriously, you almost glow in the dark—it doesn't mean you don't look good in it."

"Everyone on the beach will go snow-blind, and then I'll just burn. You've seen it, you know it's true!" Trying to keep her laughter in check, Anne gave up her attempt to steal the bikini back. "Okay, okay. I'll wear it. But if I look like a tomato at the end of the weekend, I'm blaming you."

"Sunscreen is a thing, you know." Her friend rolled her eyes, rooting around the floor of the closet for the worn duffel Anne had packed for every sleepover at the Barrys' house during the last six years. "Come on, let's see what other cute things I can torture you into wearing this weekend."

Which is how Anne came to be standing on the sand, in a pair of denim shorts cut several inches higher than she'd normally wear, and one of her best friend's many designer T-shirts. Diana kept insisting that redheads *could* wear pink, it was all about the shade. Seeing as she was the rising fashion major of the two of them, Anne opted to finally take her advice. She fingered the edge of the pale rose-colored cotton, secretly pleased to be wearing a color she'd told herself was off-limits.

"Lookin' good, Shirley," someone called from behind her. Recognizing the lightly mocking tone, Anne's back stiffened. Of course. *Of course* he would be here.

Turning away from her view of the ocean, she watched Gil climb the dune she stood on. They hadn't seen each other much since graduation. He looked good, but then, he always did. Summer suited him, the sun had streaked his brown curls with dark gold and bronzed his skin. As he stepped up next to her, she caught a glimpse of annoyingly adorable freckles marching across his nose. Clearly, he'd managed to get time off from his part-time job at the ice cream shop and decided to join them for the last night. A rolled-up tent, closed camp chair, and over-sized duffel bag leaned against his car like he'd dumped them there and walked directly to the dunes as soon as he arrived.

A discomforting sensation fluttered in her belly at the thought that maybe he'd done it because he'd seen her. Which was ridiculous, obviously. They just barely tolerated each other, a fact that exasperated their shared group of friends to no end.

"I didn't know you were going to be here," she said, cursing her lack of foresight in not asking Diana for a full list of kids who'd be camping out. It wasn't like Gil's presence would have kept her home, of course. But she'd have been better prepared to deal with the way he always seemed to knock her off-balance lately.

"But I knew *you* would be. Despite the threat of fresh air."

Anne turned her head sharply at his words, but the hand closest to her blocked most of his expression as he shaded his eyes to look over the crowded beach. What exactly did that mean? Not that she was going to ask. Gil wouldn't give her a straight answer, he never did. It was one of the more irritating things about him, how he always made her chase down answers. It wasn't that she didn't know what he was doing, driving her nuts for his own amusement, one of the reasons she'd been one of the few people in school who *didn't* seem to have some sort of crush on him.

"Are you packed and ready for next week?" Gil asked idly, as he pulled a battered baseball cap out of his back pocket, un-rolled it, and plopped it on Anne's head. She started to protest, recognizing the hat from years of him wearing it practically everywhere, and God *knows* the last time he washed it, but he batted her hands away. "You're gonna go up like an ant under a magnifying glass if you don't figure out some cover this weekend, ghost girl. Hope you brought a bottle of SPF 1000."

"Thanks, Dad, you know, I *have* been to the beach before." She rolled her eyes but left the hat alone. It didn't smell from a decade of sweat like she'd been afraid it would, all she got was the faintest whiff of laundry detergent. And she wouldn't admit it, but the shade on her nose did feel good. It was hot enough her shirt was already sticking to her back, and she was starting to wonder why she was still standing here listening to Gil lecture her on sunscreen when she could be out there swimming in the cold Atlantic water instead. Swimming sounded like an *excellent* idea. Pulling an elastic off her wrist, she scooped up the hair spilling out from the bottom of the cap and twisted it into a messy bun.

After a moment of hesitation that made her fingers fumble at the hem of her shirt, Anne steeled her nerves and pulled it over her head, taking care not to dislodge the hat. Gil went still beside her as she popped open the button on her shorts and shucked them off in one movement. Scooping the clothing up, she balled the shorts together with her shirt, and shoved them toward him. Automatically he took the bundle, eyes still stuck somewhere south of her neck. Amusement suddenly bubbled up inside Anne, it was hard not to laugh at the way his gaze jerked up to her face again when she cleared her throat.

The faint pink spreading over his cheeks was both fascinating and hilarious.

"I'm going swimming."

"Uh. Okay."

"Can you just take my stuff back down with you and drop it off with Diana?"

"Yeah. Sure. I can do that. No problem."

She was definitely going to laugh in his face if she didn't leave soon. His usual smartass quips seemed to have deserted him. Who knew a bikini could scramble a boy's brain so thoroughly, even Gil's? Maybe Jane and Diana had been right after all, if the glazed-over look in his eyes was any indication. Turning, she allowed herself a private grin as she made her way down the dune, picking her way across hot sand toward the water. An itch between her shoulder blades made her look back, just as the foamy surf rolled up over her toes. Gil was still standing on top of the dune, watching her. He spun around when she gave a little wave, quickly disappearing down the other side. Anne finally gave in to the urge to snicker as she waded out into the ocean, telling herself it was the frigid waters of the North Atlantic that took her breath away and definitely not the arrested expression in his eyes when she'd shoved her clothes in his hands.

She didn't examine the memory of that look when she watched him setting up his tent later, shirt tossed on the ground without care, the muscles in his back bunching as he pushed the poles into place. She didn't think of it as he sat down next to her when the group gathered around the huge bonfire they'd built and offered her a slightly charred hot dog from his plate. And she definitely didn't think about it when he wandered off to socialize after and a very tipsy Josie Pye put her hand on his bicep, giving it a squeeze as she flirted up at him through her lashes.

She *did* think about it, however, when he gently extracted himself from the other girl's grip and his gaze collided with Anne's across the fire. This time she couldn't blame freezing water on the way the air in her lungs deserted her in a rush. His eyes narrowed, and one side of his mouth tipped up in a smile she recognized as a precursor to him doing or saying something that would get her all riled up. Except this time, it wasn't annoyance that filled her, but something she'd never thought she'd feel for Gilbert Blythe.

A full-blown, rampant desire to kiss him until he couldn't remember his own name.

Oh, no, no, this was totally unacceptable. He was awful and she didn't like him.

Of course, she didn't have to like him to want to kiss him.

When he set down the beer he'd been nursing for the last hour and started around the bonfire toward her, Anne pushed herself to her feet and escaped to the beach, determined to avoid him. Yes, it was the end of summer and they'd all be splitting off into a million different directions for college, but that didn't mean she had to throw all good sense to the wind.

But she should have known he'd follow her. Gilbert Blythe never missed an opportunity to get under her skin.

Although, this time it felt different. She glanced over at him, but he wasn't looking at her. He stood with his hands shoved into the pockets of his hoodie, staring out at the water, eyebrows furrowed in thought. She chewed her bottom lip, confused by his silence, and even more by how comfortable it was. He'd been here almost two full minutes and they weren't bickering. She wasn't sure what to do with that. After a moment, she decided to leave it. She'd come out here to get some clean air, away from the bonfire smoke, not to talk. Especially not to talk to him.

Dark waves crashed against the shore, leaving a thin sheen of silver over the sand as they retreated. The cool, end of summer wind sent Anne's hair flying in long ribbons behind her, and she wrapped her sweater around her torso just a little tighter. To-morrow would be torture, dealing with the knots and tangles, but right now, she couldn't bring herself to care all that much. Soon she'd be leaving this all behind to live in the city, and she wanted to soak up as much as she could.

A few more minutes passed, and she forgot her resolution to ignore him, the quiet between them finally making her fidgety. "It was so hot back there. I don't know why they built the fire so high." This was torturously awkward, searching for something innocuous to talk about. But she didn't know how to navigate this uncharted territory, where they weren't sniping at each other. "Smoke got to you too?"

"No." Gil's eyes locked on hers. The brilliant light from the full moon threw the sharp angles of his cheekbones into high relief, gilded the long, tousled curls that kept blowing into his eyes, and kissed the perfect bow of his upper lip in a way that sent desire shooting through her again. What a horrifying re-alization, that she wanted the one boy she needed to stay away from if she had even a shred of self-preservation.

"I came out here because you're out here." Then, if that wasn't shocking enough, he did something *else* he'd never done before, and reached out to tangle his fingers with hers. Bringing their joined hands up to press a kiss along her knuckles.

She sucked in her breath, shocked as he smiled, no trace of the usual mockery behind it.

A storm of butterflies swirled in her belly, battering the inside of her rib cage. Frozen by the sight of him dropping airlight kisses on the back of her hand, she didn't notice how far he'd gotten until he turned her arm over and rubbed his lips against her wrist. The intimacy of it, the potential exposure of how her pulse was hammering under his touch, had Anne jerking her arm out of reach. She pressed it to her chest without thought, struggling to clear her mind.

This was . . . what was he thinking? He *lived* to make her life difficult, he couldn't possibly want this.

Except it seemed he did.

Even if Anne had ever expected Gil to kiss her, much less any part of her body besides her mouth, which of course she never had, the feel of his mouth against her skin would still have been overwhelming. The care he took, the delicacy in which he'd held her arm captive while exploring what little territory he could cover before she'd pulled away, was nothing like the clumsy fumblings of the few boys she'd let get close before. She didn't know how to handle the weakness loosening her knees or the floaty feeling that was making it hard for her to concentrate.

Or the way he watched her with those coffee-colored eyes. Even in the pale light she could feel the intensity of their focus.

"Anne." His voice was low, rough with an emotion she couldn't name. Wasn't sure she wanted to name.

This was ridiculous. This was *Gil*. He didn't make her shiver and want to be touched; he was a thorn in her side. An annoyance. A nuisance. Stepping back, she sent him a wide smile that felt just this side of manic. "I should go back. Diana will probably think I wandered into the surf and drowned."

"I doubt she's going to notice anything for a while, she left the fire with Hannah," he said, that annoying dimple deepening. "You might just have a tent to yourself tonight, if that's what you want."

The image of him lying back on her sleeping bag, the taut muscles of his naked abs flexing under her fingers, flashed through her mind. A flush heated her cheeks at that thought, so strong there was a distinct possibility of passing out. It was like the campsite bonfire had taken up residence inside her body.

Make good choices, Anne Shirley.

"Good for her. For them. That's been a long time coming." She gathered what was left of her rational mind, keeping her voice as distant as possible, not acknowledging the insinuation in his words. This whole thing had taken a sharp left turn and she desperately needed to get them back on familiar ground. "I thought Hannah would never notice she was being aggressively flirted with."

"Funny how that happens more than you'd think." Gil took a step in her direction, the controlled, fluid way he moved in contrast with the idle tone he used. She reflexively moved backward in response, recognizing the danger at allowing him within arm's reach again. Danger of losing her mind and wrestling him to the ground, maybe.

The way he watched her set off warning pings in her brain. It was a struggle to remember what they'd been talking about before he began to stalk her across the sand. And she needed to get it together. She wasn't the kind of girl to be chased around a beach, driven silly by lust for a boy she could hardly stand. Okay, she would admit he'd made her laugh once or twice lately without her wanting to hit him in his smug face with a notebook again. But that didn't mean she wanted to spend any sort of prolonged time in his company. Drawing up her shoulders, Anne blew out a breath and halted her absurd backward progress. It was time to put a stop to this insanity and—

Without warning Gil was in front of her, his dark silhouette blocking out the moonlight.

She swallowed, gaze drawn upward to meet his, forgetting what she'd been about to do. Their bodies were close enough now that she could feel the warmth emanating off him, right through his Avonlea Prep hoodie. His hands closed around her upper arms, reeling her in slow enough for her to protest, if she really wanted to. But she didn't say a word, even though she *knew* she should, and then suddenly they were pressed together from knees to belly. Her hands kept their chests apart just a few vital inches, trapped between the two of them, clenched into fists because what was she supposed to do now?

Touch his shoulders?

His *chest*?

She was without a doubt out of her depth now, and it made

her uneasy. Gil always called her bossy, said she always had to be the one in charge, and he wasn't exactly wrong. Per se. It was just . . . loss of control was very hard for her.

The moment stretched out and Anne realized he was waiting for her to look up. When she finally raised her eyes, she almost jerked away, his gaze was so intense. It dawned on her that the rapid beating of a pulse against her fists wasn't hers. It was his. And that was oddly reassuring, to know he was as affected by this as she was. Whatever this strange thing that was happening to them, she wasn't alone in it. Tentatively, she spread her fingers, finally letting her palms rest against the hard planes of his chest. It was almost imperceptible, the way he twitched when she touched him, but she felt it. His fingers flexed once, pressing into the flesh of her upper arms.

Maybe she wasn't as powerless as she'd thought.

She stilled, thinking, a ribbon of curiosity winding its way through her. In experimentation, Anne let her hands slide downward just a bit, the thick cotton of his hoodie shifting as he held himself in check while she explored. After looking up to make sure she had Gil's complete attention, she slowly pulled the zipper of his sweatshirt down. He made the most *interesting* sound when she slid her fingers around to his back and eased up under the edge of his T-shirt to touch bare skin. The knowledge that she, of all people, had caused that reaction in him made her bold. As she brushed her thumbs across the rigid muscles along his spine, she leaned in, just far enough that her breasts pressed against his front.

The way his whole body jerked made her smile.

With a choked laugh, Gil reached back and captured her hands, pulling them down to their sides and lacing their fingers together again. Anne's breath stuttered as he bent his head, stopping only a whisper away from her lips.

Gaze trained on her mouth, he murmured, "You should probably stop me now."

A little voice in the back of her mind agreed, absolutely, 100 percent, she probably should, but the rest of her was dizzy with wanting him too much to care about the unavoidable fallout.

"I'd rather not."

"You sure? Because—"

He came out here after her, clearly with this in mind, and now he was backing off? Honestly, some days she just wanted to strangle him.

"For God's sake, kiss me already." Out of patience, Anne yanked one hand free, wove her fingers into the curls at the base of his head, and tugged him down toward her lips.

Without another word, Gil closed the gap, taking her mouth with an urgency that shocked her.

Letting go of her other hand, his fingers dropped to grip her hips, holding her in place. They dove deep into the kiss, pushing forward, then retreating, but never ceding ground. Anne rose on her toes as he broke away, his kiss-swollen lips tracing a path across her skin to the sensitive place just under her ear. The squeak she let out when he bit there, then sucked on the tender flesh, would have been embarrassing if she had any sense of pride at that moment. But she was too absorbed in getting her hands on as much bare skin under his shirt as she could to worry about it. One of his hands left her hip to tangle in her mass of loose hair. Tugging her head back for better access to the column of her neck, Gil's grip tightened when her fingernails spasmed into the muscles just above his ass. Mind hazy, she was wondering how much she'd regret sand-burn the next morning when he spoke again, his lips moving across the skin of her throat.

"Finally—proof you *do* like me. I knew you couldn't hold out forever."

Anne came back to herself with a thud, blood turning to ice in her veins. For years, Gil had insisted that she liked him and was just too stubborn to admit it, and she did her best to convince him that, no, she really did think he was just that irritating.

So, was all of the flirting and tender kisses only about winning their six-year standoff, because Gil couldn't stand the idea that not everyone who met him fell in love with him instantly? Was this a *game* to him? Did he feel smug right now, that she'd kissed him back, that she'd exposed exactly how much she wanted him in this moment?

She was so naive to think this could be anything else.

Mortification burned as she tore herself from his arms and wrapped her own arms tight across her stomach to contain a lurch of nausea. Gil stumbled back, the genuine confusion on his face making her want to kick him in the shin. Hard. It must be mind-blowing to him that there might be a girl who wouldn't fall for him the moment he kissed her. Anne felt sick that she'd almost, *almost* been that girl. Nearly allowed him to keep kissing her, to touch her body, to go even further than that—she should have known it was about settling the score between them once and for all before they both left Avonlea.

The relief that she'd never have to see him again after tomorrow was dizzying.

When he reached out to take her hand, forehead creased in consideration, Anne backed away swiftly. "No," she said, ignoring the tears creating a lump in her throat. It was unthinkable she'd allow him to ever see her that vulnerable now. "I'm going back to the tent. I'm . . . I'm tired."

"You're tired." He repeated her words slowly, like they were a puzzle he was trying to piece together.

"That's what I said." It came out sharper than she'd have liked, the edges a little wobbly, but neutral was so far beyond manageable now.

His gaze narrowed, searching her face. Whatever he found there didn't seem to be what he was expecting, his lips flattening into a tight line as he locked eyes with her again.

"Did I do something wrong?"

Oh, so he was going to keep up the pretense this wasn't all just for the satisfaction of *winning*? It was infuriating how close she'd been to letting him have that victory.

"This—" She made an abrupt gesture between the two of them. "This was a mistake, and not one I plan on repeating."

A cloud slid across the moon, dimming the silver light just enough that she couldn't be sure if the flinch she thought she saw was just a trick from some foolish part inside her still hoping she'd misunderstood, or not. But when the shadow passed, his body was once again relaxed into the sort of lazy arrogance so familiar to her. Hands that had only moments before been pressing her body against his had found their way into the frayed pockets of jeans, casual, as if nothing in the world could bother him. His transformation back into the Gilbert Blythe she knew, confident and self-satisfied, the kind of boy who would never even think about kissing her, had been near instantaneous. She hadn't realized how much that would hurt.

"You said you wanted to go back, let's go back." He caught her staring and threw a smirk her way, his brown eyes cool. "Good call, really. That would have been awkward in the morning."

Bastard. She should have known better. She did know better; this was what she got for ignoring her instincts.

"Happy to save you from that horrifying situation," she muttered, stomping away as well as she could when the sand kept shifting under her feet, her sights locked on the distant pillar of smoke from the bonfire.

Out of the corner of her eye she saw him flip his hood up, moonlight-gilded profile disappearing from sight. "I mean, I wouldn't go that far. But you have to admit, we're the last two people anyone would imagine hooking up. Us together? It would be a disaster, obviously."

That stung, even though she agreed.

"You know, I'm not really in the mood to talk." *Why* had she wandered so far down the beach? The trip back was interminable as he matched her stride, never letting her outpace him. Irritated, and eager to escape his company, Anne ignored her burning calves and pushed herself to move faster, but he still refused to drop back.

Because of course he did.

They couldn't even *walk* without it becoming a competition, for God's sake.

Flat sand gave way to the swell of the dunes finally, the sound of laughter intertwined with music becoming clearer as they approached the campsite. Light from the bonfire just out of sight beyond the hills made crazy shadows dance along to the song blaring from someone's car. At the start of the path cut between the two grassy humps that would bring them back to the others, Anne halted and drew in a deep breath, needing a moment to compose herself.

She would rather throw herself into the ocean than let him see how upset she was.

Gil slowed to a stop next to her, his face unreadable within the darkness of his hood. She hadn't realized how many of his expressions she knew until she searched this one and came up empty. The tiniest, slightest, near microscopic sliver of doubt wormed its way in. Did she overreact?

But maybe she *should* check. Just to be sure. That way she could have a clear conscience for shutting him down like that, not even a bit of wiggle room for uncertainty, and she would know without question he was at fault for this entire fiasco.

"So that was a mistake, right? Definitely a mistake," she said, cautiously, searching his expression as she did. All that got her was a weird look, like he thought she was just messing with him now.

"Yeah, I think we covered that. Definitely a mistake."

"Right. Obviously."

Anne gritted her teeth. Okay. Good. Now she could forget the whole thing had ever happened. Still, it was harder than she'd thought it'd be to force a smile. Making the decision to be the bigger person, and to take back control of the situation, she stuck her hand out in a gesture of civility.

For one long moment Gil just looked at it, then back up to her.

"No one knows what just happened. Or almost happened," she qualified, continuing to hold her hand out steady. "We tell no one. I think we can both agree it would be *incredibly* embarrassing if any of our friends found out."

"Jesus, Anne. You really are something, you know that?" Partially turning away, Gil shoved his hood back to scrub one hand through his hair. She ignored the part where he gave it a short, sharp tug. What was he all cranky about? Everything was back to normal now and they could erase this night from their memories, if he would only just *shake her hand*.

"I'm only trying to come up with a solution that works for us both."

"Right." He let out an incredulous huff of laughter. "I'm not going to fucking shake on it, like a business deal. I guess you'll just have to trust me, impossible as that probably sounds to you."

The bitterness in his voice made her chest tight. Why did he have to make this even worse by being so disagreeable? She bit back a reply that would probably just send them into a new round of bickering. There was a headache brewing behind her eyes and she just wanted to be done. Just . . . done.

It must have come through on her face, despite her silence, because Gil's jaw clenched tight as he let out an explosive hiss of air. Then he turned his back on her and walked away without another word.

Which was fine. This was what she wanted.

That was what she *needed*.

So why did it feel so awful?

Chapter 3

Now

"I hope you wanted a hard cider, because the only other options were beer, more beer, and also, beer. Which I know is not really your thing." Diana appeared at Anne's elbow with a foamy glass of amber cider in one hand and a dark brown bottle in the other, eyes widening as she noticed their old classmate. "Gilbert Blythe!"

She thrust both drinks into Anne's hands and threw her arms around Gil. Some of the other patrons made noises of irritation as her momentum pushed him back a step, bumping into people. But he just laughed, steadying her as she planted a loud, smacking kiss on his cheek. The unguarded, warm affection for her friend was so different from the way he had always looked at Anne.

Why couldn't she find her mad? After how he'd acted, shouldn't the sight of him disgust her? But it didn't. It didn't and she couldn't understand why.

After another tight hug, Diana took her beer back from Anne, then nailed him in the shoulder with her fist. "Where have you *been*? You don't call, you don't write. Not cool."

"Ow, geez." He dramatically clutched the spot she'd hit. "What, are you still playing field hockey? That's some punch, D."

"I'm sure you're in agony," she said, rolling her eyes. Anne stood in silence as they started chatting, awkward with a lack of anything to add, taking a sip of her cider instead. Bubbly foam coated her upper lip, and without a thought, she swiped her tongue across it. Gil abruptly shifted next to her, their arms bumping, and she looked up to find his eyes on her again. For a second, they flickered down to watch her lips, then darted away as he turned back to listen to what Diana was saying.

Oh.

Breathe. Anne let air out on a slow, measured exhale.

It was just nostalgia combined with a dearth of non-self-induced orgasms in the recent past, combined with the slight buzz of alcohol, combined with being confronted by sinewy, tanned forearms dusted with a light coating of wiry hair. Forearms that looked like they would have no problem holding his body in a plank position. For a *while*. Any girl's libido would be doing an internal mamba in that situation, it had nothing to do with the actual man involved. She pulled her gaze away from said forearms and took a much larger gulp of cider than before.

Too large, as it turned out. The liquid stuck in her throat and she choked on the sting of carbonation. Thank God, she managed to swallow it down instead of spitting it all over herself, eyes watering from the herculean effort.

Up and to her left came an almost imperceptible snort of amusement.

"Gonna make it?" One of those indecently capable-looking hands patted her between the shoulder blades. Clearing her burning throat, Anne sidled out from under the touch of his palm against her back, before something terrible happened. Like her shivering.

Letting his hand drop away, Gil shoved it into the front pocket of his jeans, his gaze going thoughtful. She just concentrated on avoiding eye contact and sipping her cider instead of aspirating it. Oblivious to the thrumming undercurrent of tension between the two, Diana grabbed their third roommate around the wrist and hauled her forward.

"Hey, you haven't met Phil! Gilbert Blythe, Philippa Gordon. She was Anne's first-year roomie and now we all share a place." The impeccable manners he always used around everyone but her kicked in as he shook the other girl's hand with an expression of polite interest on his annoyingly handsome face.

Diana turned to Phil, explaining, "Gil is from Avonlea, we all grew up together, but he lives in Cali now."

"No one who lives in California calls it Cali, D."

"LL Cool J did."

"No one who lives in California calls it Cali, D."

Diana opened her mouth to retort, but Phil beat her to it, ever the peacemaker. She smiled warmly at Gil. "So, California. My aunt lives in Pasadena, it's a pretty area. But how funny that we ran into you in Brooklyn, then, of all places."

"Ah. Yeah, well . . . my dad has cancer. Prostate. He got the diagnosis in the spring, but I had to finish last semester before I could come home. The doctors are pretty optimistic, but we won't know more until he starts chemo." If Anne hadn't spent years glaring at Gil across a classroom, she would have missed the way the smile left his eyes, even as it lingered on his lips. Accepting the noises of sympathy from Phil and Diana, he hitched one shoulder up in a "what can you do?" gesture. "I figured I'd just hang around and drive the old man crazy until he gets well enough to boot me back to California himself."

Anne raised her eyebrows. "Oh, well, if that's the plan, then don't worry. I'm sure you'll be back in Berkeley in no time flat."

"There's the girl I know, never passing up an opportunity to give me shit." The grin that flashed across his face was real again, even if it settled more into a smirk than a smile.

"You wouldn't know what to do if I was sweet to you," she scoffed.

"Oh, I don't know about that."

Her face heated at the teasing tone. Well, she'd walked right into that one.

"But I am sorry to hear about your dad," Anne said in a soft voice, resolved to ignore his last comment. "He always asked how school was going and actually seemed like he didn't mind listening to a fifteen-year-old girl passionately condemn algebra as the devil's invention. If he found it annoying, he was too nice to show it, anyway.

"Not sure what happened here," she tacked on, gesturing to all of Gil purely out of habit. Like muscle memory, their insult volleys were.

"And just when I thought you were going all soft on me for a minute."

She almost *had*, God help her.

Diana let out a gusty sigh. "Phil, don't mind these two. They've always been like this."

"Have they?" Philippa looked between the pair with a gleam in her eye Anne *did not* like.

"Bickering like children." Gil made a noise of protest, but Diana rolled over it. "Or cats and dogs. Or I don't know . . . what other things needle each other constantly until one of them flounces off?"

"I have never in my life *flounced*." Anne narrowed her eyes, offended at the imagery.

"I said what I said."

"I, on the other hand, enjoy a good flounce," interrupted Gil, leaning in toward Philippa as if confessing a great secret. He started to say something more, but a hand with the Puerto Rican flag emblazoned across the back of it came down on his shoulder, cutting off his next words.

"I was wondering where you'd run off to, but now I get it." The tattooed man who'd been with Gil when he'd spotted Anne stood there, not looking particularly upset at being deserted. His eyes lingered on Diana, before he turned back to his friend with raised brows. "You owe me twenty, by the way, for your half of the stall."

Gil rubbed at the back of his neck sheepishly. "Yeah, dude, sorry about that. Let me introduce you . . ."

The group snagged a table and stayed for what turned out to be a surprisingly good couple hours. Anne immediately liked Fred Wright, who had become friends with Gil in California before he decided college was not his thing, packed his stuff, moved to Brooklyn, and began an apprenticeship at a local tattoo parlor. He kept them all laughing, knew all sorts of nerdy, obscure space facts, and didn't mind when Diana wanted to look at his body art. In fact, he didn't mind it so much that he offered to take his shirt off for her, but when she looked him up and down with a speculative gleam in her eye, Gil practically tackled his friend in an effort to keep his clothes on.

It finally got late enough that Anne had to call it a night. She had an early-morning shift at the bookstore she'd worked in over the last few years. The bar was still as crowded as it had been when they'd arrived, the group squeezing through the press of people to get to the front door. When she was jostled by a man gesturing broadly as he talked to his friends, Gil's hand came up to steady her. The heat of his palm, where it settled low on her back just above the curve of her bottom, seemed to burn through the thin cotton of her dress. They were almost to the door when he rubbed his thumb against her back, the half-circle motion bringing it to rest in the divot at the base of her spine. The feeling was electric, streaking up her spine, causing an involuntary shudder.

Sucking in a lungful of air, Anne practically leapt forward, spilling out onto the sidewalk right on Diana's heels. Her friend glanced back, giving her an odd look, but she avoided eye contact and concentrated on pulling in the cool night air. It had been stifling in the bar. That was why she felt like she was overheating. Not because of the way Gil had touched her.

The way he touched her.

No. She was not starting this cycle again. The constant exchange of witty barbs, the competition to always come out on top, the irresistible urge to antagonize each other beyond sanity. Throw in lust and it was a powder keg waiting to be lit, and not in a good way.

Diana had been truthful when she told Philippa the two of them were always at each other's throats, through middle and high school. They'd quarrel about who was better at frog dissection in biology. They would argue over the best way to get the answer to a math problem in calculus. Then there was that time they feuded for an entire semester of sophomore year because Anne had stated that probably half of the inventions and discoveries credited to men over the centuries were actually by women, but the patriarchy had swept them under the rug, because *God forbid* a woman be better at something than a man. The part Gil seemed to take offense at was that she glared at him all through the last half of that sentence. Looking back, Anne wasn't sure why she'd done it, but she was positive it had been justified.

The point was, given the opportunity, there wasn't anything they couldn't find a way to fight about. From the first day she and Gil had met, excepting that lone summer night, it had been nothing less than war between them. And that's the way Anne liked it. In safe territory.

Chapter 4

Gil paid the cabdriver, then joined Fred on the sidewalk in front of the narrow brownstone where they were renting the second floor. It wasn't new and shiny, but it was home—at least for the next year. Fred's tattoo shop was just starting to break even, and right now, Gil was living on what money he'd managed to squirrel away in California. The old apartment was the best they could do at the moment. It wasn't what he was used to—which made him sound like the worst kind of snob, he knew. That sort of thinking was a by-product of growing up the way he did, going to an elite private school and living in a house with a pool and tennis courts.

He was working on it.

So, once he left high school, he started waiting tables and then bartending to support himself through college and into grad school. It was important for him to stand on his own two feet now, and not rely on his parents' money. And he'd been doing okay before the move; once he found another job here, he'd be doing okay again. He already had an interview set up the next afternoon at a little family-owned bar called Kindred Spirits. But even if he did struggle a little, it didn't matter. He belonged *here* now, not three thousand miles away. His dad had been diagnosed with cancer, Redmond had accepted his transfer application, and Fred had needed a new roommate. The decision to move back east was easy.

Well, maybe not *easy*. But it was the right thing to do, coming home.

Home . . . where Anne Shirley was.

He wasn't going to lie; he'd known long before he'd made his decision that she'd moved to the city after high school. (And what she was majoring in, and how often she came back to Avonlea, and that she lived with Diana now, and a whole host of other things his mother felt were imperative he know over the last five or so years.)

Not that being near Anne again had been a deciding factor in Gil's application. He'd also applied, and been accepted, to NYU and Queens College. But Redmond had the program that was closest to Berkeley's, and their program had the least number of supplemental courses required to complete his degree in New York. The switch from one university to another was already pushing his graduation out another year. The possibility of seeing Anne again was just a bonus. Nothing more. Gil had gotten over her years ago. Dated plenty in California, some women more seriously than others. He'd been with Christine Stuart, a girl he'd met in economics class in sophomore year, for almost a full year before realizing their relationship was about as much fun as watching wallpaper paste dry. She'd been safe. Lovely and sweet and calm, and he knew she'd never hurt him. It took a while to figure out the reason she'd never hurt him was because she didn't have the capability, since he'd never given her anything real to work with.

That epiphany made him extremely uncomfortable and the relationship had died a quiet, unremarkable death soon after.

From then on, Gil kept it casual, never going out with the same woman more than a handful of times. There would be plenty of time to find something more meaningful after he finished school and was firmly established in his career. His new direction had served him well so far—which is why it came as such a shock to spot Anne and have his heart immediately want to leap out of his chest and throw itself at her mercy.

Again.

He'd thought it had learned its lesson in seventh grade, and then again that summer after their senior year, when she crushed it underfoot without a thought. Apparently, his heart was a glutton for punishment.

She'd been nearly lost in the rowdy Friday-night crowd of bar hoppers, but the thick mass of copper waves tumbling over one shoulder caught his attention like a beacon. Still, he'd thought, there were probably hundreds of willowy redheads in Brooklyn. It was just reflex by now, that his gaze would snag on red hair, briefly assessing before moving on. But then their eyes met, and he was sure. After years of unconsciously searching for her in every crowd, it was almost a shock to finally land on the *right* redhead.

The way his heart slammed in his chest, as the undeniable compulsion to be closer to her had him hauling open the safety cage's door, neatly answered the question of whether his feelings for her were truly gone again. It had registered in the back of his mind that Fred said his name, pitched to be heard above the noise, confusion in his voice. But Gil's focus had been singular, the gleam of burnished copper curls in his sights as he wove through the crowd. Even halfway across the bar he could see the moment she became aware of him, eyes the color of rain over the ocean widening with shock. Amusement at the flash of something that looked almost like panic on her face, followed quickly by suspicion as he got closer, helped temper the urgency to reach her. It was so *Anne* to assume he was up to something. He'd spent years trying to coax that look out of her, because then he had her attention. It was embarrassing how many hours of his life had been dedicated to getting those big gray eyes to turn his way.

Gil thought he was prepared to see her again; he'd had the months spent arranging his transfer to New York after his father's cancer diagnosis to get used to the idea. But he wasn't, not by a long shot. It was laughable, how not prepared he'd been.

Unlocking the front door, he moved aside just in time to not get stepped on as Fred ambled past, kicking off his boots as he headed toward the kitchen at the back of the apartment. Neither of them was exactly known for their housekeeping, so Gil just knocked them up against one wall with his foot as he followed the sound of his drunk roommate's off-key singing. Every time Fred drank more than three beers, he started in on Broadway's greatest hits. It never got less funny.

Leaning against the doorframe to the kitchen, Gil raised his eyebrows. "Didn't you eat nearly an entire pizza *and* a full Caesar as a side earlier?"

"Dude." Fred looked wounded as he balanced half a hard salami, a bag of shredded cheese, and a questionable box of mushrooms on top of a carton of eggs. "That was five hours ago. I work out, I gotta eat a lot of protein."

Snorting, Gil moved into the kitchen, kicking a chair out from under the table and dropping into it, suddenly tired. Fred sniffed the mushrooms, then gagged and lobbed them into the trash by the back door. They were quiet for a couple minutes, Fred slowly slicing salami with the careful, precise movements of a man just a hair past buzzed, and Gil enjoying the silence after the noise of the bar. If he didn't move, he could still feel his ears throbbing along with the music.

"So," Fred said.

Fuck. Well, he'd known this was coming, he just figured he had until tomorrow, at least.

"Yeah?" Gil rose, grabbing a sports drink from the fridge and twisting off the cap. Better to have something to do with his hands. He took a small sip as Fred slid diced salami into the pan, the pieces making a sizzling noise and filling the room with the fragrant aroma of cooking meat.

"What's up with you and the redhead?"

From the sideways grin his friend sent him, Gil knew he hadn't forgotten Anne's name, he just liked to mess with him. Gil capped the bottle again and hoisted himself up on the counter next to the sink, thinking of how to condense a decade of not-quite-friendship, not-quite-enmity into bite-sized chunks.

"We have history," he said, finally. Rolling the bottle between his hands, he watched the bright blue liquid slosh back and forth, still a little dizzy from the last round of shots they all did before calling it a night. "You know we're from the same town. Went to school together, with Diana."

Fred just nodded, cracking a couple eggs on top of the salami and scrambling them around.

"Well, except Diana and me, we grew up together. It's a small town, everyone knows everyone, right? Anne didn't move there until we were in seventh grade, and . . ." He paused, scratching the back of his neck sheepishly. "We didn't exactly get off on the right foot."

"What did you do?" Fred dropped a handful of shredded cheese into the pan.

"Why do you assume *I* did something?"

"Because I know you."

Gil laughed, caught out, and leaned back until his head rested on the door of the hanging cabinet behind him. "Yeah, okay. Fair. I, uh. ImighthavecalledherCarrotsandpulledherhair."

"Dude, what?" Confusion wrinkled his friend's brow as he flipped his witching-hour breakfast onto a plate.

"I might have called her Carrots and pulled her hair." Gil hopped off the counter as Fred choked and sprayed bits of salami and eggs across the table and tossed the paper towel roll to the other man. "I *know*. It was immature and mean, which she absolutely let me know at the time."

"I bet." Fred made a face as he wiped the table surface down, then tucked back into his eggs. "You have some sort of death wish as a kid, to mess with a ginger? I know a ginger with a temper is a stereotype, but my cousin Macey is a redhead, and she will fuck you up."

"No, just the usual middle school boy dumbassery. The kind I'm going to make sure if I ever have a son, he knows not to pull any shit like that. I regretted it almost immediately and apologized, but it didn't do any good. Damage done. Believe me, she hasn't forgotten it—and she'll never let me forget it either, no matter what I do."

"Wait. Hold up." Putting his fork down, Fred gave him a hard stare. Gil took a long swallow from the bottle to avoid eye contact, knowing his friend had made the connection he'd hoped to avoid. "Is she *the girl*? The one who messed your head up so bad, you haven't managed a real relationship since I met you four years ago?"

"To be fair," Gil started, tossing the now empty bottle into the trash with regret. There went his tool of avoidance. "It was never her fault. That's on me. I don't think she really believed I liked her, even after we hooked up that one summer. *Hooked up.*" He snorted, the sting of missed opportunity still as sharp now as it was six years earlier. "We kissed. Once. Then it all went sideways, like it always did whenever we tried to call a truce."

"So, is that it? You guys hated each other because you made a crack once about her hair?"

"Well, it sounds dumb when you put it like that."

"Seriously?"

"No, not seriously. I never hated her. Sometimes I wished I could, just so I could stop *caring* so damn much, but I never quite managed it." Gil stretched his legs out, feeling the last week catching up with him. A cross-country move, then meeting his mom and dad for his dad's first chemo treatment, plus unpacking. It was a lot, and he could feel the weight of it trying to drag his eyelids down. Yawning, he slumped down in his chair. "And I mean, I don't think she actually hated me either. She just thought I was obnoxious, which was accurate about fifty percent of the time. Maybe seventy percent."

"Did you tell her you're at Redmond now too?"

"No."

"Why?"

Letting his head drop back, Gil stared at the ceiling. "I don't know. I was going to, but . . . then I just didn't. Maybe because I know her, and if I'd told her tonight, she'd probably spend the weekend mapping out routes around campus to avoid me.

"And I really don't want her to avoid me," he added with a resigned sigh.

Fred heaved himself out of his seat and brought his plate to the sink, giving Gil a couple moments of silence while he washed up the dishes. Wiping wet hands on a towel, his friend turned around and leaned back against the counter, eyeing him.

"Is this going to fuck you up again?"

"Maybe."

Probably.

"Damn." Fred threw the towel to the side, mouth twisting in a wry grin. "I really liked Diana. Cute girl. Funny. Great legs. Too bad, I'd have liked to get to know her a little better."

Gil sat up, feeling guilty. "We can still hang out. Diana is cool, and Phil seemed cool. Anne and I can be . . ."

"Cool?"

"Shut up." He aimed a kick at his friend's shin, but Fred danced out of reach with a laugh. "Yeah, we can be *cool*." He waved away a decade of animosity as he stood, cracking his back. "We're twenty-four—high school was almost six years ago. It'll be fine."

"What could go wrong?" muttered Fred, sotto voce, as he disappeared down the hall toward his bedroom.

Well aware his friend was being sarcastic; Gil nonetheless couldn't help but feel a sense of optimism. His rivalry with Anne was in the distant past and they were both adults now. It shouldn't be that hard to put aside their differences and figure out how to be friends, especially since it looked like they'd be hanging out some time in the near future. So what if he was still wildly attracted to her and had never quite forgotten the feel of her soft, perfect mouth under his?

He knew how to compartmentalize. It would be *fine*.

Chapter 5

Then

Anne stepped into her first class of seventh grade at Avonlea Preparatory Academy with the same sense of determined optimism she carried everywhere. A new school, a new academic year, a new home, and new friends—there sat Diana Barry in the second row, the girl who lived next door to her most recent foster family—and Anne was ready to jump in with both feet.

Again.

Because for the first time in a long time, her good luck seemed to be holding. Due to a paperwork mix-up, in which the adoption agency sent the Cuthberts a girl when they'd requested a boy, what was supposed to have been a very brief temporary placement had turned into what just might be a permanent home. Her new foster parent Marilla had agreed to a trial period, instead of returning her to the group home she'd been living at before. Being that the older woman had first been vehemently opposed to Anne staying, it was more than a surprise, although a happy one. Apparently, Marilla's brother, Matthew, had been "moping about" the house at the thought of the young girl being sent back into the foster system when they themselves had so much to share. The older woman had insisted that she was only offering the probationary period so that he would stop driving her crazy with sad faces and deep sighs.

But when Anne threw her arms around Marilla's waist in gratitude, the woman's returning hug was just as firm, her hands gently patting the young girl's back.

So, the unlikely trio settled into a comfortable summer routine. Anne would get up at dawn and wolf down breakfast, then head out with Matthew for the morning. He never seemed to mind her tagging along, even though she had countless questions about . . . everything. Once a week, she'd stay back with Marilla instead and they'd clean the house from top to bottom. Anne wasn't sure why they needed to do it every single week, because nothing was ever out of place under the older woman's eagle eye, but she grew to appreciate the sense of precise order.

The summer flew by, evenings becoming chilly enough that Anne had to throw on a sweatshirt to sit on the porch after dinner. Her favorite time of day was when the sun started to set behind the trees, flooding the sky with brilliant pinks and oranges. It was quiet there, except for the crickets, a kind of quiet she'd never experienced before, and she was able to let her mind wander far and wide. Too soon, however, Marilla was talking about school enrollment, and the next thing she knew, Anne was signed up for the *fanciest* school she'd ever seen in her entire life. The older woman explained it was a private academy, one that would challenge her, so she could make the most of "that big brain, endless curiosity, and disturbingly extensive vocabulary." It was almost too late to apply, especially for an academic scholarship, but Marilla went into the front office with that determined expression that the girl had already come to recognize as her no-nonsense face. She came back out an hour later, welcome packet in hand, and thanked the slightly shell-shocked headmaster, then swept out with Anne in tow.

Marilla Cuthbert was a force of nature.

So here Anne was, dressed in the school's regulation tan shorts and white polo shirt, which did *nothing* for her pale complexion, her new sneakers making a squeaking noise on the linoleum as she crossed the room to Diana. The dark-skinned girl looked up and sent her a wide smile, jerking her thumb toward the seat she'd saved with her backpack. Anne felt a wave of gladness that she'd met Diana over the summer and they'd had an immediate connection. Even with only one good friend, nearly anything else was bearable. After handing Diana back her bag, she fell into the seat with a gusty sigh, untangling her long braid from the straps of her own backpack before dropping it at her feet.

"I was almost late!" Making a face, she laid out several sharp-tipped pencils with military precision. "Marilla insisted I eat a full breakfast, even though I told her there's a *definite* possibility I might puke from anxiety this morning. She said I was being a drama queen again, which—I guess that's fair. But then Matthew realized his truck was running on empty when we were supposed to leave, and I wanted to *die* at the idea of walking in on the first day with everyone already in their seats, staring at me."

"Well, you made it with five minutes to spare," her friend replied as the final bell rang and the rest of their classmates spilled into the room at the last second, talking loudly. She propped her chin on her hand, brown eyes amused as she watched Anne pull out a pristine notebook and center it exactly on the desk. "Do you need a ruler or something?"

"Ha ha ha, you're hilarious," Anne said in a dry voice. "Listen, I have a *lot of feelings* about organization now. Marilla corrupted me over the summer, it's not my fault."

"Riiiight."

As the other kids jockeyed for seats in the back of the class, Anne subtly gave her desk one last critical survey, the feeling of new girl nervousness making her chest tight again. Shoving it deep down inside where she could pretend it didn't exist, she turned back to Diana. She felt a stab of envy at her friend's height; the other girl had to have grown two inches since they'd met at the beginning of the summer. One of Anne's former foster moms had said she must have been the runt of the litter, being skinny and short, which was really rude and kind of mean. It was hard not to let people like that get in her head, especially on bad days. But her nose was pretty cute, and her freckles were tolerable. Hopefully someday the shocking fiery color of her hair would darken to auburn, like her mother's had been. There wasn't much Anne remembered from before her mother died, when she was five, but she would never forget how fascinating the dark, fiery curls looked wrapped around her small fingers. Hopefully, one day she would be able to look in the mirror and see some piece of her mother looking back at her. But until then, she'd just have to make the best of what she had to work with.

Even if there wasn't even a *hint* that someday in the next decade she might get boobs.

"I like the new hair," she said to Diana instead of continuing an internal lament of her flat chest, gesturing to the long, thin braids streaked with vivid blue in the front.

"Thanks." Her friend ran a hand gently over the top of her head, looking pleased. "My mom didn't want me to get them, she's obsessed with me competing in the Prix des States in October. She says the judges will take points for not having the traditional bun or French twist. She says everything has to be perfect, that I can't give them any excuse."

"Will they? Give you a bad score just for that?" Anne knew nothing about competitive horse jumping except that Diana had done it since she was a little girl and seemed pretty into it, regardless of how hard a time the judges seemed to give her.

Her friend shrugged, mouth turning down for half a second before her expression smoothed out again. "Probably. If it's not my hair, it'll probably be something else. It always is. But I don't care anymore. I wanted something different this year and the straightener was killing my hair. The chemicals just fried it. But, ugh, I was in the chair *forever.*"

Their teacher entered then, forestalling any further conversation, followed closely by a tall, broad-shouldered boy with a mess of dark curls. As the teacher made his way to the whiteboard at the front of the room, the boy looked around, flashing a grin toward a few kids who called out greetings. His eyes passed over Anne as he searched for a seat, then snapped back, narrowing. The way he studied her, as if cataloging every detail, had her dropping her eyes, unsettled. She bent to rummage through her backpack, like she was actually looking for something and not just trying to cool flushed cheeks.

A bright red face and orange hair was never a good look.

As soon as his shoes passed her desk, she sat upright again, shifting uncomfortably when she heard him slide into the empty desk behind her. Going all twitchy over a boy just wasn't something she *did*. Ignoring the skin prickling on the back of her neck, Anne opened her notebook and tried to pay attention to the teacher as he introduced himself. Mr. Philips enumerated the many, many rules he expected them to follow as his condescending gaze drifted over the students. Then he picked up a piece of paper from his desk and scanned it before looking right at Anne.

"Class, we have a new student this year. Anne Shirley, please stand up and tell us a few things about yourself."

This was always the worst part, but she had perfected a short speech over the last few years, moving from school to school, and was able to recite it smoothly.

"Hi, I just moved here from Deer Park. I like to bake, love to read, and my favorite color is blue." She started to sit, then popped back up. "Oh, and my name is spelled *A-N-N-E*."

Mr. Philips looked down at the paper again, then raised one brow. "Your transfer form says *A-N-N*."

"That's the official spelling, but I like 'Anne' with an *E* much better. If you leave the *E* off it feels really short and unfinished, so that's why I always add it to the end."

"Well, the correct version of your name is spelled without the *E*, regardless of how you feel about it. That's the one I intend to use."

Anne swallowed a sigh, knowing already that she and Mr. Philips were *not* going to get along well. His sort never liked her; she was too talkative, too loud, too enthusiastic, too full of imagination. Just *too much*, she'd been told. But she focused her entire attention on him anyway, as he directed them to open the books that had been passed out and launched into a dry, monotone lecture on the Napoleonic Wars.

After a couple minutes, the eraser tip of a pencil prodded her right shoulder from behind.

A loud whisper followed. "Hey, can I borrow some paper?"

It was the brown-haired boy who'd sat in the next seat back, she realized with a blink of surprise. Next to her, Diana seemed to be trying to tell her something untranslatable using only her eyebrows when a second nudge came. With a sigh of irritation, Anne ripped out a couple sheets of paper and passed them back without turning around. It was the first day of school and he didn't remember to bring a notebook? Seriously?

Leaning forward, hopefully out of pencil-poking range, she refocused on what Mr. Philips was saying, copying neat notes down of what he'd written across the board. She had no time for boys right now, even really cute ones, but most especially ones who thought jabbing someone with a writing tool was the best way of getting their attention. This was the best school Anne had ever gotten to go to, with its pristine books and new computers lining the tables along the wall. The dizzying possibilities of what she could do here were endless. At first, she'd been apprehensive about going to a private school, but Marilla staunchly informed her that she had just as much right to be here as any of the other kids. Maybe more, since she was here on merit and top grades alone. Never in a million years had she thought she'd end up in a school like Avonlea Prep, things like that just didn't happen to her. She wasn't about to waste even a single moment of it. Marilla had said if she kept her place at the school until the end of eighth grade, she had a good shot at making it into the upper school as well. Which, the older woman stated, would give her a solid foundation to build on, so she could get into a good college.

Then Anne would never have to rely on anyone else's goodwill and charity again.

Absorbed in the writing assignment the teacher had given, she almost missed the bump of a sneaker against one of the back legs of her chair. That boy *again*. Gritting her teeth, she bent over her work and ignored him. The next nudge was a little harder, making the chair squeak against the linoleum.

"Knock it off," she hissed, whipping around in her seat to glare at the boy behind her. He just sent her an innocent smile, one cheek dimpling. The little dent only made him cuter, which annoyed Anne even more in the face of his obnoxiousness. She'd

met boys like him before; every school had their good-looking popular boys, so sure of their place at the top of the social pyramid. And she'd learned to steer clear of them, because too many times they turned out to be jerks who liked to make fun of her. They'd pick on her for being a foster kid, for being a "nerd," for her bright hair, for being too easy to wind up.

"I'm Gilbert Blythe. Everyone calls me Gil, though," the boy clarified, unaware of her thoughts as he slouched back in his seat, clearly pleased he now had her attention.

"Fascinating." She rolled her eyes. *Honestly.* They really were all the same. "Just knock it off. Some of us are actually interested in learning something."

"I'm interested in learning," he protested, then winked at her. Of all the . . . "Like who you're going to sit with at lunch."

Oh, for—

"I'm going to eat with Diana," she whispered furiously in return, hoping to shut him up. "Who *doesn't* jam her pencil in my back. Now can you please hush!"

"Anne Shirley." Mr. Philip's voice cracked, whip sharp, from the front of the room. A chill of humiliation washed over her. "Would you care to share with the class what could possibly be so interesting that you feel compelled to hold a conversation with Gilbert rather than complete the work you're supposed to be doing?"

Ignoring the guilty look Gilbert sent her as he mouthed "sorry," Anne squared her shoulders and turned back to face the teacher.

"I wasn't having a conversation, because that would mean

he had something to say that I was interested in, which I am *not*."

"Hey!"

The teacher ignored the boy's exclamation, eyes narrowing as he stared her down. "Is that sarcasm I hear, Ms. Shirley?"

It definitely was, but she hadn't *meant* for it to come out like that. Adults like Mr. Philips just put her on the defensive. Their opinions were formed too quickly, as fixed and immovable as cement. She was always and forever the outsider, too smart-mouthed for her own good, too proud for her circumstances. All she could do was take the hit, put her head down, and suck it up.

"No, sir. I'm sorry," Anne said, resigned to apologizing for something that was absolutely not *her* fault.

"Not as sorry as you will be if you don't respect the rules in my classroom."

She nodded, mute with embarrassment. Maybe some of her former teachers had taken a dislike to her, but she never got in trouble in school. *Never.* Pretty much everywhere else, due to the curse of having no filter when she spoke, but not in *school*. Seemingly satisfied, Mr. Philips returned to his desk and re-sumed typing on his laptop.

"Sorry. Didn't mean to get you in trouble."

The sound of Gil's low voice had Anne closing her eyes briefly, reaching deep down into her soul for patience. Was he talking to her *again*? Some people should come with a mute button, and it was clear he was one of them. In her head, she counted to ten. Unfortunately, there was no mute button, so she'd just have to be the bigger person and ignore him.

"Psst. Hey. C'mon, Carrots, don't be mad—"

Carrots? Carrots?!

Anne sucked in a sharp breath, shocked to the absolute core by his insult to her hair, forgetting her resolve to stay calm and composed. Furious, she snatched up her notebook, whirled around, and whacked that *horrible* boy over the head with it.

"Ms. Shirley! I have never had such a disrespectful student in my ten years of teaching, your behavior is unacceptable!" Mr. Philips rushed up the aisle toward them, his face red, eyebrows pulled down into a scowl. Anne felt a surge of dread, but refused to flinch, lifting her chin stubbornly.

"I *had* to do it, sir. Did you hear what he *said*?" Surely, he'd see *she* was the innocent one here. *Anyone* with an ounce of pride would have reacted the same way when *attacked* like that.

"I don't know what you were allowed to get away with at your other school. Here at Avonlea Prep, however, we do not assault other students."

That awful boy spoke for the first time since the teacher had stormed over. "I'm okay, it's not really a big deal. It didn't even hurt."

Anne glanced back at him, narrowing her eyes. "I don't need you to defend me, thanks."

"Look, I already said I was sorry."

A hand held up in front of his face blocked any further words. "He called me Carrots, Mr. Philips. *Carrots.*"

"Not in a mean way!"

"Not in a mean—" She threw her hands up as he defensively crossed his arms over his chest. "How exactly is that *not* mean?"

"Enough!" Mr. Philips raised his voice over Anne and Gilbert's bickering, the whispers and snickering that had started up from the other students during their argument going silent. He made a sharp slashing motion through the air with one hand. "Ms. Shirley, congratulations on earning detention on the first day of school. And Mr. Blythe, since you seem so eager to continue your conversation with her, who am I to stand in the way of what's sure to be a charming reunion? Both of you, three o'clock on Friday, in the media center."

Anne snapped her mouth shut, face flaming with mortification and fury as she realized the entire class was staring at them. So much for making a good impression at her new school. She wanted to sink through the floor. She wanted Gilbert Blythe to sink through the floor.

He was an awful, horrible boy and she would *never* forgive him.

Chapter 6

Now

The Redmond Writers House, a shared space for all M.Ed. courses under the umbrella of the fine arts parent program, was tucked into a block of buildings catty-corner to Washington Square. An unobtrusive three-story walk-up, it was sandwiched between a famous recording studio that produced some of the seventies' biggest hits and a set of overly expensive apartments. Before the school had bought it, the building was home to a famous songwriter/poet/beatnik, who hosted parties known as much for their spectacular array of drugs as they were for the famous faces that showed up night after night. Then the man got tired of his fame, sobered up, and if rumors were to be believed, moved to Montana to start a cattle ranch. The school snapped the building up for, well, a song.

But now the top two floors were rooms for lectures, rooms

for studying, rooms set up for casual group discussions. It was an interesting setup, not at all what Gil had been used to in Berkeley, where classes were held in a sprawling, gothic-style building that had been built to hold hundreds of students at a time.

This place probably couldn't hold more than seventy-five, elbow to elbow.

He made a point of arriving early on the first morning of classes, right as the doors opened, to give himself time to explore the first floor. It had been love at first sight, when visiting last spring, before transferring; the entire ground floor was a dedicated library. Three original fireplaces had been bricked over decades before, and now contained arrangements of silk flowers or sinuously twisted clay sculptures. Bookcases lined the walls, and although the rooms were small and crowded, with intimate seating arrangements, tall arching windows let in plenty of natural light tinted by multiple verdant green plants spilling out of hanging baskets. The entire library had an airy, bohemian feel to it, which suited Redmond's more relaxed attitude down to the ground.

He imagined Anne felt right at home. It probably gave her hives to walk through the rooms with their overcrowded, jumbled bookcases and windowsills cluttered with forgotten pencil nubs.

Wandering into one of the library's back rooms, Gil grabbed a seat next to a narrow window overlooking the small courtyard the school shared with several other buildings in the block. Grateful the building had excellent air-conditioning that seemed to be holding up well in the middle of a late-August heat wave, Gil ignored the way his T-shirt clung damply to his back from the short walk from the subway and pulled out his laptop. He spent the next hour catching up on email, checking to make sure he'd ordered all the materials he'd need for each of his courses, and reminding himself he absolutely wasn't going to be distracted on the first day of classes by the possibility of seeing Anne again at some point during the day.

Surely, they would have *some* overlapping classes, since the program was tiny.

His lips curved in anticipation of her reaction when she realized he'd transferred into her program. Was it immature of him, at age twenty-four, to still relish the prospect of seeing that little scowl she'd always seemed to save just for him? Absolutely. Was that going to dampen any of the enjoyment he was about to get out of it? Not particularly.

A glance at his phone told Gil he needed to get going or risk walking into class late. He packed away his laptop and the books he'd been glancing over in anticipation of that morning's course on ancestral word-of-mouth storytelling traditions and the impact they'd had on modern literature. Making his way up the narrow staircase to the third floor, he exchanged nods with some other students squeezing past on their way down. Checking out the brass nameplates next to each door as he walked, it didn't take long to find the room quirkily dubbed the Dashiell Hammett. In honor of the building's former owner, each room was named after a famous writer or poet. Tomorrow morning's class would be in the Octavia E. Butler, on the second floor. He'd passed the room on the way up and caught a glimpse—it was filled with long, cushy couches and comfortable-looking chairs, with multiple coffee tables scattered throughout. The difference between that room and this was striking.

Pausing in the doorway, Gil took in the long, curved tables and wooden chairs that created a half circle of rows that fanned out from a lecturer's podium, partially filled with students either chatting in quiet voices or setting up their laptops. Finding an open seat at the end of the second row back, he drew out his own laptop again, and was setting his phone on silent when a flash of red in the doorway made him glance up.

There she was, stalled out halfway across the room, fingers clenched around the strap of the backpack she'd been swinging off her shoulder.

Gil offered her a crooked grin and patted the empty chair next to him. She stared at him for a moment, her expression inscrutable. Then her shoulders dropped, the strain of her muscles loosening a fraction, and she moved to his side. Sitting down, she lined up her own laptop and phone on the space in front of her with precise movements, then turned to Gil with raised eyebrows.

"All right, spill."

"Spill what?" He held back a laugh as Anne's eyes narrowed predictably at his innocent question.

"*What* are you doing here, of all places? Are you stalking me, Gilbert Blythe? Because honestly, this is weird." Her fingers drummed on the Formica table surface as she stared him down.

Now he did laugh, holding up both hands, palms out. "I'm not, I swear. I won't lie, I knew you went here when I transferred in, but that isn't why I'm here. Redmond had the closest curriculum to Berkeley. I won't have to make up credits like I would at NYU. Plus, I liked the vibe here."

"Marilla calls it artsy-fartsy." She sent him a little grin.

"Marilla's a national treasure."

"She really is," Anne agreed. "But why didn't you tell me at the bar that you'd be here?"

Because he wanted this excuse to talk to her again didn't seem like a thing he should say out loud, Gil shrugged instead. At least with age came the ability to filter from brain to mouth, as opposed to that humiliating time he'd blurted out an awkward invitation to homecoming in front of half their grade. Which she turned down with extreme prejudice.

"I guess I forgot." Weak, but he was sticking to it.

She sent him a flat look that projected skepticism as loudly as any words could have, but didn't challenge him. The professor came in then, cutting off any chance to continue their conversation. But Gil couldn't help stealing sideways glances at her occasionally, an odd sense of déjà vu hitting him at the familiar way she flicked her hair over her shoulder with impatience when it would obscure her vision. Once, he looked over to find her looking back, gray eyes meeting his for a moment before flicking away again. The faint red that crept up her neck after was fascinating.

When the class ended, Gil lingered, slowly packing up as Anne exchanged hugs and laughter with a few classmates she

hadn't seen since last semester. He had about two hours until the next class, it wasn't worth heading home in the mean-
while. Feeling the drag of waking too early after a restless night,
he would cheerfully kill someone for a cup of coffee. Maybe if
Anne was also free, they could catch up without having to shout
over the relentless thump of bass or dodging drunks.

Just when he was about to give up, feeling foolish as he shifted
some books around for the third time, Anne returned to scoop
her belongings into her backpack. She twisted her hair up into
a massive bun and secured it with a thick elastic band, heavy
strands slipping free almost immediately.

Shouldering her bag, she glanced sideways at him. "Heading
out?"

"Yup."

He'd said "yup." God, kill him now. He was twenty-four.
Twenty-four.

In silence, they made their way down the stairs and across
the lobby; the wave of mid-morning heat hit as they stepped out
the front door in a way that Gil knew would have him sweating
within a few minutes. Stopping on the sidewalk at the bottom
of the short set of brick stairs, they shifted to the side to avoid
being bumped into by the steady stream of people going in and
out of the building.

Anne lifted her hand to shade her eyes, squinting a little.
"What's next for you?"

"Educational law," Gil said, already thinking about dropping
it. He'd still have the credits without it, and it was drier than
overcooked chicken.

"Sounds fun." She wasn't successful at hiding her amusement, although he wasn't convinced she'd been trying all that hard.

"Oh, so much, you can't imagine." He glanced at the time on his phone. "I've got about an hour and a half until I have to be at the business building, and I'm in desperate need of caffeine. What do you have? Want to grab something?"

"Sure. I actually don't have another class today." Anne crossed the street, the side shadowed by large, leafy trees, he was relieved to note. "This year is a much lighter course load, just a few classes each semester. I pushed hard the first two years so that I wouldn't feel overwhelmed when it came time to work on my thesis."

Pushing open the door of a small coffee shop not far from the Writers House, she hitched one shoulder up in a half shrug, and joined the line that stretched almost to the door. "I know myself—I get a little obsessive. I didn't want my other grades to suffer because I'm giving most of my attention to my thesis."

Gil wisely refrained from reminding Anne he knew exactly how laser-focused she could get when she wanted to hit her goals. They were doing surprisingly well; it was actually sort of nice not to fight for once. So instead, he made light conversation as they waited for their orders. Squeezing into a small table near the front window, Gil unwrapped the oversized muffin he'd ordered and broke it in half, offering her one side. Despite her insistence she wasn't hungry when ordering her drink, she took it with a wry smile.

Breathing in the sweet smell of blueberries, she made a little humming noise of pleasure, then laughed as she took a bite and had to scramble to catch the muffin as it fell apart. Watching her pinch together the pile of crumbs on her napkin with amusement, Gil solved the problem by breaking his up and eating it in three big bites. Anne rolled her eyes at the way his half of the muffin disappeared in under a minute.

"I didn't think I needed this until I smelled it, so thank you," she said. "I meant to eat breakfast, but of course I was running late, and the fastest thing was a banana. Which didn't last as long as I thought it would."

"I'm not a fan of bananas. They're so . . . " Gil shrugged. "Bland, I guess."

"Did you know that the bananas we eat today aren't the same bananas they used to eat at the turn of the last century? There was a fungus outbreak and it wiped out a whole variety of bananas that used to be bigger and more flavorful." Anne popped the last of her muffin into her mouth, holding up one finger as she chewed. Trying not to grin around his cup of coffee, Gil took a sip while she swallowed, then brushed the crumbs off her hands neatly. "So, scientists developed the banana we eat today by *cloning it*, of all things. But now there's *another* fungus threatening the new bananas, so who knows what they'll do next. Probably create some sort of Frankenstein banana monster in a lab somewhere."

"Your love of random, weird facts hasn't faded any, I see."

"Hey, that was a Quiz Bowl question! I do like weird, random facts, though," Anne admitted, as she crumpled up her napkin and threw it across the table. She just laughed when he caught it before it hit him in the face. "Did you know that most people associate the woolly mammoth with prehistoric times, but in reality, they were still alive when Egyptians started building their pyramids? And in that vein, Cleopatra's reign is closer in time to the invention of the modern car than it was to the building of the Pyramids of Giza?"

"Did you know that elephants have ten-pound brains and can track up to thirty members of their herd at one time?"

"Did you know that usually siblings share about fifty percent DNA, but if you have an identical twin, you share one hundred percent DNA, which means instead of yours and your twin's children sharing twelve percent of their DNA, as with typical cousins, they will share twenty-five percent, which makes them closer to half-siblings?"

Gil sat for a moment, then shook his head. "Nope, that one hurts my head, I'm leaving it alone. Did you know if you drove your car straight up into the sky at sixty miles per hour, it would only take one hour to get to space?"

"Obviously," Anne said in an obnoxious voice that he remembered fondly. "Did you know that a quarter of all your bones are in your feet?"

"And I think I've broken every single one over my years of playing soccer when I was a kid." Gil laughed. "Do you seriously remember all this from the Quiz Bowl sheets? Because I'm lucky if I remember what I ate yesterday for lunch."

"Not *all* of it." A light flush colored her cheeks. "I read that one somewhere just last year, actually."

Moments like this were why Gil had a hard time killing his

fixation on Anne. Sure, she was beautiful, with hair he wanted to bury his hands in, and a soft pink mouth he wanted to start kissing and never stop. If that was all, he could have moved on without difficulty. Purely physical attraction felt shallow to him and had always been easy enough to dismiss. But her quirky, offbeat intelligence, and how *funny* she was, kept him coming back long after he should have admitted defeat.

"So . . . how's your dad doing?" Gray eyes studied him, serious again, a softer look in them than he was used to being turned on him.

Gil's stomach twisted a little, remembering how pale and quiet his father had been when he had stayed at his parents' the week before he moved in with Fred. "Hanging in. You know him; when he sets a goal, he refuses to back down. And he's decided he's going to beat cancer. I'm not sure that's the way it works"—he knew his smile was more bitter than he'd meant for it to be, but the idea of losing the man who helped him catch his first fish and taught him how to make pancakes was gutting— "But everyone says a fighting, positive attitude is good, for his mental and emotional health, if nothing else. The doctors are hopeful, though. That helps too. Obviously."

"How are *you* holding up?"

"Me? I'm fine. I'm not the one with cancer," he scoffed, crumpling his empty cup with a tight fist. Why did everyone keep asking that? He was *fine*.

Even if some days he couldn't look sideways at the possibility of his dad dying from this, way too young, without feeling like there was a pile of bricks caving his chest in.

Anne didn't look like she quite believed him, but dropped the subject, clearly recognizing he was done talking about it. Clearing his throat, Gil reached for his backpack, sweeping up his trash in one hand. The cheerful mood had been broken. He didn't want to leave things on this note, but he didn't feel like talking anymore.

"Sorry, but I really do need to get to my next class." To his relief, Anne didn't look annoyed at his sudden ending to their coffee break. She followed him out to the sidewalk, pausing as he stopped and pulled out his phone. "Listen, do you want to exchange numbers? Seeing as we're in the same class and all. Makes it easier if either of us gets stuck on something and needs to hash it out."

"Oh. Um . . . sure." For the first time since they'd left Writers House, Anne looked wary again. But she pulled out her phone anyway, fiddling with it for a moment before waving her hand without looking up. "Okay, go ahead."

As he recited his number, he wondered at the way her mood had cooled by several degrees at his request, her fingers stiff as she sent a text off to his phone. Absently, he saved her number, contemplating the sudden change. It happened at the bar too, when he'd put his hand on her back, trying to use his own body to block the crowd from jostling her on their way out the door. He could understand that, he probably shouldn't have touched her without asking first. It had been instinctive, even though he knew she was perfectly capable of taking care of herself, and always had been.

Still. This felt like something different.

Putting the puzzle of Anne's abrupt turnabout in the back of his mind, to pull out later and pick apart, Gil ignored the distant look in her eyes and sent her a warm smile. "This was nice. Thanks for keeping me company."

She thawed a little at his casual tone, another tidbit he filed away, and offered him a half smile back. "Sure. If we don't have any other classes together sooner, I'll see you next Monday."

They parted then, heading off in different directions.

If Gil paused at the intersection to watch until the flash of copper curls was swallowed by the afternoon crowds, well, that was his business.

Chapter 7

Anne sat in one of the chairs outside Dr. Lintford's office, trying to balance her planner across her knees while hunched over and scrolling through the phone calendar for the upcoming guest lecture dates for her class on the exploration of eighteenth-century writing culture, in an effort to distract herself from a case of jittery nerves. The class promised to be fascinating, but it was hard to get excited about the course offerings when her extensive list of thesis project ideas kept running in the back of her mind.

This was it, the moment she and her mentor put together a plan for the most important project of her school career. It would be the make-or-break component of her degree. If she messed this up, the last two years would be for nothing.

The sound of footsteps echoing down the hall had her looking up, the sight of Gil had her narrowing her eyes. It had been a week of bumping knees every time she shifted in her seat, of sideways grins when one of the professors made a terrible joke, and of being distressingly conscious of the summer humidity creating a halo of frizzy, short curls that escaped from her ponytail no matter how tightly she bound it. A week of Gil in her way at every turn on campus. It should have been aggravating that after six years, he'd suddenly turned up again and disrupted her neat, ordered life. But for some reason, it wasn't. Instead, Anne found herself smiling back at him with a growing sense of . . . *fondness.*

It was enough to make her snippy on principle alone.

She stifled a sigh as he dropped into the seat next to her, despite the other three chairs lining the wall. He didn't say anything, just pulled out his own phone and began reading what appeared to be a news article. Not that she was looking over his shoulder. Setting her jaw, Anne turned her attention back to the planner. Her appointment with Dr. Lintford had come and gone ten minutes earlier, but she'd learned that some professors operated on what she called doctor's office hours. That's to say they were constantly inundated with work and students, and ran on their own private timetable. There was nothing for it, this wasn't a meeting she could skip, so she just kept filling in her semester's schedule, and tried to ignore the way Gil's bicep brushed her arm every time he shifted in his seat.

But after the third time it happened in as many minutes, Anne snapped her planner closed and turned to him, exasperated. "Did you have too much caffeine today? You're positively *twitchy.*"

"Sorry," he said, easily. "Didn't manage to get a run in this morning. Meds don't do everything; I've learned focus comes a lot easier if I cut my energy with regular exercise."

"Ew, running. I only do that if someone's chasing me."

"Har, har, never heard that before."

Anne sent him a tiny grin. She wasn't against exercising but was much more inclined to spend her free time lying on the lawn in Washington Square Park with a book as opposed to running the paths. It was good people-watching, especially when the dogwoods were blooming.

"Are you here to see Dr. Lintford?" she asked, glancing at her phone again. The professor was now fifteen minutes behind, and she was in danger of missing the window to grab food before her afternoon class.

"Yeah. Ten-thirty appointment, but I guess he's running late."

Ten-thirty appointment. That was *her* time.

Anne turned in her chair to face him. "I think either there's a scheduling problem or one of us got it wrong, because I'm here for a ten-thirty as well."

Before he could say anything, the door to Dr. Lintford's office opened. He ushered out a stressed-looking blond girl, reminding her to email if she needed to discuss anything more, then turned to face Anne and Gil.

"Ah, good, you're both here. Sorry about the wait, come on in."

Anne blinked as he gestured to them in welcome before disappearing into his office. Surely, he couldn't mean both of them, but Gil was already up and following the professor. Caught off guard by the development, she hastily shoved her planner into the backpack at her feet and joined them.

Taking the second of two guest chairs in front of Dr. Lintford's desk, Anne looked around the small, windowless office. Packed bookshelves crowded the walls, only broken by the occasional photo of the professor with one famous writer or another, and his multiple, framed degrees. There was an artistic interpretation of a sepia-toned world globe on a brass stand squeezed into one corner that she'd love to get a closer look at. A line of colorful, blown-glass paperweights marched across the desk, next to an expensive-looking gold pen perched in its holder. The combination should have been comforting for Anne, all the things she enjoyed best, but the low ceiling and lack of natural light gave the office an oppressive air. It didn't help that sitting this close to the older man made his heavy hand with the cologne a bit overwhelming.

Not to mention that the assessing glint in the professor's eye when he turned his attention to her made Anne want to shift in her chair with discomfort. She controlled the urge, placing her backpack on the floor before she sat on the edge of the seat and folded her hands in her lap. Determined not to let her nerves show, she squeezed her fingers together tightly, pressing them into her lap.

In contrast, Gil leaned back in his chair and crossed one ankle over his knee, looking as if he didn't have a care in the world. She didn't understand how he was so relaxed. She felt like she was going to leap out of her skin.

"All right, let's see. As you both know, I'm Kenneth Lintford, and will be your thesis departmental liaison for the year." Dr. Lintford shuffled some papers in a stack on his desk, then pulled out two thin folders. He flicked them open, one after another, scanning whatever was inside as if to familiarize himself with it. After several agonizingly long seconds, he looked up again, running one hand over his beard thoughtfully. "Anne Shirley and Gilbert Blythe. How interesting you grew up together and both wound up here. Serendipitous, you might say."

A frisson of wariness rippled through Anne. She *had* to excel in this for both her career prospects and her own peace of mind. Lumping her in with Gil just because they both came from Avonlea wasn't exactly going to give her a chance to shine.

"I'd asked everyone earlier in the week to come prepared to their meetings with several ideas for their project, so I hope you each brought a list. My time is valuable, and I won't waste it on brainstorming; this is a master's degree, not a middle school science fair," he continued. "When the first semester is at a close, I will start to evaluate progress on your project and make suggestions as necessary. But again, I'll stress, this is a student-driven project, a sort of a test-drive for the post-graduation real world, if you will."

"Excuse me," Anne broke in, her brain still stuck on one point. "Did you say 'project,' as in singular? As in together?"

Dr. Lintford frowned at the interruption but answered her. "Yes. As I've stated, my time is valuable. I wasn't expecting a last-minute transfer, so space in my mentorship program is a bit on the tight side." He tapped the folders in front of him with one finger. "I assumed, as two grown adults in an M.Ed. program, you could manage to successfully work on one project together. Was I wrong?"

By the tightness in his voice, it was clear the professor disliked being questioned. Anne bit back her instinctive urge to rise up in the face of such disdain. His approval was too important to alienate him this early in the year. Or at all.

"Not a problem for me," Gil answered calmly, and she felt the side of his foot press against hers in warning.

Instead of stomping on his toes, she dredged up a smile for their mentor. "Perfectly fine."

Dr. Lintford eyed her for another moment, then turned his attention to his open laptop and tapped a few keys before gesturing to them. "All right. Go ahead and tell what you've each come up with and we can discuss it, and hopefully get this settled before you walk out of here today. Mind the time, however, I've got several more appointments this morning."

A bit unfair considering how delayed their own meeting was, but Anne only drew in a deep breath and pulled out her own laptop as Gil started to go over his ideas. This was going to be a trying year, between being tied to him on a project she'd had so many plans for and working with Dr. Lintford. The man strongly reminded her of Mr. Philips and not in any sort of favorable way. But it was what it was, and she'd just have to make the best of it. Dr. Lintford was right—they were at the top of their class and full-grown adults. Surely, they could manage to successfully work together on this one thing.

Besides, things were different between her and Gil now. Time and space had done them well, the animosity of their younger years mellowed. For the most part. She'd just have to make sure they didn't backslide into sniping and one-upmanship. Since she'd really only have to see him in class until they started working on their thesis project, it shouldn't be that hard to keep things professional.

Of course, she should have known Gil wouldn't cooperate with that plan any more than he'd ever done at *any time* in her life. Because after he'd somehow managed to finagle her into telling him where she worked, he seemed to be constantly underfoot.

One of the biggest perks of working in the bookstore was that it was only a short walk from her apartment, tucked away in the heart of Hell's Kitchen on Forty-fifth and Tenth. The Lazy Lion Bookstore wasn't trendy, or even particularly pretty, but it had been a neighborhood staple for fifty years and had a steady stream of loyal customers. Which was great, because it meant the owners could afford to pay her enough to make rent every month, and also eat regularly. But sometimes she forgot what it was like to just stop and breathe. It turned out, shockingly, that working forty hours a week while going to grad school full-time was *exhausting*.

Gil's inexplicable decision to make the Lion his second home by the end of the week, creating a big snag in her plans to avoid him outside of their designated project collaboration sessions, didn't make things easier.

"You know this isn't actually a public workspace, right?" Anne asked as she shelved a couple of books with possibly more enthusiasm than needed. Gil glanced up from where he was working at the small wooden table shoved up against the picture window at the front of the shop. His gaze followed her as she crouched down to find space for the newest installation of a science fiction novel she'd tried, and failed, to muddle through. Considering how quickly they sold copies, however, it seemed to be a singular problem.

"There's free wifi, cheap coffee, and a table with decent light. Not to mention the staff is easy on the eyes. Seems pretty ideal to me." From her viewpoint, she could see him tip his chair back on two legs and nearly gave into the temptation to kick it out from under him.

"Easy on the eyes." Anne rose, rolling her own eyes. "Am I supposed to be flattered?"

"Bold of you to assume I was talking about you. Maybe I have a thing for octogenarians with a permanent scowl."

Despite herself, she snorted, glancing over her shoulder to where the other bookseller on duty was standing at the register. Ken was eternally grouchy, and while she didn't think he was quite into his eighties, he had been working there as long as anyone could remember. Anne had been an employee for most of the last two years and he still referred to her as the "new kid," and not in a fond way.

She turned back to Gil, eyeing the pile of books at his elbow. "Are you actually buying any of those or am I just going to be reshelving them all later?"

He shrugged, a lazy movement that drew her gaze to the way his T-shirt clung to muscular shoulders. How he kept in shape when he seemed to spend all his time split between classes and the Lion, she didn't know. Annoying. Biting back a sigh, Anne grabbed the handle of the book cart and pushed it over to the next aisle. The shop was quiet, the sound of traffic and pedestrians beyond the glass window muffled, the loudest sounds the air conditioner clicking on and Gil tapping away on his laptop. She lost herself in the task of shelving books, occasionally pulling down a title that caught her interest and reading the back copy. Her collection was already a bit out of control, but the call of a new book was irresistible. Engrossed in the first page of a romance novel, she jumped as Gil spoke from behind her.

"Excuse me, miss, I'm looking for a book. Maybe you can help me."

Pressing the book she was holding against her chest, trying to quiet the sudden thump of her heart, Anne turned to glare at him. A man his size should *not* be able to move so quietly.

"Not enough to come in and pester me at my job, now you're actively trying to kill me?" she said, willing the heat in her cheeks away. Having skin as pale as hers was a trial at times, especially when she was embarrassed. Or angry. Or . . . She cleared her throat, fingers clenching and unclenching on the soft cover of the book. This constant awareness of him, and the way she couldn't seem to turn it off, was becoming quite inconvenient.

"Sorry, I thought you heard me."

She didn't believe *that* for a minute, her theory supported by the little grin that flirted at the edges of his mouth.

"Moving on from your near brush with death . . . I really was wondering if you can help me find this book. Promise I'll buy it this time." He brandished the page pulled up on his phone browser at her.

Grateful for something to focus on other than how the green T-shirt he was wearing made his eyes look warm and golden like honey (and didn't that overused cliché make her want to smack herself in the forehead), Anne considered the title of the book. She didn't recognize it, but that wasn't unexpected. The bookstore housed a surprisingly high volume of items for such a small shop. Skirting around Gil, she headed to the old computer at the front counter. Ken gave her a dark look as she squeezed past where he was tagging a new shipment of novels, but she ignored it, used to his suspicions she was somehow shirking her bookseller duties. Stepping up to the counter to rest his forearms on the worn wood, Gil leaned forward, craning his head to watch the screen as she searched the database. Which put him much too far into her personal space for comfort.

She tapped the down arrow rapidly with one hand, pressing the other one to his forehead and pushing him back to his side, trying not to smile when he made a noise of protest.

"We don't have that one," she said, after a minute. "But I can order it, if you want."

"How long will it take?"

"Maybe a week."

Gil tucked his phone into his back pocket. "Yeah, okay, that's fine."

Pulling up the digital order form, Anne squashed the urge to ask him why he didn't just order it online. It would definitely be faster. But Ken was nearly falling over in an effort to eavesdrop on their conversation, so she wasn't about to sabotage a sale and give him a reason to complain about her again. Not after the incident with the pastrami sandwich.

After hitting *send,* Anne turned back to where Gil was idly flicking through the small display of New York City guidebooks they kept in case any tourists wandered into the Lion on their way to some new trendy restaurant down the block that they'd read about in the *Times* food section. She didn't have the heart to tell them they'd probably have more luck in Tribeca or Soho.

Searching for familiar ground, she pulled her own phone out and pulled up the calendar. "When are we meeting up to talk about the thesis project? I still don't understand why Lintford would pair us on this. I've never heard of a joint thesis. It seems counterproductive; how will he know we each put in an equal amount of work?"

"Are you worrying I won't hold up my end of the project?" Gil didn't look offended by her bluntness, just curious. "I'd like to think by now you know I don't work like that."

"No, I do," she conceded. "Still, it's a strange arrangement."

He shrugged. "But it's one we have to work with, so let's figure it out. I'm free tomorrow afternoon."

"Tomorrow's no good for me, I'm the TA for Professor Kerry's Shakespeare Lit class."

"Yikes."

"Hey, I like Shakespeare!" Anne protested with a laugh. Rude.

"He created some of my favorite words. 'Fathomless.' 'Reprieve.' 'Never-ending.' As in, 'it's fathomless to me that I get no reprieve from your never-ending presence in this bookstore.'"

"All right, all right, I know where I'm not welcome." He pushed away from the counter in mock indignation and headed back to his table. Once he'd packed up, he slung his messenger bag across his chest and headed for the door. One hand on the door handle, he paused. "You free Friday night?"

Anne blinked at him, brain stalling out. Was he asking her out?

"Friday night?"

"To make a final decision on the project topic, divvy up research?" Gil's expression was bland, but she got the feeling he was laughing inside at her.

"Oh." Well, that was embarrassing. "Um. Yes, my weekend nights are usually free." Oh God, did she just admit to having no life to speak of? She hastily added, "I work morning shifts here, the store opens at eight. I have to be here early to neaten up and dust. That sort of thing."

With effort, Anne snapped her mouth closed, cutting off the mortifying, directionless babbling spilling out.

With a nod too solemn to be genuine, Gil hauled the door open. "Great. See you at the library at seven? There's a study space in the back of the fiction section I found that never seems to be occupied."

"It's a date," Anne said, unthinkingly.

"Perfect. See you then."

By the time her words registered, the door was closing on Gil's back. With a groan, she leaned forward and thumped her forehead onto the wood counter. *Ow.*

"If you're done with the dramatics, there are a few dozen new books waiting to be shelved." Ken's tart voice piped up from the right of her. With a sigh, Anne straightened, managing not to bobble the box the older man shoved into her arms.

Chapter 8

It occurred to her she might have miscalculated how much exposure to Gil's annoyingly broad shoulders she could handle as she made her way through the library stacks that Friday night to where he sat, his half of the table already strewn with several books, a laptop, and what looked like a contraband bag of trail mix. Her traitorous pulse stuttered when he smiled wide enough for his dimple to make an appearance.

It smoothed out again when she sat down and pulled her things out, the ritual of placing everything just so, within reach, perfectly ordered, as calming as a chamomile bath. Also dampening the wild attraction to Gil was the realization that he still hadn't managed to shake some of his bad habits from high school. She watched with morbid fascination as he tipped his chair onto its back two legs, as he did habitually, chewing on the end of his pen.

"Okay, so what do you have on your list?"

Once again Anne could only hope to see the day he lost his fight with gravity. She absolutely would say she *had* warned him.

"First, ugh, stop doing that. It's gross. And unhygienic." Ignoring the way he tossed the pen back on the table with a roll of his eyes, Anne folded her hands on her day planner and leaned forward. "I read over the ideas in your email, and then mine again, and honestly? I think the one that appeals to me the most was your number three."

Gil lit up, nodding. "After-school programs and the role they play in creating healthier, happier students? That's my favorite as well."

"Perfect. That was easy," Anne said, making a note in her planner.

"Now I'm nervous, because that was easy. Painless, even." Gil smiled at her over the edge of his laptop screen, eyes crinkling at the corners, and wasn't that annoyingly charming? Eye crinkles. Of all the things her libido decided to find attractive in that moment. What kind of word was "crinkle" anyway? It didn't sound sexy at all, and yet.

"Anne? Earth to Anne?"

She blinked to find Gil's sexy eye crinkles were out in full force, along with his cute dimple, as he slowly waved a hand in front of her face. *Ugh.* She was failing at this "be cool and unaffected" thing.

"Sorry. I was just thinking," she spoke quickly, dropping her gaze to her planner, "what about offering a creative writing after-school program? It's a skill that gets overlooked too often in English classes, and it's one we're both very qualified to teach. Also, I think we should stick to middle school–aged kids. Younger, and it's closer to an after-school camp. Any older and we'll probably spend most of our time convincing them we *are* old enough to teach."

"Solid point."

"Even if the main focus is on the writing part of creative writing, I still think we need to include at least two assigned books. As they read through them, we can break down what works and what doesn't. Talk out themes, structure, characters . . . it could give them a little insight into their own writing project." Anne paused, thinking. "It'd be easier to catch, and keep, their attention with books that were made into a movie we can watch afterward. That gives them something fun to work toward."

She waited while Gil studied the ceiling for a long moment, chewing on that damn pen again. Dropping back onto all four chair legs, he pulled his laptop close. "Not a bad idea. If we can make the program fun, or at least interesting, there's a better chance they might retain the information."

While he typed, she eyed the short stack of books at his elbow, reaching across to pull the nearest one close. Furrowing her brow, she flipped through the first chapter, skimming a couple paragraphs that caught her interest.

Gil shrugged when she raised her eyebrows upon realizing she was holding a book on child psychology. "I figured, if we're going to be working with kids, especially middle school kids, we probably don't want to walk in unprepared. I took a class at Berkeley, but that was years ago, so I figured it wouldn't hurt to brush up."

"Okay. And same. I think it was maybe sophomore year, but since it wasn't my focus, I never took anything beyond the base class," Anne said slowly, working his reasoning out. She closed the book, turned it over, and studied the back copy. "'Juvenile psychology and therapy techniques.' Feels a little like overkill for a supplementary, after-school writing program."

"Do you remember what *we* were like in eighth grade? Complete dicks."

"Speak for yourself, I was a delight." She ignored his loud snort. "But . . . good point."

Puberty was like precariously negotiating a twisted path through a minefield of mood swings and social disasters waiting to happen. She wouldn't go back to being a teenager again for *any* amount of money.

They spent the next hour negotiating the structure of the yearlong program, sometimes arguing over specifics, such as which books they planned to assign the kids, which movies they'd like to add in for fun content, and which schools to prioritize in contacting to host the program. Thankfully they both agreed the Herschel Public School for the Arts, Brooklyn, was the top choice for both of them. It was a magnet school, with a curriculum split nearly evenly between academics and the arts. The only way to be accepted for the magnet program itself was by completion of a rigorous application and a demonstration of their chosen art medium, then a lottery; their student body drew kids from all over the borough.

The school had experienced some unfortunate budget cuts over the last few years, however, and from what information

Anne and Gil were able to unearth, an after-school program like theirs would fit neatly into those underfunded areas.

The longer they worked, the more excited Anne became. She'd done some tutoring over her summer breaks from college, back in Avonlea, but nothing on this scale. The project was going to be as much a mentorship program as it was an extra creative writing class. It was firmly in the overlapping middle of her Venn diagram of interests, and she was eager to really get going. She and Gil worked up a list of schools besides Herschel to contact for appointments to talk about their idea; teaching grants to research; and the materials they'd need to price, then split those costs down the middle.

A sense of optimism buoyed her as she left the library an hour later. They'd come up with a good plan and a workable time schedule, and she'd only lost her train of thought two times while looking at him. He'd been wearing another one of the T-shirts that hugged his shoulders and chest, this one a mossy green that only served to highlight the golden flecks in his eyes. All in all, Anne was proud of herself for only being distracted twice. It was a relief to know she was building up a resistance to Gil again. Soon she wouldn't even wonder if his hair would be as soft to the touch as it looked, if his stomach was as flat as it looked through those T-shirts, or if he was a cuddler, after, well . . . *after.*

Determined to put Gil out of her mind, Anne took a chance on the subway's spotty wifi on her ride home and called Marilla's cell. The older woman would be just completing her nightly routine of reviewing sales and profit margins, that sort of thing.

She'd tried to instruct Anne more than once over her high
school years, hoping to train her as a sort of assistant, but for
all Anne's academic achievements, math was the subject she'd
liked least. Finally, the older woman had thrown her hands in
the air and relegated Anne to filing. It had been a bit of a mind-
less task, but that had just given her more time to plot which-
ever story she'd been working on at the moment.

On the third ring, Marilla picked up. "Anne-girl. How did
you know I was thinking of you?"

"Great minds and all that," Anne replied, smiling. She tucked
her backpack farther under the seat with her heels, then crossed
her ankles, relaxing on the bench. Thankfully the subway wasn't
elbow to elbow at this time of night and she had the short row of
seats to herself. "How are you?"

"Same as always. Good."

"Don't take this the wrong way, but you sound tired."

"Well, it's been a long few days. There was a hiccup with payroll. Nothing too disastrous, but it took some untangling with
the bank to get the funds transferred in so I could get payroll
in on time for next Friday." There was a moment of static as the
train moved through a tunnel. "—and Ruby cut her hours to
part-time, so now Matthew has to find someone to replace her.
It's a bit of a mess at the moment, but I'm sure it'll be sorted
soon enough."

Picking up enough of what she'd missed to follow the thread,
Anne frowned. Although Marilla insisted she and Matthew
were just as capable of running their business now as they were
in their twenties, Anne couldn't help but worry that they carried

too much on their shoulders now that she wasn't there to share the load. She made a quick decision in the moment to get back home for a visit soon, mentally flipping through the autumnal events Green Gables hosted every year. It shocked her to realize how close to the winery's annual Autumn Jubilee they were.

"I'm on the roster for the Jubilee, right? We can talk more about this then," she said. "I'll come home Thursday and stay until Sunday evening. I don't have classes on Fridays anyway."

"You don't have to do that. I know this year is a busy one, Anne-girl. We can get on fine without taking you away from your studies."

"I know I don't *have* to, but I want to do it. It's tradition, Marilla. And I'll show up whether you add me or not, so you might as well just do it." The announcement for Anne's stop drowned out her voice for a moment, and she pulled on her backpack, then moved to hang on to the pole closest to the doors. "I miss you all."

The smile in the older woman's voice was clear, even though her voice was gruff. "We miss you too. If you think it's going to be a conflict, don't hesitate to cancel . . . but I'll be glad to see you again. Seems like August was forever ago."

October at Green Gables was more beautiful than anywhere else in the world, in Anne's opinion, and she was glad she wouldn't miss it this year. Or the apple cider doughnuts Marilla's longtime, close friend Rachel Lynde only made this time of year, steaming and rolled in sugar and spices. Just the thought of them made Anne wish she had more than store-bought lasagna waiting for her in the freezer.

"On the other hand, I can't believe I'm halfway through the semester already," Anne said. The train rolled to a stop, the doors whooshing open, and she made her way quickly across the platform and up the stairs. The autumn evening air was a relief after the stale, warm atmosphere in the subway stop. "Oh! I haven't even had a moment to tell you. Remember I said that Gil had moved to the city and transferred into Redmond?"

"How could I forget," Marilla said dryly.

"Hey." Anne laughed, remembering her long, annoyed series of texts about his sudden resurfacing directly into the middle of her life again. She had omitted the bit about how the brief touch of Gil's hand on her lower back made her entire body tingle. "This might sound weird, considering, but we're actually getting along fairly well now. Which is good, because get this: Dr. Lintford paired us together on a thesis project."

"Oh Lord."

"I know, right? I'd have thought by now we'd have murdered each other, but it's working. So far, anyway. We're only a quarter of the way through the year. There's still time for homicide."

Marilla laughed, then there was a pause so long that Anne thought for a moment they'd been disconnected. The older woman cleared her throat, sounding uncharacteristically hesitant as she spoke. "I also have something I meant to tell you last time we spoke. Rachel is moving in."

Another pause.

"With me."

"Oh," Anne said, momentarily caught off guard. She'd suspected over the years that Rachel and Marilla were more than just friends, even close friends, but they were so circumspect it was difficult to know for sure. Anne had figured if there was anything to tell, that Marilla would let her know in her own time. She'd always been a very private person with her emotions. Anne wouldn't dream of forcing her to share something like this before she was ready.

Marilla continued, "I know you and Rachel didn't get off to the best start, but things have settled since, haven't they?"

This made Anne chuckle, remembering how it had taken a few years after she arrived at Green Gables to get used to Rachel's unflinching commitment to the truth, even if it wasn't very sensitive at times. But that was a long time ago, and she'd become genuinely affectionate of the older woman since.

"No, of course. We're fine now. She's lovely . . . and I'm really happy for you," Anne hastily reassured Marilla. "I just didn't realize things were moving this way, but actually, I think this is going to be really good for both of you. When is she moving in? Is she selling the house? Are her sons coming into town to help pack up? I haven't seen them in *forever*—what are they up to now?"

They talked for a few more moments, Marilla filling her in on the details and assuring her that in no way was anyone going to allow Matthew to move Rachel's heavy, antique furniture, Anne only saying her goodbyes as she unlocked the door to the apartment. It had been good to catch up; she wasn't the best at remembering to stay in touch regularly. Which reminded her she probably owed Jane a call as well. She tried to see her old childhood friend whenever she was home, but it seemed that time passed so quickly when Anne was away from Green Gables. Each year, when she went back to Avonlea, it felt like the space between her and Jane was just a little bit wider.

It was a shame that people had to grow up, and move on, and drift apart.

Calculating how much work she had ahead of her over the weekend, Anne passed through the kitchen just long enough to heat up her subpar lasagna and give Phil a loud, smacking kiss on the cheek that had the other girl squealing and rubbing at the damp spot. Settling on her bed, balancing her food on one folded knee and her textbook on the other, Anne spent the next two hours buried in coursework. When she finally lifted her head, she was shocked to see it was after midnight. Cracking her stiff neck, she set aside her work, pleased with the progress she'd made. That was a big dent to give her a bit of breathing room over the next few days.

The quick shower she took relaxed the last of her sore muscles, tensed from spending hours hunched over her laptop. Toweling her hair quickly, she braided it with deft fingers, and threw on a knee-length, old T-shirt from one of the events at Green Gables years ago. Finally climbing into bed was like heaven, the thick comforter a soothing weight as the fan perched on the edge of her desk blew cool air across the room.

Her mind grew heavy, thoughts drifting.

For the most part, she loved her life. She had the girls, Marilla and Matthew, school, and the bookstore. Dating wasn't really a priority right now, and that was fine. There was an order to things, a routine that Anne was content with. *Had* been content with, until Gil came back and complicated her life, as he was wont to do. She wondered what the universe found so amusing about throwing the pair of them together again and again.

Maybe one day she'd figure it out.

Chapter 9

Pub night out! Sat, @ Kindred Spirits, 10pm. Bring Fred.

Amusement lifting one corner of his mouth, Gil read the text from Diana that had just come in, the vibration loud enough on the library study desk to have a girl halfway down the table from him glaring. He lifted his shoulders into a shrug, mouthing "sorry," before starting to pack up.

Bossy, D. How do you know I'm not already working the bar?

He kept one eye on the wide marble steps of the library he jogged down as he typed. It wasn't uncommon for students to slam directly into each other on campus, heads bent over their phones, but he tried not to do it himself. Nothing like trying to explain away a black eye from walking into a traffic post—Fred would never let him live it down.

Are you?

No. BTW, the shop's open until 12, but I can ask Fred if Lacey can close. Hit you up later.

He lasted another five minutes but paused just before ducking down the stairs to the subway, his self-preservation skills losing the battle against not being a slightly obsessed weirdo. As always.

Who else is going?

Whyyyyyy do you ask? HMMMMM??

What?

What.

YOU'RE MAKING ME GO INTO THE BAR I WORK AT ON MY NIGHT OFF, JUST TELL ME FFS.

Yikes, okay, calm your moobs. Prob not Phil, b/c night shift. A couple of my friends from Parsons. You, Fred, meeeeeeeee.

Fuck. She was going to make him ask. Somehow, Diana had always been able to look right through him and call him on his bullshit. Why he thought that would change just because he hadn't seen her in six years, he didn't know.

Anne too?

Yes, lover boy.

AM OFFENDED. Nice. And here I am, just trying to help and I
   get this, WOWWOWWOW.

I'm going now.

To daydream about a certain redhead?

I'm blocking you.

No, ur not, LOL.

I'm going to tell Fred you said your body's a temple and tats
   are gross.

Too late, already made appt to get my 1st one done. But he's
   welcome to worship at the temple of my body anytime.
   wiggles eyebrows

JFC, I'm def blocking you.

Love you too.

Bye, D. Go do some work or something. Gotta go before I miss the train.

Byyyyyyyyye.

After hearing Diana had asked for him by name, Fred was very much on board with the plan, secure in Lacey's competence in closing up shop. Gil tried not to think too much about the impending hangout over the week, burying himself in schoolwork. He and Anne didn't talk about it in class, or even while solidifying the proposal for Herschel; hopefully the school board would be interested. It was good, staying busy. Helped keep him out of his head. He really didn't have time to be messing around, getting all tangled up in feelings he probably shouldn't be having in the first place. The longer he forced himself to chill about it, the easier it got, until he was able to flash Anne a careless smile as he and Fred slid into the booth with everyone on Saturday night, and actually mean it.

His knee pressed against hers, the horseshoe-shaped seating a tight fit, and he was encouraged when she didn't shift away. "Hey. Sorry we're late, Fred had a guy come in at the last minute for a touch-up. Took longer than he'd thought."

"We've only been here maybe half an hour," Anne reassured him, then paused while he ordered a lager from Mia, one of the career waitresses who worked the weekend night shifts.

"You on tomorrow night?" she asked him quickly as she waved to acknowledge the guy two booths over calling to her.

"Yeah, five to close."

"Good." The older woman looked satisfied. "Tips are better with bartenders who know what the fuck they're doing. You got a good face for pulling in the extra cash too."

She said the sweetest things. If she wasn't married, and also extremely gay, he'd offer to run off with her in a minute. "Right back at you, beautiful."

Mia cackled and swatted him on the shoulder before moving off, and Gil looked back at Anne to find her chin propped in her palm, the curve of her slender fingers not quite covering her grin.

"What?"

"I didn't say anything."

"Not out loud, but you're definitely saying something inside that head of yours."

"I just thought it was cute," she admitted, gray eyes sparkling.

Cute. Great. "I can't help it if she's madly in love with me."

"Weird, because I'm pretty sure that was a pink, red, and white Pride flag pin on her apron."

"It is, and I'm always happy when a pretty girl notices, thank you." Mia winked one heavily mascaraed eye at Anne as she thumped down Gil and Fred's drinks. "This one here thinks a dimple and a tight pair of jeans makes a personality. Which, to be fair," she continued, to the table at large, "I might be into if he had the right equipment."

"The path of true love is never easy," Anne murmured as she leaned in close, the curve of her smile against the shell of Gil's ear making him want to shiver. She straightened away when

Mia left to check her other tables, resuming their conversation as if she'd never been interrupted. "So, I was thinking we should talk to Julie in Admin about a field trip next month, something fun that might inspire the kids to—"

"Stop," Gil groaned, holding up one hand. The last thing he wanted to do tonight was plan their thesis. It seemed like every time they were together for more than a minute, she was bringing it up, and he was tired of it being the only thing they talked about. "My brain needs a breather for a few hours."

"Yeah, no shop talk tonight!" Diana chimed in from across the table, using two thin dreads to tie the rest of her long hair back into a low ponytail. She turned to the two women next to her, a pair of transfer students from London whom she'd befriended at the beginning of the semester. "She's really fun when she lets loose but is also the most gigantic nerd I've ever met."

When Anne made a noise of protest, Diana just laughed and playfully stuck her tongue out at her best friend.

"Like this swot. Practically impossible to pull her arse out of a book once she gets going," said Perdita, the woman closest to Diana, the deep brown skin of her smooth face creasing into humor lines as she jerked her thumb at her girlfriend. Winnie just shook her head, sending the ends of her dreads dancing across her shoulders, like she'd heard this complaint a thousand times before.

Gil half listened to the swirling conversation as the night wore on, peppered with laughter, too aware of where he and Anne were touching. It felt like a line of fire, from his hip to his knee, where they were pressed together. It occurred to him at one point that there was enough space between her and Winnie that she didn't need to sit so close. Darting his eyes sideways, he felt a thrill go through him when he caught her looking at him. Gray eyes widened, then skipped away, as a light flush began to work its way up her neck. Unable to drag his gaze away, he watched as she lightly placed her hand on the side of her throat closest to him.

He bit his lip, wondering how she'd taste there, the soft hollow at the base of her throat, where her clavicle dipped. What sort of sound she'd make if he did press his mouth against that tempting bit of skin.

When Fred flicked his knee hard, Gil managed to tear his gaze from Anne, his friend raising his eyebrow silently. Which meant Gil was probably being more obvious than he wanted to be. Picking up his beer, he took a long swallow and tried to listen to Perdita and Diana complaining about one of that term's guest designers, who was apparently a huge fucking drama queen.

He was doing pretty good at staying focused on the conversation until a slender finger poked him in the ribs. Looking down, he found Anne's nose scrunched up, something that made him want to squish her cheeks between his hands and pepper her face with kisses.

"What?"

"Out," she said, giving him a little shove. "I have to pee."

Sliding from the booth obligingly, Gil held out a hand to help her to her feet, ignoring the exaggerated cooing from the rest of the table. Freckled face pink again, she took it, let him haul her up, and quickly disappeared into the crowd. He dropped back into his seat, reluctant to face the music, turning back to their friends with narrowed eyes.

"*Such* a gentleman." Diana batted her eyes.

"D, I swear to God—"

"Diana, let that poor boy alone, look at his face," Winnie interrupted with a laugh. "Although . . . it was pretty cute. Is this a new thing?"

Gil dragged a hand down his face, wondering if it was too late to transfer back to California. "It's not a thing at all."

Fred snorted. "And it sure isn't new."

"*It's not a thing.* It's just . . ." Gil waved his hands, growing irritated. Getting teased about his clearly transparent crush (like he was twelve again, it was humiliating) was starting to get old, fast. "It's nothing." Jerking to his feet, he threw an excuse over his shoulder as he strode off, knowing he was probably overreacting. But there was only so much a man could take when he'd been chasing the same girl half his life and getting nowhere, only for his friends to find it a source of amusement.

He bumped into Anne in the hallway outside the bathrooms, annoyance still riding him.

"Hey, everything okay?"

He made an effort to relax his scowl when she looked concerned. "Yeah, it's . . . nothing." Unable to smother the sharp bark of laughter that slipped out, Gil leaned against the graffitied wall, suddenly wondering what he was even doing there. A linebacker of a man lumbered down the hallway, forcing Anne to step closer to Gil to avoid being squashed, and he put one hand on her hip to steady her.

Eyes shadowed in the dim light, she turned her face up to his, lips parted as if she was about to say something, but nothing came out. The urge to trace the soft line of her cheekbones, and count the freckles scattered over her nose, had him lifting his hand halfway before he dropped it again, clenching it into a fist at his side. The noise from the pub was muffled in the hallway, their harsh mingled breathing the only sound.

Gil swayed forward, the pull of her irresistible.

The bathroom door banged closed like a shot, shattering the moment.

He blinked, pulling back as Anne flushed and looked away. The same large man pushed past them again, muttering an incoherent apology; as soon as he passed, she backed up a couple feet.

"I, um, I should get back to the table, so Diana doesn't ask me if I fell in in front of everyone. She's used that joke for years, but still thinks it's hilarious." Words tumbling over each other, almost too quick for Gil to decipher, Anne stubbornly kept her eyes on the end of the hallway, where it opened back up to the rest of the pub. "Should I tell them . . . ?" She waved one hand toward the bathroom.

"Tell them I'm not feeling good and went home," he said, suddenly tired of this complicated dance they'd been doing for over ten years. It wasn't untrue, he *wasn't* feeling great anymore, and kind of just wanted to bury himself in his bed for the next twelve hours.

Looking startled at his abrupt change in mood, Anne nodded. "Okay. Well. See you Tuesday, then."

Right. They were starting with the kids at Herschel on Tuesday, he'd forgotten. That was fine. It gave him two full days to get his head on right, then the buffer of twelve middle-schoolers between them.

"Yeah, okay. See you." Not waiting for her to say anything else, Gil brushed past her, pushing through the crowd, toward the exit.

He had two days to think about what he wanted, really wanted, and what he was going to do about it. Because this shit? The hot and cold, the push and pull? He couldn't do it anymore. Because his feelings this time around were more complicated than the need of a thirteen-year-old to get his crush to notice him or the youthful lust of a seventeen-year-old. Back then he would have settled for anything she'd give him. A smile, a kiss, a date.

Now he wanted as a man wanted, with the urge to take her apart with his hands and put her back together with the words he'd whisper into her hair, afterward. He wanted her to come home with him at the end of the night, and to have her full and complete concentration. He wanted everything she had to give—he was hungry for it.

But if he finally made a real move, there was the possibility of being rejected. Again. Or not being rejected, but having the whole relationship blow up in their faces after a couple months, ruining the tentative friendship they were building. Not to mention, they had a yearlong joint thesis to work on, which wouldn't go away if they messed up things. It would just make it a miserable experience for everyone involved.

So maybe it was better *not* to go there, to keep things cool between them. He'd been in love with Anne for as long as he could remember and wanted her friendship even longer than that. Shouldn't that be enough? *Could* it be enough?

Gil shoved his hands in the pockets of his coat and sighed, putting his head down against the wind as he walked the long blocks to the subway.

Chapter 10

Working alongside Gil wasn't *terrible*, Anne concluded after their second week at Herschel. He still thought as fast on his feet as she remembered, which was interestingly less annoying now than it used to be. She had laughed more in the last ten days than the past two months combined, the kids all loved him, and the genuine effort he put into co-running the group had come as a surprise. Although maybe it shouldn't have; he'd always been patient with younger kids, giving them his full attention, none of the sly humor he seemed to save for her on display. Diana's kid sister Minnie May had followed him around for years with heart eyes and Anne couldn't recall one time he'd brushed her off or made fun of her painfully obvious crush.

It wasn't the *worst* thing to spend six hours a week together, all in all.

Anne bumped her heels against the wooden wall of the auditorium stage, perched on the edge next to Gil while they waited for the kids to finish the micro fiction assignment they'd given them that afternoon. Wordlessly, he held out the bag of pretzels he'd been working his way through. With a sigh of relief, she took a small handful, too aware that she'd skipped lunch in favor of extra time working on a paper for a different course at the library. Pulling her phone out as she munched on the salted, carby goodness, Anne checked the time. They only had the kids for another forty-five minutes, and it'd be nice if the ones who wanted could share their stories before the group disbanded.

"It's four-fifteen," she said, tucking the phone away again.

"Give them another five."

"That's only forty minutes for sharing and feedback."

Gil shrugged, unbothered as his gaze skipped over the room. "Most of them are done."

A couple of the kids were still working, but the majority had moved off to the side to lie flat on the scuffed linoleum floor or talk in small groups while they waited for the others to wrap up. Anne was pleased to note they were all making the effort to keep their voices low so their fellow writers could continue to concentrate, a huge change from the first few days of barely controlled chaos. A trio of girls in the corner started giggling, shushing each other as they darted glances over to Gil.

Sometimes she missed Janey with a vicious ache. It had been her, Di, and Anne since seventh grade, tight like the girls still trying to muffle their laughter at the back of the auditorium. She really needed to convince Jane to make a weekend trip into the city soon. The way her friend talked, it was like she considered riding the train in from Long Island and flying to Paris required the same level of planning and energy, instead of a few hours of travel time and a rolling suitcase.

"Okay, let's call it." Gil hopped down from the stage, pulling Anne out of her musings. He clapped his hands together loudly, drawing the kids' attention. "We've got less than an hour left, people, let's make it count. C'mon, circle it up."

Some of the kids bounded forward with enthusiasm, some wandered over at a more apathetic pace, and a couple were definitely dragging their feet. Anne made note of the pair, a tall, slightly awkward boy named Damon, and Jenna, a curly-haired girl with hard eyes. Damon seemed to be struggling with the work, and probably needed a little one-on-one time with her or Gil. Which was fine; one of them could swing by a couple Friday afternoons to get him up to speed.

Jenna, however, was a different story.

Maybe her problem was writing-related, but maybe it was something else. She sat off to the side, apart from the others, looking at them with barely concealed scorn. As if the other kids were beneath her, to be tolerated until she could escape their presence. But the fingers that relentlessly worried the edge of her T-shirt told another story, and it was one Anne wanted to unravel.

She wasn't surprised when neither kid volunteered to share their stories, the girl sitting with a defiant lift of her chin that positively *dared* someone to ask her, and the boy slowly folding in on himself as time went on. Both pinched the heart in different ways, because Anne recognized each reaction in her younger self, in turn.

One of the other girls raised her hand after her friend shared their story. "Mr. B, I still don't get how we're supposed to write a whole story in three paragraphs. Like . . . how is that even possible? Won't it just automatically suck? Because mine *definitely* does."

Gil waited for the laughter to die down, the girl's included, before answering, and flashing her a dimpled smile. There was a melting from nearly half the room's occupants that was practically audible. Anne would have laughed, if she hadn't found it so relatable.

"Yeah, sometimes it does. That's writing. You're not always going to get it right on the first try. Or the second, or sometimes even the sixth. But you keep going and eventually you'll get there."

Anne tucked away a smile at his earnest expression. He was unbearably cute sometimes.

"The key is to remember that just because it's micro fiction doesn't mean it stops following basic story structure."

"There's still a beginning, middle, and end," Anne jumped in, slipping off the stage to lean back against it instead, legs crossed at the ankle, her palms braced against the edge. "You have to establish the story, build up the tension, hit a crescendo, and slide down the other side of it. The trick of it is to scrape the story down to the bare bones without losing all the interesting bits."

"Ugggghhhhhh."

"It's too hard!"

"I don't get why we even have to do this, you guys said we'd learn how to write a book. This isn't a book. It's a waste of time."

The last comment came from Jenna, her expression mulish as she folded her arms over her rib cage.

Okay, so apparently, they were going to do this now.

Anne waved two fingers at Gil to let him know she'd take this one. "Learning story structure is important, whether it's a micro fic or a book. But writing a novel is infinitely harder, and not something we can probably accomplish in an after-school program, which is why we figured we'd start small. So to speak."

A couple kids groaned theatrically at her pun, but Jenna just ignored it, her narrowed gaze focused on Anne. Anne sighed internally, recognizing that look. It said that the girl had decided that Anne was the perfect target, deserved or not, to take her problems out on. Wonderful.

"I'm not here because my grades are *bad*," the girl said, her scorn directed at the other kids, some of whom scowled back at her. "I'm here because I want to be a real writer. Mrs. Matling said you guys could help us with that, but I know all of this already. I only want to learn how to write a *book*."

She tossed her hair over one shoulder, her expression pinched. "Like I said, this is a total waste of time."

Breathe. She was just a kid, even if she was acting like a brat at the moment. Clearly, there was more churning beneath the surface here.

"I'm sorry you feel that way." Anne was proud her voice came out even and calm as she addressed the girl. "Next week we'll be moving on to short stories, maybe that will interest you more." She turned away to look at the rest of the students. It was important to listen to a student's frustrations, but it was another thing altogether to let them derail the entire class. "Over the weekend, we'd like everyone to pick out a photo or some other art you want to use as a prompt to write a short story about. If possible, bring an image of it on paper. It's easier to work with your prompt in front of you, and I'm sorry, but there's still no exception to the no cell phone rule. If you don't have access to a printer, email the image to one of us, and we'll see if they'll let us use the one in the teacher's lounge. Or cut something out of the paper or a magazine instead."

As the kids began to disperse, heading out to the carpool pickup area or off to catch a city bus, Anne blew out a breath. She watched as Jenna slammed out the door, her stride aggressive enough to send the few kids in her path skittering out of the way.

"That one's going to give us hell."

Ruefully, Anne glanced over at Gil. "I was thinking the same thing."

"I don't get why she signed up for the program if she doesn't think she'll learn anything. She seems kind of pissed off to be here, to be honest."

"She does seem like she's made a choice to be as difficult as possible. I think I'm going to try to dig a little deeper, see if I can figure it out." Anne stared at the closed door thoughtfully, tapping her lip with a pen. She looked up to find Gil watching her, his eyes fixed on her mouth. Flooded with the sudden memory of the other night at the bar, when she'd been almost positive he was about to kiss her before they were interrupted, Anne felt herself flush. Dropping the hand holding the pen back to her side, she cleared her throat, not looking at him as she picked up her bag and slung it over her shoulders.

Out of the corner of her eye, she saw him turn away abruptly, reaching for his own bag. Which gave her a perfect view of his excellent rear, clad in worn jeans that molded lovingly to his butt and that looked so soft she positively itched to run her fingers over the material.

Clearly squats were a regular part of his workout routine.

They walked to the subway together, lingering by the railing at the top of the stairs. She was headed back to Hell's Kitchen, but lucky Gil, the place he shared with Fred was only a few blocks away.

"I talked to Marilla, by the way, and I'm headed home the weekend after next for the festival. Are you going?" Anne fiddled with one of the straps of her backpack, trying not to notice how close he was standing.

"Yeah, actually." Gil ran a hand through his curls, ruffling them even more than the wind had. "I want to visit my dad, see how he's doing, but it'll be nice to see everyone again too."

The weekend was an annual draw for Avonleans, even those who'd moved away, alongside the hordes of tourists there for hayrides, apple picking, and the food and wine tours. It would be a big deal for Gil to show up this year, she knew; he hadn't been back since moving to California.

"Everyone's going to freak."

He grinned, looking pleased. "You think?"

"I know." Not wanting to be late for her shift at the bookstore, Anne started toward the stairs. "You should tell Charlie. He's going to want to put together a thing."

"Maybe that's exactly why I *don't* want to tell Charlie. I remember what his nights out were like, and I don't want to spend my weekend with my head in the toilet."

Rolling her eyes, she said, "You're twenty-four, Gilbert Blythe, surely you can handle a little pushiness."

"You'd think," he replied, with a pointed look. "And yet."

"Oh, go home." Reluctantly amused, Anne started down the stairs.

"Still telling me what to do," drifted down the stairs after her, and she rolled her eyes once again, even though he couldn't see it. Somewhere along the line Anne had started finding comments like that funny instead of offensive, and she still wasn't sure when things had taken a turn. Maybe it was because the edge to his jokes that had always rubbed her the wrong way, they made it feel like he was laughing at her instead of with her, had been missing since he'd come back.

It was possible they'd both grown up while separated.

And it was possible, *im*possible as it seemed, that they were friends.

What a bizarre, pleasing thought.

Chapter 11

Anne shifted in her seat and tried not to be obvious in her discomfort. Dr. Lintford's gaze lingered on her legs where she'd crossed them, and she resisted the urge to tug down the hem of her shorts. Not for the first time since their meeting had started, she wished that Gil hadn't gotten stuck covering for his sick friend's shift. When she argued that their project was infinitely more important, he'd countered that the manager had told his friend to find someone to pick up the shift or not bother coming back for his next. Which made it impossible to continue to insist that Gil come to see their mentor with her instead, obviously.

Besides, Anne reminded herself silently, she shouldn't need to use Gil as a shield. She was a grown woman, more than capable of dealing with . . . whatever it was Dr. Lintford was doing.

Leering, maybe.

But just subtly enough she couldn't be positive. Since it would be academic suicide to call him out without being sure, instead, she adopted a brisk, no-nonsense attitude in an effort to end the appointment as quickly as possible.

"The kids at Herschel are responding well to our curriculum so far, and we're working on putting together a field trip to the Brooklyn Book Festival. The only hitch is finding chaperones, because even on a Saturday, a lot of the parents are working. Some of the local Big Brothers Big Sisters clubs said they might be able to send some people." Scrolling down the page of notes she'd put together for the meeting, Anne pursed her lips. "We're also working on putting together some donation money so all the kids can buy at least one book while there. At least half are on scholarship, and since they'll already need to bring money for lunch, I . . . we thought it would be better to provide a book for *every* kid as a gift. A gift for everyone isn't singling anyone out."

Anne knew, from firsthand experience, the stomach-roiling anxiety of being the only one who couldn't buy something just because; having to pretend she didn't want whatever it was, so no one would feel sorry for her. It had felt so unfair that some people had almost nothing, while others had *everything*. This festival was supposed to be a fun day, about books and writing and learning—a time to inspire the kids to fall in love with stories, even just a little bit. She didn't want anything to take away from that.

"Sounds great," Dr. Lintford said indifferently, his impatience to move on obvious. Anne clenched her jaw. He was so much more engaged when Gil was there, it was beyond frustrating.

"And have you picked a date for the first draft of your thesis paper? You know you'll need my approval before sending in the final version.

"Well," he amended, his eyes drifting over her again, "you will if you want to complete your degree with a decent average."

A decent average! As if she'd ever gotten anything less than 3.9—and only then because she'd had a group project that year in high school biology. Every cliché about group projects was true. Atlas had done less heavy lifting, to be honest. She might as well have been working alone. She'd have preferred to work alone.

But at least Gil pulled his weight.

Feeling silence was the better part of valor, Anne merely gave the professor a tight smile and began to pack up. Thankfully, the half hour he'd allotted for their meeting was almost up. There were so many other things she would rather be doing than sitting here, practically *steeping* in misogyny. Like cleaning the public bathroom at the Lazy Lion.

As she stood to leave, Dr. Lintford rose and came around the desk, brushing close enough to bump her elbow as he moved toward the door. Willing herself not to let the inward grimace at his overpowering cologne show, Anne started to follow, then drew up short as he paused, one hand on the knob. The older man's smile was positively oily as he casually held the door closed.

"It occurs to me that it might be helpful for us to meet again, to go over some of the . . . techniques you're using with the children. I have classes until late afternoon, but perhaps Thursday evening? The building will be closed, but it's not a problem. I can let you in." His tone was light, but she didn't like the look in his eyes. Not at all. "I feel you would benefit greatly from the experience I can share."

"Oh, I can't. Sorry. I'm working that night," she lied glibly, willing him to just open the damn door. She had no intention of setting up another appointment with the professor any time in the near future. Situations like this were why God invented email.

"Of course, my dear. No problem at all. We can schedule something for another time." Anne didn't miss the fleeting look of annoyance, however, before Dr. Lintford quickly smoothed his expression out again. He paused, hand *still* on the knob. "Of course, you understand this invitation is just for you. I'm quite selective with who I give extra mentorship to, as you can well imagine."

Extra mentorship, her butt.

"Of course," Anne echoed, mentally sighing.

Finally, the professor opened the door, stepping back just enough for her to squeeze through. It was infuriating. She drew in her limbs tight to avoid touching him and walked down the corridor at a fast clip. Technically, he hadn't said or done anything she could report, but he would. Men like him always did, sooner or later. They couldn't help themselves, so sure in their power.

Dr. Lintford didn't know her very well.

If he did, he would have recognized the steely glint in her eye and the determined set of her slim shoulders. If he understood her, he would have known she never did anything without a plan, once she knew all the variables in play. He also would have been aware that she had little tolerance for bullies, and even less for those who abused their power.

If he knew her at all, which he didn't, he would have known the grim set of her mouth as she strode down the sidewalk meant he was about to come up against the immovable wall that was Anne Shirley's sense of justice.

Chapter 12

Then

"Y ou are a horrible bully and I loathe you," Anne cried out as she held up her only Barbie, now bald in patches and covered in dark green marker. Tears ran down her face as she confronted Lillie, the oldest of the three foster girls Anne shared a room with at Poplar Grove. Yes, she was too old for dolls and she knew it, but that wasn't the point. It was hers, the only toy she'd had since she was little, and it had been at the bottom of her underwear drawer. Which meant once again, the blonde had gone through her personal things. At Anne's accusation, Lillie climbed off her bed and flipped her hair over one shoulder with a nasty look on her face, then sauntered over to where the younger girl stood rigid, skinny arms now akimbo. She towered over Anne, folding her arms over her chest as she cocked out one hip.

"And *you're* a little freak and no one likes you."

That hurt more than Anne had thought it would. She knew the other kids thought she was strange, and she wasn't close with any of them, preferring to spend her time writing stories or playing imaginary worlds in a corner of the backyard. Mostly, they just left her alone. But for some reason, since Anne had come back to the home from the Hammonds' house, Lillie had decided she was a prime target and hadn't stopped needling her since.

Anne clenched her jaw, trying to ignore the other two girls snickering at Lillie's words from their beds. "If you don't stop picking on me—"

"What? What are you going to do, cry about it?" The blond girl smirked. "Go tell the director? Let me know when, so I can get a front-row seat to that."

And that was the problem. Anne wouldn't get any sympathy from Director Adams. She knew it, Lillie knew it, *everyone* knew it. He saw her as a problem child. One of the ones who just couldn't stay gone, and he never believed her in instances like this, even though it would make no sense for her to mutilate her own Barbie. Because she liked to make up stories about imaginary adventures and people, he pinned her as some kind of compulsive liar, and that was that.

Thank God she was leaving tomorrow again. Anywhere had to be better than here.

Anne just threw Lillie one last disgusted glare, then retreated to her own bed. She turned her back, ignoring the way the other three whispered and giggled, clearly laughing at her, and used the corner of her sheet to rub off as much of the marker as possible. A good amount of color came off the smooth, hard plastic body, but the face was a loss; the porous rubber had soaked up the green. With a sigh, she tucked the doll under the far side of her pillow and tried to lose herself in the book she'd started the night before. It was engrossing enough to allow her to tune out the other girls until it was time for lights out, keeping her occupied as she waited for them to drift off to sleep.

Once there was no sound but that of even breathing, Anne silently threw back the covers and crept out of bed. With slow movements, she reached into the front pocket of her backpack and fished out a blue pen. She tiptoed across the room, one eye on the sleeping girls, then opened the door in increments, careful not to trigger any squeaking of the hinges. Once it was wide enough for her to slip through, and she'd checked thoroughly to make sure no adult was patrolling in the immediate area, she moved down the hallway toward the bathroom on swift feet.

It only took a moment to locate Lillie's shampoo, and a moment more to unscrew the pen cap and shake the blue ink out into the open bottle. When the pen was as empty as could be, Anne tossed it in the trash, closed the shampoo bottle, shook it well, and stole back to the room she shared with the soon-to-be-not-quite-as-blonde.

Sometimes a girl had to take justice into her own hands.

As she slipped into bed again, tucking her feet, icy from the linoleum, up under the blankets, Anne smiled. She burrowed into her pillow, sleepiness finally overtaking her, now that her revenge was complete. Tomorrow would be another adventure, hopefully one that would lead her away from Poplar Grove, and Lillie Kent, forever.

She couldn't wait.

Chapter 13

Now

Fall on the island was Anne's favorite time of year, when the mornings became too cold to step out on the porch without thick socks. Always an early riser, she'd made it a tradition during her visits home to sit on the steps with a cup of milky tea, watching as the autumn sun came up over the harbor. The burgeoning light crept across the bay, changing dewdrops on the lawn into tiny diamonds and, and her favorite tree, Gloriana, all crimson and gold.

Although Anne was home just for the winery's fall festival weekend, this morning was no different from those of her childhood. She wrapped her fingers around the mug she held, trying to leech some warmth from the hot tea to heat up hands chilled by the brisk breeze coming off the water. The marsh grasses offered some protection from the wind, but she had still needed to steal Matthew's coat from where it hung by the door before venturing outside, a wool blanket tucked under her arm to sit on. She'd been sitting only a few moments when the door opened behind her. The familiar sound of the scrape of wood against wood where the top corner always stuck in the frame, and Marilla's subsequent *tsk* of irritation, made her smile into her mug.

"I need to get Matthew to fix that damn door," the older woman said as she tugged some of the blanket out from under Anne's butt and sat down on the step next to her with a grunt. "I don't understand why you like to come out here and freeze every morning, but it is nice to look out the kitchen window and see that head of red hair again."

"It's nice to be here again." Anne leaned against Marilla's shoulder, offering her the mug of tea. The other woman took a sip, then handed it back over, her face screwing up in distaste.

"Too much milk, as always."

"The *perfect* amount of milk."

The retort was easy, automatic, and familiar after years of arguing with her adoptive mother over how to make a good cup of tea. The older woman preferred hers strong and black, same as she drank her coffee, something that never failed to make Anne feel like her tongue was shriveling up dry as a raisin. She sent Marilla a sideways grin, pleased when it was answered with a huff of laughter, then was immediately distracted by the sound of meowing. She blinked as a sleek gray cat appeared from under the porch, bound up the steps as if it owned them, and wound itself around the ankles of a rather embarrassed-looking Marilla.

The older woman pursed her lips, gently nudging the cat from her with one leg. "Don't look at me like that. He started coming around a few months ago, ribs showing, clearly a wild thing by the state of his patchy fur. So, I put out some food and water in the mornings for him. But he'll never be domesticated, after so much time on his own."

"Mmm, I can see that. Not attached to you at all," Anne teased, letting her fingers trail over the cat's back as it pushed against Marilla's legs again. There was a tear on the tip of one of his ears, long healed, but he showed no fear, butting his head against her palm when she stopped petting him. "I already knew you had a soft spot for strays. Have you named him?"

"No, why would I?" Marilla raised his eyebrows. "He's not a pet."

"Just a new friend?"

"Hush, you." Her voice was gruff, but the corners of Marilla's lips turned up, knowing she was caught. The older woman wasn't one to display her emotions for all and sundry, but she did in fact have a special sort of sympathy for lost creatures. There was an elderly horse in the barn, rescued from a breeder who no longer had use for her. The house had never had fewer than two dogs, taken in from one shelter or another, snoozing in patches of sun in the front room the entire time Anne had lived at Green Gables. Now there was the nameless gray tom.

And of course, herself.

Marilla liked to think she hid her tender soul well, but one only had to know where to look to uncover a streak of kindness a mile wide and long.

They sat quietly as the sky changed from patches of purple and pink into a pale blue, Anne stroking the now-purring cat, both women lost in their own thoughts. Finally, Marilla sighed, then slapped both palms on the tops of her thighs before rising, signaling an end to their dawn escape from reality.

"C'mon, Anne-girl. There's quite a bit of work ahead of us today."

Anne gave the tom one more brisk scratch behind his ears, then stood and scooped up the blanket they'd been sitting on. "See you soon, old man." She headed back into the warm kitchen, letting the screen door smack closed as she shrugged out of Matthew's coat and hung it up.

The work Marilla spoke of *was* why she'd come home, after all, to help with the fall festival. All the weekends from April to late October were busy on the island, first with the summer tourists and then with the wine-touring and apple-picking crowd, but the three days the winery held the Autumn Jubilee at Green Gables were a madhouse. The last six years Anne had overseen running the events staff. Most of them were temporary workers hired just for the weekend, which meant she spent most of the three days directing hay bale placements, making sure they didn't run out of caramel apples and plastic tasting cups, and praying none of the local musicians they'd booked to play by the cluster of folding tables outside the main building would bail at the last moment. Thus far her track record was spotless, and she intended to keep it that way . . . which meant another fortifying cup of tea was in order before she could even think about getting her day started.

Pausing only to drop a kiss on Matthew's head where he sat at the kitchen table, his face creasing with pleasure at the gesture, Anne crossed the room to refill the electric kettle, then leaned back against the counter to wait while the water boiled.

Tapping her fingers idly against the edge of the counter, she asked, "Do you have the list of people working today? Anyone I know?"

"Ah, yes. I meant to get it to you yesterday, but it was hectic. Sorry about missing dinner on your first night back, I hated that." He shuffled around the stack of paper on the table in front of him, pulling out two pages, and handed them to her with a look of apology.

"That's okay, my schedule was all turned around too. I'd wanted to catch you on your lunch break, but Diana wasn't able to get off work before one, so we couldn't catch the last Jitney like we'd planned. We barely made the train." She scanned the names, noting several previous workers had signed on for the weekend again this year. That was good; it would make her job a lot easier to have people she trusted to know what they were doing and didn't need her hovering over their shoulder. Late-season events like theirs gave locals a chance to make a little extra cash before the tourists deserted the island for warmer climes. Winter on the North Fork wasn't exactly easy for any of them but it was hardest on those who made their living house-cleaning or landscaping for wealthy summer vacationers, when the homes were closed up during the cold weather.

Anne smiled to see her friend Jane's name on the list, same as it had been for the last decade. It would be good to catch up, they hadn't seen each other since the summer. She penciled Jane in to run the raffle booth; they could use the lulls between customers to chat. Sipping her second mug of tea, she went upstairs to shower and get ready for the day. Thankful she'd left her galoshes behind when she'd headed back to school, she paired them with worn jeans and a long cable-knit sweater, twisting her hair up into a careless bun on the crown of her head.

The ends were getting a little ragged; maybe she'd have time to squeeze in a trim before the weekend was over. Every time she'd thought about it over the last few months, the resolution to deal with her hair had gotten lost in all the madness of balancing schoolwork, the Lion, and the project at Herschel.

And the . . . well, she couldn't lie to herself anymore. The *flirtation* between her and Gil, and her subsequent microanalysis of it, took up a significant amount of whatever time she had left over. This new thing was unexpected and mystifying, but also kind of nice.

Anne spent the next two hours helping the festival crew set up tables and chairs, the raffle booth, and the small, low stage where the band would play later. She confirmed the musicians' arrival for mid-afternoon, checked to make sure the popcorn maker was working, and helped troubleshoot a problem with the fairy lights strung on poles around the front lawn of the winery. Eventually she had to give up and send one of the workers out to get replacements. Priorities—not one of them was stressing out over a half wire of lights that had died sometime in the last year.

An old truck bumped its way down the drive, turning in at

the house instead of continuing around to the employee parking lot behind the winery, and she grinned as a familiar brown-haired girl climbed out of the cab.

"Janey!" The two women met in the middle and hugged each other tightly. Anne pulled back, holding her childhood friend by her upper arms and studying her face. "You look so good! I wish I could come home more often. I miss you."

"I know, I miss you too," exclaimed the other woman, falling into step with Anne as they made their way inside the winery. "If work wasn't always such a nightmare, I might actually get into the city to see you sometime. If not this fall, though, I'll definitely come up after New Year's."

They dropped Jane's purse in Matthew's office and headed out to set up the raffle booth for business, Jane telling her some of the funnier stories about the pair of twins she nannied. Time passed swiftly as the pair laughed and chattered, but the urge to tell Jane about Gil's resurfacing in New York lingered in the back of her mind.

Focusing maybe a little more intensely on sorting tickets for the drawings than was necessary, watching out of the corner of her eye as Jane double-checked the prizes that some local businesses had donated against the list Matthew had printed out, Anne lightly said, "So, I have news. Of the boy variety."

"Really?" Jane glanced over, her eyebrows raised, pen hovering above the paper. "Hit me."

"Gil Blythe is back from California. He transferred to Redmond for his last year of grad school, into my program, and we're working on our thesis project together."

"You and *Gil*?"

"I know!" Anne threw up her hands, marveling again at the craziness of the universe. "What's even more bizarre? He's flirting with me. No, more than flirting. Janey, he's definitely putting out signals. Of the sexy kind. I'm ninety percent sure we almost kissed during a night out with some friends. I think."

"*What?*" Her friend just sat for a long minute, digesting this, then started laughing. "How are you even handling that? He used to drive you nuts, completely around the bend. You would spend hours ranting about him taking first place in the spelling bee or whatever you two were competing for that week."

Jane paused, then a look of speculation came over her face. "Actually, now a *lot* of things suddenly make sense."

Anne's cheeks heated. Sometimes she would almost forget how much he used to irritate her, when he would smile at her over their books or compliment her on how she handled a particular sticky moment with one of the Herschel kids. It was like knowing two Gils. The one before, whom she could barely tolerate, who seemed to go out of his way to get under her skin. And the Gil now, whose brown eyes lit up whenever he got her to laugh at one of his jokes, like it was the best thing to happen to him all day.

"He's not so bad," she mumbled, sweeping the tickets into two separate bowls. At the swat of Jane's pencil on her arm, Anne rolled her eyes. "Okay, so I might be enjoying it. A little. Who doesn't like it when someone hot flirts with them?"

Jane just shook her head, smiling. "Maybe I'll have to come up to the city sometime after all. I'm going to kill Diana for not texting me about this."

"Brat," Anne said, fondly. "All right, I have to go make sure the Mitchell brothers don't overfill the hay wagon. Last year it was practically up to my hips."

Jane waved her off, already turning back to her checklist.

The crunching of gravel had her bringing her hand up to shade her eyes, to watch the first car of the weekend drive into the winery parking lot. Drawing in a deep breath, Anne pushed away any lingering tiredness and went looking for the two rowdy teen boys in charge of the bales of straw.

Chapter 14

Gil had been home a grand total of thirty-two minutes before his father brought up the possibility of him continuing on for a doctorate degree.

"Dad, I told you," he explained, the tortilla chip that had been halfway to his mouth now steadily dripping salsa back into the bowl. "I'm not interested in becoming another Dr. Blythe, even if it is of the academic variety, not medical."

"What's so wrong with that?" Bushy, silvered brows lowered in irritation. "It's tradition. Your grandfather and great-grandfather were also Dr. Blythe."

"I know." Gil sighed, putting the now soggy chip onto his napkin. They'd been over this before, several times. "I don't want to break tradition. But I also don't want to spend another two years in school. I'm twenty-four, Dad, it would be nice to experience life without homework."

His father came around the counter from where he'd been

leaning on his cane and lowered himself into a chair next to Gil at the kitchen table. "All right. I just hope you don't regret it later, but all right."

"If I regret it later, I'll go back to school then."

"So smart, you think you have all the answers. Smart enough to be a doctor," the older man muttered under his breath.

"Dad."

"Fine. Not another word." His dad mimed locking his lips and throwing away the key. Gil just managed to refrain from rolling his eyes. Doubtful. John Blythe was not known around Avonlea for holding back when he had something to say.

Gil picked up another chip.

"Still."

He threw the chip down.

"Dad, seriously. *Stop.* I'm only here for a couple days, I don't want to fight," Gil said, exasperated. He searched for a change of subject in the face of his father's mulish expression. "How are Fancy and LL doing?"

His dad's face lit up at the mention of the two former race-horses, Fancy Britches and Lord Light, that he'd bought a few years ago. They weren't for riding, like the other three horses the Blythes kept—mostly they fat-catted around the pasture west of the horse barn and formed a mutual admiration society with his father. Dr. Blythe had had a deep love of everything equine since he was a child; he'd almost become a farm vet, before his own father put an end to that idea. It never occurred to Gil growing up that his father might have wanted to be anything but what he was, one of the most well-respected reconstructive plastic surgeons in the country. He never complained within his son's hearing, but as an adult himself now, it wasn't hard for Gil to see that his dad was never happier than when he was with "his babies," as his mom called them.

And they wondered why Gil wanted to follow his own path, instead of the one his family was trying to carve for him.

Having successfully diverted his dad's attention, they went for a walk down to the barn to see the horses in question, then an even slower walk back. It worried Gil, how easily his father tired these days. A year ago, they would have gone running together in the morning, but now his father needed a nap after only one short, leisurely stroll. This, if nothing else, really drove home the reality of his dad's illness. After making sure his mom was there to help her tired husband upstairs to lie down, Gil just stood in the middle of the living room, staring at a bit of chipped plaster on the wainscoting. He took a deep, shuddering breath and pressed the heels of his hands onto his closed eyes, hard enough to see starbursts in the darkness behind his eyelids.

Seriously—fuck cancer.

Dropping his hands, Gil shook his head, and went to find his coat.

The festival was starting the next morning, so a ton of hometowners were back, and Charlie had put together a meetup at The Widow's Walk, just like Anne had predicted. Named for its position high on the hill that overlooked the bay, where all the fishing boats docked, the bar itself was unremarkable. It was a long, squat building with scarred plastic booths, two ancient pool tables, and so much nautical paraphernalia on the walls, Gil was shocked they hadn't collapsed under the weight of it all. Everything on the menu was fried, the beer watered down, and the tequila even more so. Half the time the toilets were broken and the customers had to resort to peeing out back by the dumpster, and if you sent back food (God help you), the cook would appear at your table to cuss you out personally.

The place was a hellhole, and Gil loved it.

But he hated himself the next morning, when his alarm went off at eleven. He'd told Anne he would drop by Green Gables at noon, a decision he almost regretted now.

The inside of his mouth tasted like something had crawled into it and died, and he could practically smell the vodka sweating out of his pores. It took him two tries to get out of bed without falling, and into the shower, where he just leaned against the wall and let the hot water wash over him while attempting not to vomit. The downside was that he was dying, definitely dying; his head felt like it was splitting like an over-ripened tomato. The upside was that maybe it would hurry up and happen soon and put him out of his misery. But unfortunately, he was still alive, if not kicking, by the time the water began to run cold. Shivering in only a towel slung around his waist, Gil rummaged through the medicine cabinet until he found a bottle of aspirin that was miraculously still in date. He swallowed two of the pills with a handful of faucet water, then leaned against the doorway for a long moment before gathering his strength to find clothes that would keep him warm while working outside all day.

He really should have listened to Anne . . . not that he was going to *tell* her that.

Which was why he stopped at the local coffee shop to pick up the largest latte known to man, with as many espresso shots as they were legally allowed to put in. Even if he still felt like he'd been dragged backward through a hedge, twice, he could cover it with a caffeine high and Anne would never know the difference. An Anne ignorant of the humbling experience of his vicious hangover was an Anne without the ammunition to send him smug looks that practically screamed "I told you so."

After adjusting his sunglasses to cut down on the eye-searing rays of the noonday sun, Gil drove across town with one hand, while drinking the inky nectar of the gods with the other. He was a little shocked, but also pretty proud of himself, to find he'd managed to slug back twenty ounces of the coffee equivalent of high-octane jet fuel in under fifteen minutes.

The winery lot was nearly full when he arrived; he finally found a space under a couple of old chestnut trees out back. Winding his way through the other cars, he kept an eye out for red hair, but Anne was nowhere to be found. He did stop by the raffle ticket table on the way in, however, and was reunited with Jane Andrews, who just patted one of his biceps and smirked, then pointed him in Anne's direction.

Wandering toward the start of the dirt path the hayride truck would use to wind through the fields, Gil was sidetracked when he spied Marilla next to a long table, unloading cases of cider from the back of a push dolly. Sliding in between her and the dolly, he picked up the next case, trying not to grunt at the weight. Embarrassing. Might be time to find a new gym.

"Gilbert Blythe," Marilla exclaimed, her raspy voice the same as always, despite her hair having gone almost completely gray since he'd last seen her. "Look at you. It's been, what, six years? First visit home since you graduated high school, isn't it?"

"That's right." He smiled when she patted his shoulder before she turned back to start breaking open the cases. That was about as affectionate as the older woman got in public, and he was sort of honored she even thought fondly enough of him to bother. "Figured I should finally visit for the weekend, good son of Avonlea that I am."

Her eyes crinkled at the corners with amusement. "Well, I'm sure Anne will be glad to see you. She's somewhere over near the hayride."

"If you need help, I'm more than happy to do whatever. My schedule's pretty loose this weekend," Gil said, willing himself not to automatically look past Marilla for a glimpse of the redhead. "I told Anne I'd swing by today, but I can stay for a while if you want a hand."

"Anne knew you were coming home for the weekend?" The older woman's eyebrows rose.

Ah. It bothered him more than he'd thought it would that his reentry into Anne's life didn't even warrant a passing mention to the older woman. He knew how close the two were, and he couldn't imagine anything important happened in Anne's life that Marilla didn't know about.

Gil smiled, a bit of his good mood dimmed. "Actually, I moved

back to the city in August. We share some classes, and my roommate and I have hung out with her and Diana a few times." The
truth of it was that he was now seeing Anne every other weekday,
and at least once on the weekends, if he managed to swing by the
bookstore.

"Anne did mention you were working together with her on a
joint thesis project," said Marilla, her gaze shrewd.

So he hadn't been completely cut out of Anne's reports home.
Feeling better, Gil stood a little straighter. "It's been really interesting, and I think we're both learning quite a bit. It's been . . . an
experience so far, anyway."

"Hmm," the older woman hummed. The urge to shift at
Marilla's scrutiny was strong, her poker face was incredible,
but years of sitting under his mother's stern eye in church had
drilled fidgeting right out of him. "Well, thank you for the offer to help, but I'm just fine here. Why don't you go find Anne?
She should be taking a break about now anyway, if she hasn't
already. Maybe you can get her to sit down for five minutes and
eat something that isn't coated in caramel."

She gave him one last steady pat on the shoulder, then shooed
him on.

It didn't take long to find Anne once he made it down to the
line for the hayride. She was off to one side, crouched down and
chatting with a small girl wearing a plaid dress that looked a
little fancy for sitting in a wagon bed full of straw. The girl's
mother was busy wrangling her other child, a boy with a devilish grin, who was clearly just waiting for his moment to bolt.

"Davy, I swear to God, if you don't behave!" he heard her

hiss as he got closer, tugging her son back to her side when he strained away to pet a dog someone was walking past. Anne glanced up from her conversation with the young girl as Gil stopped next to her, something like relief flashing across her face.

"Welp, it looks like I'm needed, folks." Her smile to the stressed-looking mother was apologetic. "Enjoy the ride!" He followed her as she began to walk away, amused at how quickly she was moving.

"Are we in a rush to get somewhere?"

"Yes. Somewhere that's not here. Jane may love those kids, but honestly, Davy is a little terror."

They dodged two kids running to catch the ride before it left, then veered off toward the back door to the winery.

"A sweet terror, but a terror nonetheless," she amended, looking guilty as she hauled open the heavy door. Gil caught it with one hand before it swung shut, and followed her in, blinking to adjust to the dim hallway after the strong afternoon sunshine.

"Marilla wanted me to get you to take a break. She seemed concerned your only calorie intake today was going to be in the form of candied apples."

Anne glanced back at him, over her shoulder, gray eyes flashing in the subdued light. His stomach did a funny little flip, but he was getting used to those and was able to send her an easy smile.

"That means she's going to be on me for the rest of the day unless I eat something of substance. Which means I have to run up to the house." They passed through the staff-only door, out into the public tasting room. She waved at Matthew, who was behind the counter listening to a young couple talk. He smiled, eyes sliding over to where Gil was walking next to her. They exchanged polite nods before the older man turned his attention back to his customers. "Want to come with me? I can make you something if you're hungry," she offered.

The idea of food still sat uneasily. "Maybe just some water."

"You went out with Charlie, didn't you?"

"I'm not talking about it."

Her laugh rang out, loud and clear.

They fell into casual conversation as they walked up the hill toward the house. He'd only been here once, a long-ago Halloween when they'd both been part of the same group going out to trick or treat. Once they'd hit all the houses in the area, they trooped back to Green Gables, where Marilla and Mrs. Barry gave them popcorn balls and hot chocolate. He'd loved the big, old Victorian on sight, so different from the sharp angles and straight lines of his parents' modern house.

The braided rug by the door and the faded wallpaper of the entryway were the same as he remembered, the kitchen still looking like it had been frozen in the 1970s. He dropped into a chair at the table as Anne pulled open the door to the avocado-colored refrigerator and looked inside.

"Not much changes here, huh?" he said idly, turning the mason jar of mums in the middle of the table to look at it.

"Nope. Just the way I like it." Anne pulled out the makings of a sandwich. "Sure you don't want anything?"

"I'm good."

Gil didn't miss the way she turned away to hide her smile. *Smug*, just like he knew it would be. She spent the next few minutes spreading brown mustard on every inch of the bread slice with methodical care, like the idea of a bare patch was personally offensive, then added four precisely folded pieces of salami. It was adorable, the way Anne added a handful of baby carrots to the plate, then debated adding one more with deliberation, before returning the bag to the crisper.

Finally, she brought her lunch to the table and sat down across from him, handing him a glass of water as she did. The cool liquid felt amazing going down his parched throat, reminding him he was probably still dehydrated from the night before. This was why Gil hardly ever drank beyond a beer or two anymore; feeling like this after wasn't worth the buzz.

"So," Anne started, then took a big bite of her sandwich. Taking another sip of his water, Gil just raised one eyebrow and waited. She grimaced in apology, then swallowed. "Sorry. Rude. I meant to ask, how's your dad?"

"Hard to say." Gil watched a drop of condensation slide down the outside of the glass, catching it with the tip of his finger before it could hit the table. "Worse than I've ever seen him, but in pretty decent condition according to his doctors. We walked down to the barn today and he needed to stop twice on his way back."

"That's rough," Anne said, her eyes wide and guileless when he looked up again. "It's hard to watch a parent struggle. Marilla just got news she might need eye surgery in the not-too-distant future. The upside is that it pushed Rachel to finally move in, so she won't have to worry about getting around at night, since Matthew doesn't drive after dark anymore either."

"Yeah, I don't know what I'd do if my mom wasn't around to help." Probably he would have moved back to Avonlea instead of the city and wouldn't be sitting here with Anne. Suddenly, he needed to know, and asked, "We're friends, right? Now. We're friends now."

Anne put down the half sandwich she'd been holding. "I like to think so. Don't you?"

"Yeah," he replied, relief making the grin he flashed her bright. "Just making sure I've finally redeemed myself."

Her eyes widened, just a fraction. "Redeemed yourself?"

"From being such a pain in the ass to you in high school."

"Oh. Right. Yes, we're fine now."

Unsure at the flat tone of her voice, Gil pushed on. "Because you'd tell me if we weren't cool, right? I like this new hanging out thing we do."

"I promise I will tell you." She didn't smile, but the look in her eyes softened, then she got up and put her plate in the sink. "C'mon, I have to get back. I don't think I've taken this long a break in the last six years I've been in charge of the staff. Let's hope no one set anything on fire while I was eating lunch."

He rose from his seat, following her to the door. "Somehow, I think Marilla and Matthew were probably able to handle it for half an hour."

"You don't know." A smile played around Anne's mouth as she locked the door behind them. "It could be chaos when we get back down there. Madness. A drunken bacchanal."

"At"—Gil looked at his watch—"one-thirty in the afternoon?"

"You've been gone for a long time. Maybe Avonlea got wild while you were in California," she said with a laugh, as they lingered at the end of the driveway. "Are you coming back down or heading out?"

"I'm going to go back, see if my dad's awake. His brother and a couple of my cousins are coming over tonight to play poker. We used to do it once a month, so I figured we should do it while I'm here this weekend." It had been a long time since Gil had participated in *that* family tradition as well.

"Sounds like a good time. Tell your dad hi for me, okay?"

Anne's question only faintly registered in Gil's brain as he watched the wind tug loose a couple of pieces of hair from her braid, the long strands glinting copper in the sunlight. Without thinking, he reached out and tucked them behind her ear, only realizing what he'd done when she sucked in a breath.

Gil started to drop his hand, then paused when he looked into her eyes and saw his own desire reflected back at him. So instead, he turned his hand to cup her jaw, dragging one thumb over the line of her cheekbone. Leaning down, he caught her mouth with his. It wasn't rough, but it wasn't gentle either. He showed her what he wanted, made sure she understood this wasn't a spur-of-the-moment decision. The kiss was deliberate, his lips moving over hers with purpose.

They broke apart, Anne's breath coming quickly as she searched his eyes.

"Is that part of your definition of what friends do?"

He laughed, pulling her in for a hug, resting his chin on the top of her head. The feel of her arms going around his waist, firm and sure, eased any doubt that she might reject their kiss. Thank God.

"Kissing is pretty friendly, don't you think?" he teased.

"Is it?"

He heard the sliver of doubt in her voice and drew back far enough to look into her eyes. "Sure. But I don't go around kissing all my friends, you know."

"Fred probably appreciates that." She tucked her head back against his chest. "So, it's just me, then?"

"Just you," Gil reassured her.

"Kissing friends."

"Maybe occasionally going to dinner or the movies. Possibly hanging out with our non-kissing friends."

"That sounds an awful lot like dating to me." Anne's voice was slightly muffled by his coat.

He hummed. "Does it?"

"It really does." She drew her head back to look up at him again, hesitating for a moment. Making his expression as encouraging as possible, Gil waited for her to sort her thoughts. God knew he'd flirted enough with her over the last few months, she had to know what he wanted by now.

"So . . ." she said slowly, her clear gaze lifting to his. "What you're really saying here is that you want to date. Exclusively?"

"I don't share well, so yeah, I'd appreciate it." He bit back a grin at her eye roll.

"Be serious."

Sliding his fingers into Anne's hair, he drew her into another lingering kiss. "I am very serious right now."

"Okay," she said breathlessly, pulling back. Her lips parted, as if she wanted to say more, or possibly kiss him again, but then her gaze landed on his watch. "Oh my God, Marilla's going to kill me! I'm so, *so* late."

She slipped out of his hands, face apologetic. "Call me later? Or I can text you when we close up."

"Poker night," Gil reminded her, cursing himself now for setting the damn thing up. He'd have much rather spent the night with his fingers buried in that mass of fiery hair.

"Oh. Right. Well, you know where to find me for the next two days." Her expression was uncertain. That was no good. Gil snagged her wrist and pulled her back into a kiss, moving his mouth against hers until they were both panting slightly. Then he released her, satisfaction coursing through him at the dazed look in her eyes.

"I'll come by tomorrow again."

"Okay. Um. Good," she said faintly, then sent him a shy smile as she turned away that arrowed straight into his heart. "So I'll see you then."

"See you then," he echoed, watching her until she walked the rest of the way down the hill and disappeared around the corner of the winery. Rubbing one hand over his chest in an absent gesture, Gil started off to find his truck.

Once he climbed into the cab, he had to sit for a moment, a little stunned at how very differently his day had gone than he'd thought when he woke up that morning. To be honest, he hadn't even decided if he was going to push things between them beyond friendship or not, or at least he hadn't thought he had. Then she'd looked at him like that, her gorgeous eyes full of some soft sort of feeling, and Gil only knew he *had* to kiss her. And look what his boldness had brought him.

It had taken over a decade to get here, but he finally had a date with Anne Shirley. Or he would soon.

Shaking his head, a small grin in place, Gil started up the truck and backed out of the parking spot. When things changed, they sure changed fast. But what didn't change was his father's love of poker night, so he better stop sitting around with a dorky smile on his face and get his ass into gear. And maybe brush up on his play, because his cousins had never held back from ruthlessly taking all his money.

Feeling entirely pleased with the way his weekend was shaping up, Gil drove home whistling.

Chapter 15

Then

Gil ate his chicken sandwich and tried not to watch from across the dining hall as Roy Gardner slipped his arm around Anne's waist. He absentmindedly laughed at Charlie's joke and tried not to watch Anne offering Roy some of her baby carrots. He took a large swallow of his sports drink and tried not to watch the way Anne's eyes lit up as Roy spoke to the rest of the kids at their table, his hands sketching his story in the air. He tried not to watch as Roy rose, slung his messenger bag over one shoulder, then leaned down to brush his lips across Anne's cheek. And he tried really, *really* hard not to watch as she lowered her eyes and blushed and went soft in a way she'd never done in Gil's presence.

He tried not to watch, and he failed, and he hated himself for being so weak.

"Are Anne Shirley and Roy Gardner dating?" Gil asked abruptly. When he realized his table had fallen silent, he finally tore his eyes away from the small, private smile on Anne's face as she packed up the remains of her own lunch. Moody Sturgeon, one of his track teammates, gave a baffled shrug and went back to his tuna sandwich, while Charlie chewed thoughtfully, but in the end, shrugged as well.

Farther down the table, Ruby let out a big sigh, rolling her eyes. "Only for the past two months. You seriously haven't noticed until now?"

Two months?

"No," Gil said, missing the next thing she said. He dropped his sandwich on the wrapper in front of him, not hungry anymore.

Two months of dating, and now public cheek kissing, could only mean one thing: Roy Gardner was officially Anne's boyfriend. Frowning, he stared down at the table. Roy was cool; Gil didn't have a problem with him, in general. But he couldn't see a relationship working between them. Anne was so full of energy and bounce, flitting from one thing to another, never alone. In contrast, Roy was reserved and quiet, found more often by himself in the corner of the classroom or back tables of the library. Although, he *was* tall and lean with perfect teeth and had skin that, unlike that of every other *normal* kid in this school, never seemed to break out . . . so if she liked that kind of thing, then yeah, Roy was the guy for that.

On top of all that, it was hard not to hate Roy, because the guy was a genuinely nice person. Which, ironically, kind of made

Gil want to hate him a little bit more. If he'd been a jerk and treated Anne like crap, Gil could be smug, wishing they'd have a horrible, public split any time now. But Roy was nice, and he was nice to Anne, and they were nice together, and everything was just *super nice* . . . and now Gil felt like the shittiest kind of person for hoping they'd break up.

Ugh, the worst part was that once he became aware they were a couple, he couldn't stop noticing them.

There they were holding hands in the corridor. Or snuggling during the first football game of the season. Whispering in the library, their heads bent together over a book, knees pressed together under the table. Canoodling in the local Denny's, eating fries together. (Why did he even *know* the word "canoodling"? It was a terrible word. Awful. Should be stricken from the dictionary for the rest of time. *Canoodling.* What the fuck.)

All this togetherness was why, almost two months after he saw them being revoltingly cute together in the dining hall, Gil was almost instantly aware when Anne started once again walking alone with Diana to class and sitting several seats away from Roy in social studies.

His insides danced with glee, his shameful wish had finally come true—then he caught the constant forced smiles on her face and how she'd begun to hide out in the corner of the library, her backpack on the table in front of her to shield her from view, instead of joining her friends at lunch, where Roy remained a fixed figure at their table.

Now Gil kind of felt like a jerk for walking around whistling cheerfully whenever he thought about their breakup. (Jackass-ish.

Not completely, one hundred percent a jackass. Jackass-adjacent, maybe. What was half a level below being a jackass? A dipshit?)

God. Whatever he qualified as, it felt . . . mean. So he did his best to squash it.

After a week of watching Anne mope when she thought no one else was looking, he decided it was unnatural for her to look so sad all the time. It was really starting to bug him, that she wasn't happy anymore. Hoping like hell he wasn't about to embarrass himself yet again, Gil made the decision to try and change that.

During fourth period, he made his move, jogging to catch up as she crossed the gym to the outside doors.

"Hey." He dropped into a walk next to her, trying for casual, but wasn't sure he was really nailing it. Nobody looked good in the academy's gray-and-navy gym outfit, seemingly designed to be shapeless and baggy, but somehow Anne made it work. It was distracting. Which was *clearly* just what he needed lately.

Her eyes flicked over to take him in, disdain written in her silvery gaze.

"Hi?" she replied shortly, more of a question than a greeting. At the best of times, she tolerated his presence with a sort of reluctant amusement. This was clearly not one of those moments.

Unfortunate. Because now he'd look like a di—a jackass if he just turned on his heel and walked away.

"Are you following me?" She pushed through the heavy metal doors; he caught them before they could swing shut and slam into his face.

"Following you? No. Why would I be following you?" Gil

asked as he followed her out toward the softball fields, the late September sun warming him instantly. "Same class, remember?"

P.E. was on a rotation of softball, track, and lacrosse right now for everyone. He'd particularly enjoyed watching Josie Pye eat dirt last week when Diana came barreling out of nowhere during a lacrosse pickup game and knocked her halfway across the pitch. Diana had gotten reamed out by their gym teacher for it, but even Gil could see it was worth the lecture, considering not five minutes earlier Josie had been slyly flirting with Roy as she watched Anne out of the corner of her eye.

Remembering the unhappy tilt of the redhead's mouth as she'd stood nearby watching them was exactly why he was here now. Gil turned to face Anne, jogging backward.

"Are you going to the fair this weekend?"

"Why?"

He threw his hands up, exasperated already. "Why are you always so difficult?"

"Because it's you," she replied in a snotty voice, and surely there was something wrong with him, because he *liked* her snotty voice. It was cute. Anne let out a long sigh when he didn't walk away, like answering his question was a heavy burden. "I had planned to go. Now . . . I'm not sure."

"A group of us are going together," Gil said, turning back around to face forward, squinting off into the distance, like her answer didn't matter in the least. "You should come."

"Maybe." Her tone was dismissive.

He didn't say anything else, knowing when to let it drop.

She started digging through the pile of shoulder padding on

the edge of the field as soon as they got there, looking for some-thing remotely her size. Already dressed in his own gear, Gil followed her, rolling his lacrosse stick back and forth between his palms, the hard ball cradled in the netting as he whirled it around.

"Why do you care if I go or not?" Her abrupt question took him by surprise.

"Who would keep me entertained if you're not there to pick a fight with me over something arbitrary and meaningless?" Gil shrugged, smirking at her in exactly the way that drove her nuts. "Just come with us. I'll buy you a candy apple and you can recite all the weird facts you know about red dye number forty while we ride the Ferris wheel. It'll be fun."

"How could I say no to such a charming invitation?" Despite the dry tone in her voice, she was wavering—he could tell by the way she was nibbling her lower lip. Anne had tells, and he knew them all.

"Diana and Jane will both be there, you know," he cajoled as he reached out to help her pull the pads over her head, straight-ening them on her shoulders when she didn't smack his hands away, then tossed her a blue scrimmage jersey. "So, you don't actually *have* to talk to me if you don't want to. You can just take the candy apple like a little mercenary and go share your food dye facts with someone else."

The way her face brightened at that was kind of insulting.

"Well, when you put it that way . . . what time?"

Nice. Maybe one day he'd get tired of being kicked around by Anne Shirley's adorable little size five tennis shoes, but clearly today was not that day. "Meeting at the west entrance at seven, but some of us are carpooling." Smug satisfaction blazed inside him as Roy walked by and Anne didn't seem to notice. "I can swing by your house, if you want to catch a ride."

"I'll ride with D." She twisted her hair into a high ponytail.

"Thanks, anyway," she tacked on belatedly, like it hurt to drag the words out.

"Right. Yeah, of course," he said, feeling like a dipshit for thinking even for a minute she'd take him up on the offer. At least he'd gotten her to come, though. "Just, you know, hit me up if her car is full already or whatever."

"Sure."

"Okay."

They just sort of stood awkwardly for a moment before the P.E. teacher's whistle saved them. Anne ran onto the field without a backward glance, but it didn't bother Gil. Because she was smiling as she bumped shoulders with Diana, talking a mile a minute, like she used to do.

And she didn't look over at Roy even once.

Chapter 16

Now

"It hardly hurt at all," Diana said, carefully peeling back the bandage covering her leg just far enough for Anne to check out the tattoo she'd gotten over the weekend. Apparently, Fred had booked her for a late-night appointment at the shop, then they'd gone back to his place for an after-hours party. *If you know what I mean*, Diana had said, wiggling her eyebrows until Anne laughed.

"Don't listen to her. I have never heard someone whine so much about a surface wound before," Phil said, appearing from the hallway, peering at the tattoo. "It looks good. Don't pick at it."

"Okay, Mom."

"Hey, you'll be happy for this mom friend if you get an infection, so zip it."

"It's so pretty." Anne leaned forward to get a better view, ducking Diana wildly blowing kisses toward Phil, where she was now standing in the kitchen. The ribbons winding around the mannequin outfitted in only the wooden skeleton of a hoop shirt looked so realistic, they practically fluttered in an unseen wind. "It's so sharp and detailed. How did he *do* that?"

"I have no idea, but he's really talented. You should go down to the shop and see some of the client photos he has on the wall. Seriously."

Warmth filled Anne at the awed tone of her friend's voice. "Obviously you'd end up with someone as artistically talented as yourself. That was never even a question."

"Well, I don't know about *ending up* or anything." Diana laughed, smoothing the bandage down again, then leaning back on the sofa. "But we are seeing each other again this weekend, so that's nice."

"Speaking of dating," Anne said, hopping up and edging past Phil, into the kitchen, where she rustled around for the chips she'd hidden back behind the cereal no one ate but her.

Phil eyed her as Anne passed her again. "You do realize we all know where you keep those."

"Who cares about chips at a time like this?" Diana cried out, glaring at Phil. "Anne, finish your sentence. Now."

"Hang on, do we have any ranch left?" She fully intended to tell them both all the details, but it was so much more fun to drag it out first.

"No. Stop stalling." Diana twisted around to watch her settle back on the couch with the bag of chips, a look of anticipation on her face. "Please, just tell me it wasn't Charlie Sloan *again*."

"Nope. Charlie was too busy being hungover all weekend to actually make it to any of the island events, apparently." Anne crunched on a chip. Salty deliciousness. She didn't even want to contemplate a world where potato chips hadn't been invented. The *horror*. "Actually, if you can believe it, it was Gil. He came by Green Gables on the first day, even though he'd been out the night before too and was just as hungover as Charlie. He made a general nuisance of himself, kissed me, asked me out, then went off to play poker with his dad."

"Finally!" Phil leaned her elbow on the edge of the kitchen high top counter, looking amused. "I hardly know him and it's obvious even to me this has been a long time coming."

"Phil, you have no idea. Seriously." Diana popped a chip in her mouth, rolling her eyes. "Anyway, I can't decide if it was romantic or not. Yeah. No, yeah, it is. He braved the festival setup *and* a hangover for you."

"My hero," Anne said in a dry voice, although she did privately agree it was sweet he'd made the effort, despite looking like death warmed over when he'd first shown up.

"You could do worse."

"I have done worse. Remember James, last year?"

"Oh. Yeah."

"Well, I'd forgotten James, but now you've reminded me. Thanks for that," drawled Phil, making a face.

"So, we're all in agreement: Gil is a *huge* step up, even hungover. But agghh, this is exciting! Phil's right, I'd definitely have thought something would have happened between you two before now," Diana said, a sly smile coming across her face. "Did you know Jane and I had a running bet he'd make a move in high school? I'm still mad I lost that ten dollars."

Anne suddenly felt very dedicated to finding the perfect chip.

There was a moment of silence, then Diana slowly said, "No. No way did you hook up with Gilbert Blythe, one of the hottest guys we went to school with, and not tell me. Right? *Right, Anne?*"

Damn it.

Anne looked up to find both Diana and Phil staring at her. "Well."

"Holy shit, she did." Phil darted a glance at Diana, who was still staring at Anne. In fact, Anne wasn't entirely sure she'd blinked. It was a bit unnerving.

She waved her hand in front of Diana's face. "Hello? Did I break you?"

"Just *about*," Diana finally said. Thankfully she didn't look angry, or at least, not as angry as Anne had thought she might be. "Are you finally going to tell us what happened?"

So she did. Everything from Gil's arrival at the campout to when they parted ways, and everything that happened in between. By the time she was done, Phil had seated herself in front of the couch, on the floor, and Diana was staring off into space with a thoughtful expression.

"So." Anne spread her hands, not sure what else to say. "That's all of it."

Diana came back to herself and looked over at Anne with a

grin. "This explains why he looked at you the way he did at the arcade, and oh, I don't know, every single time we've all been out together. Because he's *already* had a taste and wants another."

"Stooooop." Anne hid behind the chip bag, her face heating up. Now was absolutely not the time to start thinking about how Gil looked at her, and what he might be thinking about when he did.

"You are such a prude," Phil said, a sense of wonder in her voice.

"I am not. You wouldn't understand. Blond hair and a blush looks cute. *I* look like a tomato."

"Never mind that." Diana smacked Anne's knee enthusiastically to get her attention. "So on a level of one to internal meltdown, how's your state of mind right now?"

"Weirdly calm," Anne replied, dropping the chip bag down onto the floor next to the couch. She drew her legs up onto the cushions and crossed them. "Given, you know"—she waved her hands around in the air—"everything that's happened between us, you'd think I'd be a neurotic mess right now."

"Don't worry, sweetie, there's still time."

Anne pointed a chip at Phil. "That's not untrue, and possibly more than a little on brand for me. I think it's a good sign that I'm not worried about what we'll talk about or if it's going to be awkward. I just like spending time with him."

"Yeah. Yeah, that's really good. Aw, I'm happy for you." An alarm on Diana's phone went off then, and she jumped up with wide eyes. "I've gotta run. I managed to book some studio time and that shit is at a premium right now."

"Go, go," Anne said, waving her off. "I have a shift at the Lion in a couple hours anyway."

Phil kept her company a little longer, but then she headed off to meet up with some friends she'd met during her residency, leaving Anne at loose ends. Determined to keep to her rule of not overthinking things with Gil, she turned the volume way up on her playlist as she showered, singing along even though the cheap Bluetooth speaker made the music a little tinny. Feeling ambitious for a Monday morning, she even shaved her legs and washed her hair. If she shampooed it more than once every few days, it floated around her head like she'd been rubbing it against a balloon. Anne had made peace with the vivid orange-red color years ago, but no one wanted to look like a walking version of one of those plasma globes.

In the middle of rubbing lotion down her arm, her phone dinged, the little preview popping up with Gil's name. Careful not to smudge the screen with greasy fingers, Anne swiped the screen open, scanning the brief message.

Good morning, freckles. <3

Unable to stop the smile at such a typically Gil sort of greeting, Anne tucked the corner of her towel more securely over her breasts, sat down on the closed toilet lid, and started typing . . .

Chapter 17

They'd been back in the city for a week and a half before Gil finally managed to take Anne out on anything resembling a date. Although he still saw her nearly every day, the only thing that had changed between them was that now when they parted ways after class or their time at Herschel, or after the hours he still haunted the back table at the Lion, he got to kiss her the way he'd been wanting to for years. She leaned into his kisses, her smile curved against his mouth, her small hands always sliding up under the edge of his shirt to touch his lower back. It was a comforting, affectionate touch, but the feel of her skin against his, even just the tips of her fingers pressed against the flesh just above the waistband of his jeans, set him on fire.

He wanted more, so much more, of her.

Their schedules finally aligned one Saturday evening, when he managed to get a swing shift at the bar, and she had an unheard-of weekend day off from the bookstore. Checking the clock over the wall of booze behind him, Gil realized his shift had flown by, and was suddenly filled with a nervous energy. To keep his mind off the clock ticking down, he started refilling the drinks garnishes, grabbing a handful of limes and setting to work slicing them into wedges. His concentration on his task was so complete, he nearly cut right into his finger when Anne slid onto the stool in front of him and tapped the bar with two fingers.

"Hello, barkeep. One iced tea with lemon, please." She grinned when he looked up.

"Welcome to Kindred Spirits, ma'am," Gil said flippantly, reaching over to grab a tall glass. "Barkeep?"

"I've always wanted to use that on someone but didn't want them to think I was weird."

"Well, I already think you're weird."

"Which is why I got to try it out on you," she explained, as if it was obvious. "Almost done? Only, the movie starts in about forty minutes."

"Yup." He finished slicing up the rest of the fruit in short order, then pulled off his apron and tossed it in the dirty linen hamper on the shelf under the bar top. Shrugging into his jacket, Gil adjusted a flat, gray cap over his curls, and threw the night shift bartender a salute before coming around to join Anne.

She swiveled on her stool as he approached, looking like something he could eat, in a pair of pink jeans and slim shirt with tiny, golden skulls printed all over it. When he stopped in front of her, she reached up and tapped the brim of his cap lightly with one finger. "Why are guys who wear cabbie hats so hot?"

"If I'd realized that was all it would take," Gil murmured, bending down to steal a brief kiss, then stepped away to let her hop off the barstool.

Grabbing a heavy hoodie two shades darker than her jeans, she slid off the seat and went up on her toes to plant another soft kiss on his mouth. He chased her lips when she drew back, needing one more taste of her sweet lip gloss before he could let her go. The shining look in her eyes told him she didn't mind that at all.

Threading their fingers together, Gil glanced at her shirt as they left the restaurant, stepping out into the chilly evening air. "A little early still, isn't it?"

"*Never.*" Looking down at the tiny grinning skulls, Anne laughed. "I found it in Avonlea last week and couldn't resist. You should see the fire escape outside our apartment. Diana and I got some of those life-sized plastic skeletons and tied them on, so they look like they're trying to climb over the railing. She's always been really into Halloween. As long as they don't block the stairs, the landlord doesn't care what we do."

"My mom's really into Halloween too. I swear, every year it gets more elaborate; the guys at the seasonal shop love her. She sent me pictures of the house this year. There's an entire fairy-tale witch's hut set up on the front lawn, complete with huge plastic candy attached to the roof."

"I can't picture it. Your mom seems so . . . don't get offended, but she seems like the type who would think Halloween decorations were too bougie to be considered."

"Don't get me wrong," Gil said, pulling Anne closer to his side as they walked, as the frigid wind whipped down the street. "Her sense of what she considers classy definitely wars with her love of the holiday. She makes up for it by decorating the house like the store displays at Tiffany's on Fifth every year. I used to tiptoe through the house during Christmas in an effort not to break any of her crystal North Pole displays. You should see it when all the lights in the room are on, that shit is blinding."

They made the movie just in time, grabbing a huge, over-priced bucket of popcorn when Anne confessed she'd gotten so wrapped up in reviewing for midterms that she'd forgotten to eat dinner. They chose seats off to the side of one of the middle rows, and settled in, elbows pressed together.

Later, if anyone had asked him, Gil couldn't for the life of him have told them what the movie was about. He'd spent most of the time being hyperaware of the way her breath would catch at a tense scene or the soft brush of her fingers against his when they both reached for popcorn at the same time.

It felt like being a teenager again; that restless, itchy feeling that made him want to touch her all the time.

It was late when they emerged from the theater, Anne cheerfully dissecting the movie as they maneuvered through the Saturday night crowds. Gil pulled her under the awning of a store advertising it was going out of business, despite the fact the discount signs had been up in the window for years now, to avoid a group of teenagers rushing down the sidewalk.

"Want to come back to mine? It's not that far from here," he asked, running his hands up and down her back in a slow sweeping motion.

Biting her lip, Anne looked hesitant for a moment, then nodded. "Okay."

The walk was short, like Gil had promised, but felt longer when all he wanted was to be behind the closed door of his apartment so he could touch her the way he had been hoping to for the last two weeks.

"I'm worried about Jenna," Anne said suddenly, pulling his attention away from more pleasant thoughts. He glanced over; her brow was furrowed in thought. "She wrote an amazing story for the prompt, but she's dragging her heels again coming up with an outline for the next short."

What went unsaid was the attitude the young girl was throwing them as well. No matter what they asked the kids to work on, there was some excuse for why she couldn't do it. Gil made a face of sympathy. For whatever reason, she saved most of her vitriol for Anne. He'd offered to deal with the girl exclusively, to give Anne a break, but she refused.

"It's not going to help either of us in the long run if I let her drive me off," she'd said, and he knew she was right. It was just frustrating to watch Anne search for things to relate to with the girl, only to be rebuffed time and again.

"Sometimes, when she thinks neither of us is paying attention, she forgets to act like she doesn't care about what we're trying to teach them." Sighing, Anne reached out and wove her fingers through his, sending an electric jolt zinging up his arm when their palms meet. "I wouldn't be half so frustrated if she wasn't wasting her talent for some reason I can't figure out. I really don't understand it."

He glanced over, resisting the urge to rub the little worry wrinkle between her eyebrows away with his finger. "I can talk to her. Not that you haven't been really patient with her, but maybe I can spell you out for a little while. You can take a break and concentrate on the other kids."

"No." A frown crossed her face, her fingers stiffening in his. "No, I can handle it, I don't need you to step in."

"No problem. Just an offer. Let me know if you change your mind, that's all," Gil said, quickly. After a couple minutes of walking, her fingers relaxed again, and the frown disappeared. When they reached the brownstone, Gil gently tugged her to a stop, hiding a smile as she looked up, startled like she'd forgotten where they were going.

Her answering smile was rueful. "Sorry I zoned out. Not very good date etiquette."

"If I got mad whenever you got lost in that big brain of yours, I'd look like the Hulk," he threw over his shoulder as he led her up the front steps. She jokingly punched him in the back of the shoulder, nearly making him drop the key. Jokingly bumping her away with his hip, Gil started laughing when she waited until he almost had the key in the lock again before jostling his arm. "I'm going to drop it in the bushes, and *then* where will we be?"

Anne held her hands up, widening her eyes in a failed attempt to look innocent. He turned back for his third go at the lock, visibly twitching when she leaned one shoulder against the doorframe next to him.

"Am I making you nervous?" She snickered, not even trying to hide how much she was enjoying herself. Gil just threw her a look, wanting to be exasperated but only feeling amused instead, and wrestled the door open. This was the funnest date he'd had in years. It felt so *easy*.

"Get inside, you menace."

Finally they were climbing the stairs to the second floor, her hand warm in his, the sound of their breathing very loud in the silent hallway. Opening the door, Gil ushered her in, taking her coat and tossing it over the side of the couch as they moved farther into the apartment. "Yo, Fred, you here?" he called, then turned back to Anne with a predatory grin when no one answered.

She giggled, a sound he didn't think he'd ever heard from her before, and backed into the tiny living room as he stalked forward.

"I don't know where you think you're going. This place is the size of a shoebox."

"Maybe I'm not that easy," Anne said as she sidled behind a dumpy old armchair Fred had inherited from one cousin or another, tossing him an arch look.

Gil stopped and threw back his head, laughing long and loud. "Oh, sweetheart, easy is one thing you are definitely not."

"Insults will get you nowhere, Gilbert Blythe."

"That's not an insult, it's a fact," he replied, drawing her out from behind the chair, kissing her full mouth. It soon turned heated, biting kisses that had them stumbling toward the couch, tumbling together onto the cushions. Sliding his fingers into the mass of hair that tumbled over her shoulders as he lifted her up to settle her straddling on his hips, Gil marveled once again that he got to touch this gorgeous woman. That she let him trace his lips down her throat, leaning in with a sigh, her body arching under his hands.

Too soon, Anne drew away, her mouth swollen and pink from his, and shoved her hair back with the hand not bracing herself upright over him.

"I hate to say this, but . . . I have to work pretty early tomorrow."

Well, shit. There went his plans for the rest of the night. But it wasn't like they wouldn't have another chance to do this again. He'd just have to make sure it didn't take another two weeks to get here. Rubbing his hands on her hips, noting how tired she looked now that they paused for air, Gil asked, "Do you want to stay?

"To sleep," he clarified at her raised eyebrow. "It's late, you're clearly wiped out. You can have my bed, I'll crash on the couch."

"I can't put you out of your own bedroom," she protested.

"It's fine." He maneuvered them both into sitting positions, needing to get her off his lap if they weren't taking this any further for the night. "I've slept here plenty of times, it's a good napping couch. C'mon."

He led her down the hall to his bedroom, trying to remember if he'd left any underwear or whatever on the floor. Thankfully, when he pushed open the door, the floor was clear. Rummaging around in his dresser for a second, he tossed her a pair of old sweatpants and a T-shirt. As he moved past her toward the door, Anne stopped him, an uncommonly shy smile on her face.

"Wait. I think we can share the bed without getting, you know, frisky."

Gil gave her a searching look, then slowly nodded. "If you're sure. I really don't mind sleeping on the couch."

"I'm sure," she said, hugging the clothes to her chest.

He nodded again, then grabbed his pajama pants and a T-shirt to change into in the bathroom, giving her a few minutes to get into her own change of clothes. When she called him back in, he came in to find her already sitting in bed, the blankets a rumpled puddle around her. Just as he'd suspected, Anne looked freaking adorable in his clothes, the T-shirt practically swallowing her. Climbing in next to her, Gil leaned over and place a light kiss on the exposed, freckled skin of her shoulder where the oversized T-shirt was slipping off.

"Ready?" he asked, reaching for the lamp sitting on his bedside table.

"Yup." She snuggled down into the blankets, tucking one arm up under the pillow. He settled on his side, facing her, his eyes tracing her features in the moonlight coming through the crack in the curtains. Her lips quirked into a smile, despite the heavy set of her eyelids, and she reached out one hand, just barely brushing his chest before pulling back. "Thanks for tonight. It was nice."

"Yeah, it was." Gil shifted over, pressed his lips to her forehead as she yawned. "Go to sleep. I set my alarm for seven so you can get home and change before having to go in."

With something that sounded like a mumbled thanks, Anne's breathing evened out, her face softening in sleep. His chest felt like it was going to crack open with the overwhelming swell of love that crashed over him. Blowing out a long breath, Gil rolled onto his back and stared at the ceiling, tracing the fine cracks that ran across it. God, she could break his heart, a prospect that hadn't felt so real as it did in that moment. He really didn't know what he was going to do if it turned out this thing between them didn't mean to her what it did to him.

It was a long time before he could sleep.

Chapter 18

Anne curled her legs up on the seat, leaving her sneakers on the floor in front of her chair in the small cafe, and cradled an oversized mug of coffee in two hands. It was a cold, blustery November day, even a knit cap and heavy jacket couldn't ward off the bone-deep chill. She sighed as the warmth of the mug slowly started to thaw her hands and burrowed into the chair as Gil came back with something that looked lethally sweet; dark and chocolatey with a tower of whipped cream, dusted with cocoa.

He caught her raised eyebrows and hunched over it defensively. "I need the caffeine; I was up half the night revising a paper for Edu Law. If I ever had an ambition to go into the administrative side of things, or become a lawyer, this class would have cured me of that real quick. My brain just doesn't work like that."

"Not judging." She caught his skeptical look and laughed.

"Seriously, we who live in glass houses . . . I had them put two shots of espresso in this coffee."

"We can text each other tonight when we're both still wide awake at three A.M."

"Speak for yourself. This is my normal functioning level of caffeine now. I'm going to sleep like a baby," Anne said smugly. "But in a selfless effort to keep you awake, I propose a game." She raised her eyebrows at him over the rim of her mug, then nodded toward the rest of the cafe. "Pick someone and give me a story about them."

Gil scratched his chin, and she tried not to blush, wondering if the slight scruff he had going on would leave marks on her skin. He glanced around the cafe. "Anyone? Anything?"

"Yup. I'll go first," she said, focusing on the game instead, willing her cheeks to stay cool. She let her gaze drift about the room, until it landed on an older lady in the corner. She wore a heavy, ankle-length fur coat, despite the warmth of the cafe, with a sweat suit and sneakers. "Ah. Okay. See her?"

Gil quickly looked in the direction Anne nudged her chin. "Fur coat or skater kid?"

"Fur coat. Which she wears because her fourth husband, Conte di Something or other, bought it for her when they honeymooned in northern Italy, where he was from. Like her other husbands, he was around for a few years, then mysteriously disappeared the night before trash day, never to be seen again."

"Gruesome," Gil commented idly. "But what about the sweat suit and sneakers?"

"What?" Anne took a sip of her coffee. "A lady likes to be comfortable. Especially when she might need to outrun the FBI or the Mob. Your turn."

Tapping his fingers against the table between them, Gil looked around for a moment, then smiled. "The couple with the little boy, sitting by the door. Instead of running away *to* the circus, they're running away *from* the circus, where they both grew up. They got married and had a little boy, whose greatest dream, ironically, is to someday become a trapeze artist."

"Very nice," Anne said approvingly.

"Well, not for them," she amended, then directed his gaze toward three teenagers loudly goofing around a few tables away. "Aliens on a scouting mission. They haven't decided if this planet is salvageable or not yet, and the oversized chocolate chip cookies here just might tip the scales in our favor. Unless they're allergic to chocolate. Then we're screwed."

"Grim." A wide grin spread across Gil's face, as he relaxed back into his chair, eyes roving the cafe for another story to tell.

They went back and forth for a while longer, until they'd run out of people to make up things about and Gil's eyes were bright and alert. Then they went for a walk in the cold, and Anne didn't even mind much, because she spent most of it tucked up against Gil's side, with his arm around her. It was funny, because the amount of time she wanted to spend around Gil now was proportionally in direct opposition to the amount of time she'd wanted to spend in his company in middle school. Which is to say, *all* of the time verus not even a single minute.

Which is how he came to be studying at her place two afternoons later, when the middle ground between their apartments was technically the school library.

Anne shifted on the sofa, her knee bumping against Gil's in the small space between where they sat facing each other. She looked up to find him looking at her, and shot him a quick smile before returning her attention to her laptop. Only a few minutes later, he bumped *her* knee as he leaned back, grimacing as he stretched out his back.

"I need a break."

"Hmm?" She tore her eyes away from the sliver of toned belly that had been exposed when his T-shirt had ridden up, only to find him smirking at her. Flushing, she snapped her laptop closed and rose from the couch. "Thirsty?"

"You have no idea."

Knowing she was now bright pink, judging by the heat in her face, Anne escaped to the kitchen quickly. She wasn't some innocent, she'd had sex before. Good sex. But one little innuendo and she was a mess. She was overly aware that they were very, very alone in the apartment, and would be for a *while*.

Which had been her secret little plan. But still.

Footsteps approached the kitchen, and she realized she'd just been standing there daydreaming about having sex with Gil. Anne hastily pulled open a random cabinet door; a shelf of plates and bowls stared back at her as he entered the kitchen. Shit. Quickly closing it again, she pulled open the right cabinet door. Glasses, thank God, just where she'd left them . . . when they'd moved in six months before. She'd just taken one down when he crowded her against the counter from behind, her eyes drifting closed as he pressed against her, his breath warm where it ruffled the hair near her ear.

A gasp escaped as Gil reached past her and took the glass from her hand, putting it down on the counter before gently turning her around.

She opened her eyes to meet his gaze.

It wasn't like she hadn't seen this coming, hadn't noticed the building tension when they kissed. It wasn't like she didn't recognize it, hadn't welcomed it. Anne knew very well where they were headed after the night they'd spent at his apartment the weekend before. But she hadn't thought it would, could, be like this.

For a moment neither of them moved, fractured breath mingling, frozen in a near embrace. A line of heat ripped down Anne's spine to pool in her lower belly, a shiver at the sensation overtaking her. Gil caught the slight movement, the focus of his gaze sharpening, his arms flexing as his grip tightened on the edge of the counter on either side of her hips. The silence filled with a thousand things unsaid, questions between them answered in an instant.

It felt like they were on the precipice of something important. Something they couldn't come back from. That moment before a trust fall, the point of suspended time spooling out as they teetered on the edge of the plunge into the unexplored territory.

The anticipation of what was about to happen, the inevitability of it, was almost too much to bear.

Anne licked her bottom lip, heart leaping when Gil's eyes dropped to study her mouth with an intensity that actually made her knees weak. She'd always thought that was something that only happened in novels, but wow, *wow*, it was a real thing. If one of them didn't move soon, she was going to lose her mind.

The feeling shifted suddenly, filling her with a tenderness that took her by surprise, Anne raised a hand and placed it on his cheek, loving the way the roughness of his stubble rubbed against her fingertips.

Her breath caught as Gil immediately turned to press a kiss into her palm, a gesture she remembered from a night long ago, cool sand under their feet, the salt-laden wind ruffling their hair. Something like relief moved across his face when the gesture tugged a breathy sigh from her lips. Releasing his grip on the counter, he stepped into her and pressed one palm against her lower back to bring her body flush against his as the other glided up and down her spine. The soothing movement banished the last of the frenetic butterflies battering her rib cage, unlocking the tension that held her still.

Sliding her hand into the silky curls that brushed the base of Gil's neck, Anne pulled him down into a kiss. He opened for her instantly, groaning against her mouth as their tongues tangled. One jean-clad leg nudged at the line of her thighs pressing together. She let them fall open, sucking in air swiftly as he rubbed against the V at the apex of her legs. Rough material scraped against the denim of her own jeans, moving the seam against her in a way that had simmering desire flaring into a blaze.

She was done pretending they hadn't been on this collision path for nearly a decade. They could do slow *next* time.

"Off," Anne commanded, yanking at the hem of his shirt, tugging it upward. Without a word, Gil ripped it over his head and threw it over one shoulder, moving back in to press her against the counter again. Anne ran her hands across his broad chest, then slid them down the plane of his abs, taking the time to press her fingers over each tight ridge. He stood still for her questing touch, head dropping to rest on the top of her head, air dragging in and out on a shudder with every inch she covered. The trail of soft hair that ran down to disappear into the waistband of his jeans delighted her. She wanted to rub her cheek against it, but one glance at Gil's face warned her that was for another time. A time when they weren't drowning in this long-denied need for each other. Instead, she tucked her fingertips into the top of his jeans, the metal of the button there pressing into her flesh.

"Come on." She tugged, turning them both, gazing backward as she pulled him out of the kitchen.

He came willingly, eyes locked on hers as they moved down the hallway toward her bedroom. She finally had to face forward again or risk stumbling into a wall, the power of his gaze making her brain short out. Twisting the knob to her door with fingers that slipped off the smooth metal the first time, she shoved it open, drawing Gil into the room behind her. A startled laugh escaped her when he kicked the door shut behind them with the heel of his shoe, pulling her back against his front with a firm grip. Her head tipped back onto his shoulder as she let herself sink into the feeling of his mouth traveling down the side of her neck, only pausing to draw her shirt up and off, dropping it at their feet. His lips were soft and full, hot and damp . . . and perfect. Long fingers slid along her torso to cup her breasts and play along the lace that adorned the edges. The featherlight touch had her arching, pressing up into his palms.

The *years* they could have been doing this.

Gil spun her around to face him again as he maneuvered them toward the edge of the bed, taking her mouth in deep, twisting kisses that had her digging her fingers into his shoulders. She had just enough presence of mind to break away to grope around the top of the bed and shove the pile of textbooks sitting near the pillow off the mattress. They hit the floor in a series of loud thuds, making Anne wince, knowing she'd hear about it later from Mrs. Hernandez downstairs. But she couldn't really bring herself to care when she had Gilbert Blythe half naked in front of her, thumbing open the button of her jeans with a look of intense concentration. It used to drive her crazy, the way he pursued what he wanted with a single-minded focus, because what he usually wanted was to show her up. But now—now it made her shudder with need, the way he looked at her, like *she* was the only thing that mattered.

Anne bit back a gasp as he ran one long, blunt finger down the metal teeth of her zipper, not bothering to drag it open in favor of following the seam of denim under it until he was touching the warm, damp patch of fabric covering the apex of her thighs. Brown eyes flashed up to pin her with a hot look, one side of his mouth edging up into a smirk.

"Is that for me?"

She took consolation at the rough, unsteady tone of his voice. "Unless you keep teasing me. Then I'll just kick you out and take care of it myself."

The smirk widened into a dimpled grin; he gave her a light shove, tipping her backward onto the bed. He cut off her gasp of mock indignation by following close behind, surging up to press his mouth to hers. Anne sank into the mattress, wrapping both arms around his neck and drawing him to settle between her thighs. Planting both forearms on either side of her head, Gil continued to kiss her until she felt like she was going to explode with the need to move. Shifting restlessly, she made an impatient noise and lifted her hips from the mattress as far as she could with his weight pinning her down, rocking them up to press her core against the hard length of him straining behind denim.

Tearing his mouth from hers as she did it again, he panted into her neck, breath hot against her skin. Goose bumps raced across her neck and down her arms, need tickling low in her belly. She was so keyed up, even her teeth were tingling. Running her tongue over them with a strangled laugh, she scratched her nails up his back lightly.

"Anne. Sweetheart. Give me a minute here." Gil pressed his hips down, inextricably holding her to the mattress and stilling her movement, desperation written on his face as he raised his head to meet her gaze. "I'm not usually—I need—just don't move for a minute or this is going to be over embarrassingly fast."

She took in the hectic flush across his cheekbones and glazed-over look in his eyes, gleeful mischief taking over as she realized how close he was just from what they'd done. They hadn't even gotten naked yet. With a laugh, Anne made the herculean effort and somehow bucked him off, rolling them over to straddle his hips. He was so beautiful; dark curls in disarray from her hands, lips swollen and red from her kisses, body tight with tension from desire.

Lifting up, she finished what he started, tugging off her jeans in a series of awkward movements that had him snickering when the bunched-up material got caught on one sock at her ankle.

She paused to point at him. "Shut up."

He raised his hands. "I didn't say anything."

"You didn't have to, I can *hear* you thinking it," she retorted, finally yanking off the offending piece of clothing and throwing it somewhere over her shoulder. His laughter died as he took in the sight in front of him, settling his hands back on her hips. Had she been thinking about this moment for the last few weeks and perhaps, just a little bit, hoped it would be tonight? With that thought in mind, was it why she'd invited him over, knowing they'd have the apartment to themselves? *Maybe.*

(Yes. The answer was yes.)

The flower-print cotton panties she wore cut high in a flattering shape, pale and thin enough to give him a preview of what lay underneath while still clinging to the pretense of modesty. His fingers brushed the wet patch at the front of the material, drawing a gasp from her lips, and she let herself fall forward onto his chest. Gil flipped them over again, kissing her deeply before pulling away to slide down her body. Anne slid shaking fingers through his hair as he placed a kiss low on her belly, then brushed his mouth over the top edge of her panties.

"I want to taste you." Looking back up at her, he ran his tongue along his bottom lip. "Will you let me?"

Need shuddered through her. "God, yes."

Refocusing on his task, Gil hooked his thumbs under the elastic and slid the scrap of material off, never looking away from what the cotton had revealed. But as he lowered his mouth between her thighs, his gaze came up, locking on hers. The intensity of the connection between them was overwhelming; she couldn't help but turn her head away, throwing one arm over her eyes as her cheeks burned.

"Look at me." His mouth lifted, leaving her aching and damp. "Anne."

She shook her head, feeling unbearably vulnerable.

"Please?" His voice was soft but undeniable, reaching deep inside her to pull her gaze back to where he waited patiently, breath hot against her fiery curls. The way he asked, like her full and complete attention was something he *needed*.

Things fell into place then, like tumblers in a lock. Oh. He did, he always had—and suddenly she wanted to give it to him. Taking a deep breath, Anne let her arm drop away, ignoring the quiver in her belly as she met his eyes again, and held them.

A slow smile curled up one side of his mouth. "Good girl."

Oh God.

In the kitchen, she'd thought their coupling was going to be fast and frantic, hot desire pushing them to abandon all pretense of gentleness. But somehow Gil had turned it around, each touch of his tongue and fingers slow torture, driving her inexorably toward the orgasm she was craving. She didn't know what to do with the emotion suddenly clogging her throat. The intensity of it pressing behind her rib cage, clawing to get free, scared her. Drowning in it, her orgasm caught her by surprise, ripping a hoarse cry from Anne's lips.

Gil made a noise of satisfaction against her core, causing her to shudder again and push him away from the oversensitive, tight bundle of nerves there. He just laughed, wiping his mouth against the back of his hand before crawling up to prop himself up on one elbow next to her. She thought he'd pull her underneath him then, but he just smoothed one hand across her belly before settling on the opposite hip. The hard length of him pressing through the rough material of his jeans reminded Anne that while she was naked as the day she was born, he hadn't even finished getting undressed.

Turning to face Gil, she scratched her nails over the bulge of his crotch, grinning when he sucked in a sharp breath. "Quid pro quo?"

"Ah—" He stuttered to a halt when she cupped him fully and squeezed. Closing his eyes, he licked his lips. "That's okay. I mean, I didn't do it so you would. You don't have to, don't feel obligated."

"*Don't feel obligated.*" Anne snickered, unzipping his jeans and shoving them down to his thighs. "While I appreciate the sentiment, I think we both know I don't do anything I don't want to do."

"I do know that—" She pumped him a couple times with one hand. "God, that's—" Then lowered to take him into her mouth.

"Fuck, that's good," he breathed, tangling fingers in her hair, resting his hand lightly on the back of her head. Anne wanted to laugh at the strangled sound he made when she hollowed out her cheeks but pushed the urge away in favor of drawing increasingly desperate noises, pleas, and panted compliments out of him instead. After a few long moments, the fingers in her hair tightened, giving the long locks a light tug, a clear signal he was close. Ignoring the way he choked out her name in warning, she redoubled her efforts, ruthless until he cried out, hips jerking helplessly.

She felt she was very much within her rights to feel smug when his hand slid out of her hair to flop bonelessly onto the mattress.

Waiting until Gil had shucked his jeans and boxers the rest of the way off and pulled the rumpled comforter over them both, Anne wriggled upward to rest her cheek on his chest. His heartbeat was loud in her ear, thumping hard as he strove to quiet his rapid breathing. Curling his arm around her, he trailed fingers up and down her back in a languid motion, the weak autumn sunlight moving slowly across the room. The silence between them was comfortable, but as it lengthened, doubts began to creep in.

They were still who they were. This new relationship could just as easily blow up in their faces tomorrow. One of them would say the wrong thing and it would all go pear-shaped. The thought made her queasy, that she could lose this. She should probably be a little more cautious, not get ahead of herself.

With a sigh, Anne rolled onto her back, dislodging Gil's arm in the process, and sat up. He raised his head to watch her pull on a pair of fresh panties and T-shirt, then scoop her hair into a messy bun, but said nothing. His gaze felt heavy where it rested on her body as she searched for clean sweatpants. Finally, he sat up too, and scrubbed one hand through his hair. She tried not to notice how charming the brown curls were, sticking up all over the place like that.

"Do you need to—should I go?" It was clear he was giving her an out, his voice neutral.

Buying herself a moment longer, Anne dug through her drawers for a pair of thick, woolen socks. If they attempted a serious relationship, she knew herself well enough to understand her heart would very much be at risk. Nothing between her and Gil had ever been casual, and she didn't know why she'd thought dating would be any different. If they broke up (again, a *very* real possibility), the fallout would be nuclear.

Unsure, she sat on the edge of the mattress to pull on her socks, glancing at Gil out of the corner of her eye. He looked calm, as if her asking him to stay would be fine and her asking him to leave would also be fine, he wouldn't be bothered either way. But then she noticed the tension his body held, and it occurred to her that he was just as nervous about this as she was.

"No, stay," Anne said as she snagged his clothes off the floor and dropped them on the bed next to his hip. The open smile he sent her did funny, fluttery things to her insides, and without thought she reached to touch his dimple with one fingertip. When he went still, she pulled back, slightly embarrassed to be caught out being so *soft*. Clearing her throat, she moved back to let him climb out of bed. "I have some leftover pasta, if Phil didn't steal it."

He combed his fingers through his hair again. She didn't have the heart to tell him he'd only made it worse. "Sounds good to me."

They spent the rest of the afternoon with their books and computers spread over her bed, plates of pizza that had replaced the ziti her thieving roommate had indeed stolen balanced on their laps. Nothing more than the occasional kiss was traded, the intense sexual tension between them for so long settled into a low burning that flowed through Anne, slow like honey, whenever she looked at him. They didn't talk about it, but she was okay with that for the moment.

For hours after Gil left, Anne found herself smiling for no reason at all, occasionally bringing her fingers up to rub at her mouth, remembering what his lips had felt like moving against hers. The fifth time she caught herself doing this, she rolled her eyes and closed her laptop. Clearly studying the rest of the night was a lost cause.

Wandering out to the living room close to midnight, she flopped down on the couch next to Diana, who immediately twisted to lie lengthwise along the cushions while not taking her eyes off the TV, and tucked her toes under Anne's thighs. But Anne knew her friend, and it wasn't long before Diana glanced over at her.

"Did Gil wind up coming over earlier?"

"He did."

There was another beat of silence, then toes dug into the side of Anne's leg hard, making her yelp. She smacked Diana's feet away as the other woman laughed. "Come on, details. Spill. If you guys had stuck to the plan and only studied, you'd be a hell of a lot chattier."

Anne shrugged, helpless to keep from smiling. "We got distracted for a while, but we *did* study."

"Biology?"

"Diana!"

"*What?* It's a valid question. That boy has been looking like he wants to study your anatomy for ages."

"Why are you the way you are?"

Diana sat up and scooted over to wrap Anne in a tight hug. "You love me the way I am. And I'm not saying anything that isn't true. On a more serious note, I'm glad you're finally giving him a chance.

"*Another* chance," she added before Anne could say anything. Letting go, Diana flopped back against the arm of the couch again and picked up the remote. "Did you guys ever straighten that whole thing out? The mess from before? I'm still not over you never telling me you kissed him that night, by the way."

"I've said sorry *a million times*. And, um, no. It didn't come up." The other woman sent her an unimpressed look. "Okay, okay, I know that's not great. It's just . . . I haven't wanted to dredge that up, not when things have been going so well."

"You have to talk to him soon. Just because it's in the past doesn't mean it's not important anymore."

"I will."

"*Soon.*"

"*I will.*" Anne threw her hands up, exasperated. "Can we just watch TV for a while? I'm tired."

"I bet you are."

The two women looked at each other, then started cackling. When she was finally able to catch her breath, Anne drew her legs up to push the bottom of her feet against Diana's. They'd done it since they were kids, and the familiarity of feeling their toes pressed together comforted her. No matter what else changed in her life, it was nice to know some things never would.

Snuggling into the lap blanket Diana tossed over, Anne settled in to watch some reality TV and resolved not to think about anything else until morning.

Chapter 19

Anne did a head count again, panicking when she came up two short, then spied the two boys she'd missed flipping through graphic novels at a nearby vendor tent. She'd have thought thirteen-year-olds would be easier to track than younger children, but every time she turned around, some of them seemed to disappear like smoke.

"Breathe," Gil murmured in passing.

"*You* breathe," she said automatically, eyes skipping over the crowd again.

He shot her an amused look over his shoulder as he wandered over to see what some of their girls were looking at. Okay, maybe she was being a little uptight. But it was so crowded, the flow of people making it hard to place everyone at once. Finally, it was time to shepherd the students over to a cordoned-off side street lined with food trucks, then find spots to picnic on the lawn of a nearby park. Feeling a bit like a collie herding cats instead of sheep, Anne plopped down on the grass, taking the bottle of water Gil handed her with a grateful smile.

"Whose idea was this anyway," she mumbled as she bit into her duck taco, tongue darting out to lick a dab of plum sauce off her thumb before it could drip onto her shirt. When Gil's eyes followed the movement, dropping to look at her mouth, she jabbed him in the side with her elbow. "Stop it! You can't look at me like that here."

His grin was wicked. "Can I look at you like that later?"

"If you get them to stop throwing acorns at those poor squirrels, you can have dealer's choice when we get home." Sighing, Anne gestured toward a couple of the kids farther down the slope they were seated on. Gil was up in an instant, yelling at them to leave the wildlife alone, making her laugh. He moved *fast* with proper motivation.

They'd spent the last four nights together, at either her place or his. She'd have thought that she'd be ready for some room by now, but it was nice. Because he already knew Diana so well, and Phil was incredibly laid-back, Gil just sort of slotted right into her life. Like how she'd talked about "home" just now, as if it was one and the same for them both. Sometimes she thought it should have made her nervous, how easy it was to assume he'd just *be there*.

How quickly he was becoming important to her.

Looking away from where Gil was now teaching the acorn-throwing kids how to juggle with them instead, Anne let her gaze drift over the rest of the class. Some were talking or reading their new books, a couple looked like they were napping . . .

and then there was Jenna. The curly-haired girl was sitting apart from everyone like she always did, bent over her notebook, scribbling away.

Anne didn't *get it*. The girl so clearly loved writing. She was good at it.

There had been a moment, last week, when she thought they were having a breakthrough. Jenna had handed in her short story and it was *good*. It was about a house that longed to be anything but a house, like a car or a skyscraper or a boat. The premise might sound almost childish to some people, but the execution was breathtaking. Jenna wasn't writing about a house's loneliness, its ache to be something impossible—she wrote it as if she *were* the house. And in a way, Anne thought maybe that's exactly what Jenna was. A house that wanted to be a car, so it could go places and do things that a house could only dream of. That story gave Anne hope that maybe this was Jenna's way of reaching out to her and Gil.

The scathing reception Anne received when she tried to sit down and talk about it with the younger girl left her reconsidering. Not reconsidering reaching out. Just her angle.

After watching the younger girl for another minute, Anne made a decision. Shoving her taco wrapper into the side pocket of the messenger bag she was using in lieu of her backpack for the day, she got up and made her way toward Jenna. The other girl didn't notice her until Anne was just a few feet away; both her notebook and expression were closed by the time Anne sat down next to the girl.

"Hey." She tried a smile, because maybe this time it would work. Doubtful. But maybe.

Jenna didn't say anything back, just stared out at the park.

"All right, I think that's enough of that," Anne said, dropping the smile, her spine turning to steel. Jenna's head whipped around at the grim tone. Anne leaned back on her hands, studying the girl intently. "What is your problem?"

"My *problem*?" Jenna's mouth fell open, looking taken aback. It was the most open Anne had seen her so far, the only expression she'd made all semester that didn't contain a sneer.

"Look, I'm going to be honest with you," Anne said. "You have a ton of talent. You're a really good writer. With practice and a dedication to learning the craft of storytelling, I think you could even be a great writer. But you don't seem to care at all. Why?"

"I—" The sneer was back, but only for a second before it faltered and fell away. The younger girl brought her legs up, wrapping her arms around her shins as she mumbled something into her knees.

"I can't hear you." Anne tapped her on the foot, willing the girl to look back up.

Jenna heaved a sigh, then tipped her head back to stare at the interwoven bare branches above. "I do care. A lot. And I know I've been a jerk. I'm sorry." Her voice sounded thick, like she was trying to hold back tears. She finally looked at Anne, holding her gaze with eyes that begged for understanding. "I care *so much*. But it doesn't matter."

This girl was in pain, and it hurt Anne's own heart to see it. She scooted up alongside Jenna and placed a tentative hand on the girl's back. "Why doesn't it matter?"

"Because being a writer isn't a real job. My mom said so," the girl said, dropping her chin to the top of her knees. "She said her dad wrote books and they never made any money, and their family was always so poor that her mom worked herself to death to support them. And then her dad left, and my mom had to raise her two younger sisters by herself. She only let me go to Herschel in the first place because I drove her nuts until she caved. So that's why she's pulling me next year and sending me to a STEM school instead. She said I need to learn how to do something useful, instead of wasting more of her hard-earned money on notebooks."

Anne blinked, head spinning from the torrent of information. She straightened and blew out a breath. "Well, that's a lot to unpack."

"I know," said Jenna in a gloomy voice. "I wanted to learn how to write better, so I signed up for the class, since my mom doesn't even get home until six on those nights. But it's pointless, because it's never going to go anywhere."

"You don't know that. You don't," Anne insisted, when the other girl rolled her eyes. "And with all due respect to your mom, she doesn't know that either. A lot of people make a decent living writing. I mean, a lot of people write and have other jobs too, so she's not wrong that it's good to learn something that you can use to support yourself if the writing thing doesn't work out. But I think she's underestimating your talent and love for storytelling."

Jenna looked uncertain. "Maybe."

"I understand where she's coming from, she just wants you to have a more stable life than she did. If I had kids, I'd probably feel the same." Maybe this was a little personal to share with a thirteen-year-old, but she had a feeling Jenna needed to hear it. "I grew up in a group home until I was almost your age; both my parents had died when I was pretty young. Well, my biological parents. I think of the people who adopted me as my family now.

"Up until I was twelve, I didn't think any of this was possible," she said, gesturing around her, including the kids, herself, and the city itself. Her gaze lingered on Gil for a moment before turning back to Jenna. "I'd been told I wouldn't be anything when I grew up, by a lot of people. That I couldn't do anything that mattered. But I wouldn't listen to them, because I *knew* I could be more than they thought I was."

"But your new family helped you?"

"They gave me an opportunity and the tools to get to where I am, absolutely." When Jenna's face fell again, Anne touched her on the arm lightly. "But it wouldn't have done any good if I didn't believe in myself. And I know that sounds like a greeting card, but it's still true."

Jenna chewed on her bottom lip, looking out over the park, her expression pensive. Out of the corner of her eye, Anne saw Gil wave at her as he started to round up the other kids. She signaled for him to give her another minute. She was on the edge of reaching Jenna, really getting her to reconsider the way she'd been thinking about things, Anne just knew it.

She bumped her shoulder against the younger girl's, prompting Jenna to look over at her. "Even if your mom does send you somewhere else next year, you can still keep writing. You never have to stop writing, that's something you could even do on the way to and from your new school. Writing is an anywhere, anytime activity. Besides, we have half a year to go and a lot left to teach. So, can I count on you to participate more?"

"I guess," Jenna said. She gave Anne a small smile, the first since the beginning of the year, and it was beautiful. "I mean, I'll try."

"Yeah?"

"Yeah."

"Awesome." Anne jumped up, then took the other girl's hand and hauled her to her feet. "Now let's go before we get left behind. I don't want to miss that young-adult panel; one of the books we're reading next semester is written by an author who'll be up there today."

When Jenna started back toward the group, Anne sent Gil a beaming smile over the girl's head. He returned the look with a discreet thumbs-up, before leading the kids out of the park. Anne brought up the rear, a buoyant feeling in her chest. Jenna's fragile self-confidence wasn't going to be fixed by that one conversation, but Anne felt she'd at least made some inroads. She'd just have to keep working at it. Gil had told her he thought she was too stubborn to walk away. Her lips curved into a satisfied smile. She'd just have to keep proving him right.

Chapter 20

"D ealer's choice?"

Something crashed off to the right, but Gil didn't bother to look as he picked Anne up and pressed her against the wall while he attacked her neck with his teeth. She yelped when he sucked hard on the soft curve of her throat, then shuddered as he licked over the bruised flesh.

"That's what I said," she managed, then grabbed two handfuls of his hair and yanked his head back, kissing him deeply. It was with a herculean effort Gil detached his mouth from hers, panting.

"So, anything's on the table?"

"Uh." She blinked up at him, her mouth swollen and shiny from their kisses. "We haven't really talked about that."

It took him a second, then he laughed out loud and let her slide down the wall to stand on her own feet. "Not anything kinky. I was just wondering if sex was on the table. *Sex* sex."

They hadn't gone any further than what they'd done that first afternoon together at Anne's place, but he knew Anne didn't just thoughtlessly throw an offer like "dealer's choice" out there without considering he'd pick sex.

She *had* to know he'd pick sex.

"If you have condoms, then sex is on the table," Anne said, then her gaze slid toward the kitchen. "Or on the bed, because I doubt Fred wants to eat his cereal where my bare butt has been."

"I just really like you." Gil hoisted her up into his arms again and carried her to his room.

"I really like you too," she laughed into his shoulder.

Undressing was less awkward now that they had practice, but still took as long as ever, because they kept stopping to kiss and touch each other. Finally, all their clothes lay on the floor in a crumpled heap, and Anne lowered herself to the bed, scooting back toward the headboard with a beckoning smile. He didn't hesitate to join her on the mattress, drinking in the sight of brilliant copper hair spilled over shoulders burnished with small golden spots.

A man could spend a lifetime mapping those freckles, and he wanted to find them all.

"Have I mentioned how hot you are?"

"Not today, you haven't."

"You're incredibly hot," Gil informed her, leaning over to kiss that soft, lush mouth, doing nothing more than that for the next few moments. When he pulled back, her eyes were heavy-lidded, and her lips just a little bit swollen from his, and he thought he could kiss her for days.

Except he really wanted to have sex now.

Stretching across Anne's body, he pulled open the drawer to his nightstand and grabbed a condom. The ones he'd brought from California had gotten lost in the move, and he hadn't bothered to replace them. There hadn't been anyone besides Anne that he'd even considered having sex with since he'd been back, and *that* hadn't been a possibility until very recently.

The morning after their first real date, Gil went out and optimistically bought an economy-sized box.

Holding the packet up between two fingers, he raised an eyebrow. "You want to do the honors or should I?" When she wiggled her fingers, he started to hand it over, then pulled back. "Are we moving too fast? Because I'm not afraid to put the work in if you're not ready."

"Gil," Anne replied, snatching the packet from him and tearing it open. "I am so ready. I've been ready for the last ten minutes. If you don't hurry up and get inside me, I might actually murder you."

The amusement at the growl in her voice was cut short by her taking his dick in one hand and swiftly rolling on the condom with the other. She gave it one short tug to make sure it was in place, rose over him on her knees, then dropped down in one smooth motion. The breath punched out of him as her heat enveloped him, their moans intermingled as Anne began to move. He gripped her hips, holding her in place, encouraging her to rock faster. She fell forward, planting her hands on his shoulders, the curtain of her hair surrounding them as her hips rose and fell. Their breathing was loud and ragged; sweat-dampened skin sliding together as they each chased their own release.

Gil could feel his orgasm building, drawing up tight within him, and he knew he wasn't going to last much longer.

"Are you close?" he panted into her neck. She shuddered as his breath blew across her collarbone.

"Yes, but I can't . . ." She struggled to push herself up, fingers biting into his shoulders as her gaze dropped to where they were joined, and he understood what she needed. Moving one hand off her hip, Gil thumbed her clit.

She whimpered, her head thrown back, eyes closed.

Then he pressed against the swollen, little nub and her orgasm rolled through her body, the sexiest fucking sound coming out of her mouth he thought he'd ever heard. When she collapsed against him, limp and shivering, Gil drew up his knees, shifting her so she was sprawling across his chest, and pistoned his hips up into her. Her mouth was hot against his ear, her little moans driving him on until his own release tore through him.

Letting his legs fall back onto the bed, he just lay there under her for one long minute, trying to catch his breath.

"Anne," he said, his voice hoarse. When she only mumbled something against his neck, he jostled her shoulder. "Anne. *Annie.*"

She lifted her head just high enough to glare at him with one eye out from under a hank of tangled hair. "I told you never to call me that."

"When I'm still in you, I think I get to call you whatever I want."

"That's not how it works, and ew, it just occurred to me how uncomfortable this is."

Hiding his smile, Gil rolled them over and carefully eased out of her. He went to the bathroom and took care of the condom, then padded back out to the bedroom with a damp washcloth. Anne caught it one-handed when he tossed it to her, gesturing he should turn around so she could deal with herself.

"Didn't we just establish that I've literally been inside you?"

"Sex does not equal intimacy," she said loftily, from behind him somewhere. "And this is about as intimate as it gets, only farther down the list from peeing with the door open."

"I think you and I have very different definitions of what intimacy means."

It seemed to be taking her an awful long time to finish up. Hearing nothing, Gil took a chance and peeked over his shoulder, only to find Anne tucked up under the sheets, looking comfortable.

Looking at him standing naked with his back to her.

"Oh, you brat."

Anne shrieked when he launched himself onto the mattress, giggling too hard to crawl away. After she choked out an apology between fits of laughter, they settled into the middle of the bed, her chin propped on his chest.

They talked for hours like that, about anything and everything, his fingers combing through her hair again and again until it was silky smooth.

Chapter 21

Gil kissed Anne goodbye at the station, hanging back to watch her and Diana climb into Mrs. Barry's Mercedes. He was going to miss her; they'd hardly slept apart since mid-November. But things were still a little too new between them to try that with their families. Sighing, Gil threw his bags into the back of the cab. Sometimes he came back here, and it was like he'd never left.

Nerves jumped in his belly, as he went over the conversation he wanted to have with his parents at dinner. It was better to get it out of the way early into the vacation; he'd much rather have the follow-up conversations in person than over the phone.

But his parents had invited the neighbors on either side of them over for the evening, squashing Gil's plans. It wasn't until the last of the stragglers left, thanking his parents for the bottles of wine they were being sent away with, which Gil was amused to see were from Green Gables, that he had a spare moment to catch them.

"Can I talk to you?" He set down the stack of dirty dishes, as his mother ran soapy water into the plugged sink. She turned to him, one silvery blond eyebrow elegantly arched.

"Now?"

"Yeah. Yes," he amended at her flat look. She'd always been a stickler for proper grammar. "Both you and Dad. I asked him to wait in the sitting room. It won't take long. I think."

"Well, now I'm curious," she said, and stripped the rubber dish gloves back off.

While his mother settled onto the couch next to his father, Gil poked the burning logs in the hearth with a fire iron, stalling for time. Why was he so nervous about this? He was an adult, he didn't need their permission to do the things he wanted to anymore.

But he knew he was nervous because their opinion mattered to him, and always would.

"Gil, honey, not to rush you, but I'd like to get the dishes done before bed. Did you have something you wanted to share?" his mother asked, sounding tired. He winced, remembering she'd not only cooked and set up the entire dinner, but had spent a good part of her day helping her husband through his.

"Right. Sorry." Gil returned the fire iron to its hook, then turned to face them. "Dad and I spoke over the fall festival weekend about me continuing on for a doctorate, and I said it wasn't something I wanted to do." He looked at his father. "I'm sorry if that disappoints you."

His father waved it away immediately. "I'm disappointed not to have another generation of doctors in the family, but I could never be disappointed in *you*."

Damn. He'd promised himself he wasn't going to get all emotional about this, but that had him swallowing past a lump in his throat. Continuing, he said, "I didn't really have a plan at the time for what I *did* want to do then, but I do now.

"The thesis project Anne and I are collaborating on has been pretty eye-opening for me. I'd always thought I wanted to use my master's in education on a more administrative level, helping reshape the current system into something that works better." He paused, then amended, "Something that works, period. But over the last four months I realized I love working directly with the kids themselves. I want to continue to do that."

"Are you saying you want to teach in a middle school?" His father sounded more puzzled than judgmental. "There's nothing wrong with that, it's just a big change from your previous plans."

"Not exactly," Gil hedged. "I want to put together a not-for-profit that works with kids who are interested in pursuing the arts but might not have an opportunity to do so. One of the things I've been frustrated with as I've become more educated on the public-school system is how little money and time are being put into the creative arts. It seems like it's less every year.

"An organization like that can really help, I believe. And it's something I'd be good at, I think."

"I'm positive you'd make it a success," his mother said. "But what will you do while you're getting it up and running? These things take a long time to get off the ground. Will you stay in the city?"

"Yes, I want to start small first, stay local in Brooklyn. And I'll keep my bartending job. Fred said I can pick up a few shifts a week at the shop's front desk. It'll be fine."

"Two jobs and starting a not-for-profit?" His father frowned. "It sounds like a lot of work."

Gil's mouth quirked into a small grin. "Yeah. I don't mind."

"What about Anne?"

There was a long moment of silence while his mother's words registered with Gil. "What?"

She looked at him with amused exasperation. "This is Avonlea, Gilbert. I hear things."

More like she was the epicenter of the gossip network. He was a fool to think the city was far enough away to escape Patricia Blythe's informants. Resigned to the shift in subject, Gil dropped into the armchair next to the sofa.

"Anne's got her own thing going on. She's going to try to stay in the city too, but she's more interested in the university career track."

They hadn't spoken about their plans for after graduation, mostly because it seemed so far away still. But the idea of her moving away for a job made Gil feel a little sick. Technically, he could set up anywhere. But he already had roots in Brooklyn, knew some people in the school system, and was familiar with the area. The idea of starting over somewhere else, *again*, didn't sit well with him.

And anyway, they still hadn't discussed exactly where they saw their relationship going. He didn't want to push her too fast and talking about him following her all over the country after graduation would definitely be pushing. Things were perfect right now; he wanted to keep them that way as long as possible.

"But you are serious about each other?" His father's dark eyes glinted shrewdly in the firelight.

"I'm serious about her." Gil shook his head at his mother's look. "She's not *not* serious about me. I think. We haven't had a chance to get into it too much yet. Which is fine. Please don't make a thing of it on Saturday."

His parents' crowded annual New Year's Eve party was the last place he wanted one of them cornering Anne and grilling her about her intentions for their baby boy. God. Just the idea had him inwardly cringing. Maybe he should warn her.

"Relax, we won't do anything to scare her off," sighed his mother as she pushed herself up from the couch. "I just decided I don't care about the dishes; they can keep until the morning. Don't the two of you stay up too late, please." She sent Gil a pointed look. "Your dad has chemo in the morning."

"Ach," his father grumbled after she was safely out of the room and couldn't hear him. "That stuff is poison. First time I went in, I couldn't shit for days. The last time I went in, I couldn't *stop* shitting for days."

"Dad." Gil let out a snort of shocked laughter. "Can't they do anything about that?"

"I'm not that worried about it, truth be told. I'll suffer a little gastro distress to get this bullshit out of my system."

"Cancer has really done a number on your vocabulary. Mom must love it."

His father's gaze softened. "Your mother appreciates a little black humor. It's how I'm dealing with all this without losing it, she knows that."

"As coping mechanisms go, it's not the worst."

"True," his father agreed, then shifted to get more comfortable. "So. Anne Shirley, hmm?"

Gil rolled his head to the side to eye him, unable to read the tone in the older man's voice.

"Seems like."

"It's been a long time."

He shrugged. "Only since October, really."

"You've been in love with that girl since high school," his father said bluntly.

Had he really been that transparent?

"More like eighth grade." He might not be ready to tell Anne, but it helped to finally say it out loud. "She used to hate me, though." Laughter spilled out as he pictured her furious little face telling him off, the most popular boy in school at the time, because he'd landed her in detention on her first day. "God, she couldn't stand me."

"Clearly, she's changed her mind."

"Yeah," Gil said, his laughter fading into a smile just shy of goofy. He rubbed his hand over his mouth, embarrassed.

His father tapped his fingers on the handle of his cane. "But you don't know if she loves you back?"

"I haven't asked, and I haven't told her how I feel yet either. It's too soon. I don't want to scare her off." Gil stared sleepily into the fire, the warmth, his hours of travel, and a full plate of food from dinner starting to take a toll. One of the logs split, sparking as the glowing pieces fell apart with a hiss.

"Did I ever tell you that I used to see Marilla Cuthbert?"

Whatever he'd been expecting his dad to say next, that wasn't it. Gil sat up, wide awake again. "No. You and Ms. Cuthbert? *When?*"

"We were high school sweethearts, actually."

Gil's eyebrows shot up. "Sweetheart" was not a word he'd ever thought to associate with the formidable woman.

"We were young once too, you know," his father said, rolling his eyes at Gil's expression. "We went together for over two years, believe it or not. Everyone thought we would get married right out of school; for a while I thought it too."

"So, what happened? Because clearly not that."

Embers popped in the fireplace, the flare highlighting the tired lines of his father's face. "I'm not sure, to be honest. A fight over something or other. We did that a lot, fighting. Sometimes it was fun, other times, not so much. This was one of the less fun fights, because I'd told her I'd been thinking about going to Duke University for college, then my doctorate. She didn't want to go with me, and she didn't want to wait for me to come back home."

"She wanted you to stay?"

"She wanted me to stay and open a horse farm with her in the fields next to the winery." His father sent him a wry smile. "But my father wouldn't have it, and I didn't have the backbone you do, to fight for what I wanted." Gil didn't remember his grandfather very well; the man had died when he was seven. But what he did recall was an unyielding face and stern voice, and the occasional pat on the back. "So, I left, and we never did make up. But I met your mother at Duke, and I think that worked out just fine."

"You'd never know it now, though—you and Marilla. I didn't even think you knew each other all that well," Gil said. He thought back over all the times the two families had run into each other around town or at school functions, the adults politely conversing while Anne acted like he was invisible, and he acted like he didn't care.

"With adulthood comes a sense of perspective. As you and Anne seem to have discovered," his father replied. "It's interesting how you've managed to fall for the daughter of the first girl I ever loved. And they may not be blood, but she's as fiery as her mother and just as fond of holding a grudge."

"You think we're going to crash and burn too?"

His father lifted one hand, then dropped it again. "Some would say it's fate, if you do.

"But not me," he added, hoisting himself off the couch with a grunt. "Because I think life is what you make of it. Don't sit around and wait for the universe to take care of things for you. Go get what you want for yourself. You've already got a good start."

Gil smiled up at him as the older man squeezed his shoulder in passing, glad all over again that he'd made the choice to come back east. "Thanks, Dad."

"Oh, and Gil?" His father paused in the doorway, looking thoughtful.

"Yeah?"

"Don't fuck it up."

Gil let out a helpless puff of laughter. "I'll do my best."

Chapter 22

Then

Anne spent her first Christmas Eve at Green Gables in a heightened state of excitement and terror.

Excitement, because there were *presents* with *her name* on them under the tree in the living room that she and Matthew had decorated a few weeks ago. Not just one present, but multiple! Enough of them that Marilla kept sending her brother narrow looks, muttering about overindulgence, while he slowly turned tomato red and hid behind his newspaper. It was by sheer will alone that Anne hadn't snuck downstairs in the middle of the night to shake or squeeze the gifts, even though she was positively *dying* of curiosity.

Terror, because she'd used all her chore money to buy them each a present (Mrs. Barry had taken her and Diana to the mall), and what if they didn't like them? What if Anne had gotten it all wrong? And then they saw how ill-fitted she was for them and they sent her back . . . ?

She couldn't bear it if that happened. Green Gables was already deeply rooted in her heart, from the musty, damp smell of the grapevines to the way Gloriana's leaves made shadows dance across her ceiling every night as she fell asleep. And she'd never felt so safe before, as with the Cuthberts. It had been a revelation, the way her soul unclenched when she didn't have to watch every step and every word and walk every line with meticulous care.

So it was with a mixture of trepidation and eagerness that she crept down to the living room as the sun peeked over the treetops, careful not to put her weight on the third step from the bottom and wake Marilla and Matthew. But her caution was for naught—both were already seated in their usual spots at the breakfast table, drinking coffee. Marilla looked up as Anne paused in the doorway, a small smile playing about her mouth.

"Well, I'm shocked you lasted this long, child." She stood, carrying her empty cup to the sink before turning back to look at Anne, who was now practically vibrating with anticipation. "Let's get on with it. I have a feeling you won't be able to eat a thing until you've satisfied your curiosity."

Anne nodded fervently, her nose finally catching the sweet scent of yeast rolls and cinnamon, making her mouth water. But Marilla was right—she wouldn't be able to choke down even a bite in her state of suspense.

Matthew chuckled and rose too, waving his hand for Anne to follow his sister out of the kitchen. She wasted no time, scurrying along on the heels of the older woman, the sight of gold and red twinkling lights strung around the fat pine in the corner once again stealing her breath. The tree was so elegant, decorated with delicate ornaments passed down through generations of Cuthberts. Painted glass balls and crystal icicles that caught the light, refracting onto the walls in mini rainbows. Thick velvet and satin ribbons twisted through the branches, occasionally dotted with fancy bows in a deep green plaid.

The strands of popcorn mixed in that Anne and Diana had spent the afternoon before stringing shouldn't have worked, but oddly, they were the perfect addition.

Stomach flopping around like a family of fairies dancing a jig on her insides, Anne seated herself on the floor near Matthew's chair, drawing up her legs at the knee and sitting with them crossed. She folded her hands in her lap politely, hoping no one would notice her knuckles whitening as she clenched her fingers together.

There was a moment of silence, then Marilla's eyebrows rose as she looked at Anne.

"Well? Go on."

The words had hardly left her mouth when the girl scrambled over to the tree and started dragging gifts with her name on them toward her. There was a huff of amusement from Marilla's corner, but the top of Anne's head was already spinning with joy as she counted five presents. Five! And not one of the packages looked like a pair of socks. It wasn't until she dug her nails into the thin paper that she remembered her own presents for the siblings.

Pulling the two gifts from under the tree, Anne shuffled over to each of them on her knees, a shy smile on her face. "These are for you. I know it's not much, but I wanted to get you both *something.*"

"You didn't have to do that," Matthew said, despite pinking up with pleasure as he turned the flat package over in his hands.

"I know, but I really did want to." Anne bent her head to work on her own presents, one eye on the way Marilla ghosted her palm over the top of the small, wrapped box in her lap. The older woman's mouth trembled once before she smoothed her expression out, her usual unruffled demeanor locking back into place.

Turning her attention to her gifts, Anne opened them one after another, exclaiming in surprise and happiness as the torn-off paper revealed a soft, pale green sweater, a thick journal and set of multicolored gel pens, a gift card for the local bookstore, a shadow box framing an artistic arrangement of shells and sea-grass, and—a jewelry box. Her brow furrowed at that, because she had no jewelry to put in it. But it was a nice thought, and someday she would put it to good use.

Marilla's voice interrupted her thoughts as she touched one finger to the ornate hinges on the wooden lid. "Open it up, that's not the entire present."

In the velvet-lined interior was a set of small emerald studs, and Anne looked back up, eyes wide as her heart thumped hard in her chest. "Does this mean . . . ?"

"Yes," Marilla said, with a gruff nod. "I thought it over, after your very persuasive and very *long* argument the other night, and decided it would be all right, I suppose, to let you get your ears pierced."

"Oh, Marilla!" Anne jumped up, nearly upending the jewelry box in her haste to fling herself at the older woman. "Thank you! Thank you so, so much! I'll be so very careful, I'll clean and twist them every night, I'll follow all the instructions, I promise." The older woman grunted as Anne hit her like a sack of potatoes, briskly patting the young girl on her back.

"You'd better, I don't want to be carting you off to the doctor to treat infections."

Anne flashed her a happy smile, hearing the pleased tone under Marilla's stern retort, before turning to give Matthew a hug too. He looked startled, but gingerly squeezed her back, then held up the informational calendar with beautiful photos of vineyards all around the world that she'd bought him.

"I'm going to hang this in my office, right next to my desk. Saved me from another year of boring calendars from the local real estate agent's office." He winked at her, and she giggled. "Thank you, Anne."

"I'm so glad you like it. I felt you'd rather have something useful, but still nice to look at." Anne bit her lip as she transferred her gaze to Marilla, anxiety pooling in her belly again as the older woman slid one nail under the edge of the wrapping, carefully folding the festive paper back from a cardboard gift box.

Marilla slipped the lid off and looked down into the box, silent, and Anne's nerves went into overtime as the older woman lifted out a compact photo album. Its hard covers were enmeshed in a deep green material, dotted with white flowers and swirls, except for a plastic-covered space on the front that showed a picture of Green Gables. Taken in the fall, Gloriana was in full glory, all brilliant reds and oranges, and pumpkins dotted the wide white porch; Anne felt the photograph encompassed the beauty of the old house. Her heart beat double time as Marilla, still silent, opened the front cover and slowly began to flip through the album.

Anne knew by heart what was in there, having agonized for hours over which photos to use and what order to place them in.

The first few pages were filled with sepia-toned photos with ruffled edges, from the stuffed manila envelope Matthew had snuck her last month. His and Marilla's parents smiled up from photos taken on their wedding day, their honeymoon in Martha's Vineyard, and their trip to the 1939 New York World's Fair. There was a slightly blurred photo of Antonia Cuthbert with one hand on her swollen belly, her face, so like Marilla's, nearly cracked in two by a wide grin, and one of Sal Cuthbert trimming vines with a chubby, toddler Matthew crouched down next to him, looking for all the world like a miniature version of his father.

Those pages gave way to a handful of photos featuring Matthew as a young man in an army uniform, the beginnings of his trademark, thick mustache covering his upper lip, and Marilla in a shockingly short, wildly patterned A-line dress and love beads. A vaguely familiar-looking, dark-haired man in his twenties was leaning against the fence next to her, one arm casually looped around her hips.

There were photos of Marilla with a bowl-shaped haircut, dancing barefoot in the kitchen with a fresh-faced Rachel Lynde, both of their heads thrown back in laughter. Matthew sitting out front of a hardware store downtown that he told Anne had closed in the mid-eighties, playing checkers with an older, liver-spotted man in denim overalls. And many, many photos of Green Gables, the lush vineyards, the construction of the winery, sunsets and sunrises over the bay . . .

Then came the photos that had a swarm of butterflies swirling around in her belly.

A selfie she'd taken with Matthew on the front porch, just a few days after arriving at Green Gables, happiness shining out of her eyes, a shy smile on his weather-creased face.

A page of shots where Anne and Diana had struck silly poses in water up to their knees, the day Mrs. Barry had taken them to the beach on the east side of the island, when she heard Anne had never spent a full day lazing around and just playing in the waves.

And Anne's favorite photo in the whole album—one she'd taken of Marilla, while the older woman sat on the back steps at sunset, unaware she was being observed. Still dressed in the mud boots and jeans she wore out to the fields, leaned back on the top step on her elbows, she wore a relaxed expression. Steel-gray hair slipped out of her usual tight bun, as a soft smile played about her mouth as the last rays of the day lit her up in golds and reds. It was a lovely photo, showing a side Marilla didn't let many people see, one Anne herself had only glimpsed a couple times.

The older woman stared down at the last photo for a long

moment, then cleared her throat, raising her eyes to meet Anne's gaze. They were dark with emotion, but she arched one eyebrow in a familiar gesture, nodding to the album.

"There's a missing photo."

Anne blinked, a surge of panic hitting her. "What? No, there can't be—I'm sure I put everything in there."

"Where's *our* photo?" Marilla asked.

Oh. Oh!

Anne grabbed her phone off the side table where she'd thrown it before opening her presents and turned to Matthew, her heart about to burst out of her chest with joy. "Can you take one now?"

"'Course," he said, taking the photo, then squinting at it sheepishly. "But, uh, can you show me how to work the camera?"

"Luddite," Anne said fondly. She showed the older man how to open the camera app, then crossed the room to where Marilla was patting the cushion on the couch next to her. Anne settled beside her, thrilling as the older woman placed an arm around her shoulders, their heads tipping together as Matthew took the picture. Afraid her smile might have been a bit manic in the first photo, Anne made him take half a dozen more before Marilla put her foot down, citing the need for breakfast.

But just before she let the younger girl go, she leaned over and pressed her lips to the crown of Anne's head, and murmured, "Thank you for the album, you sweet girl. It's a beautiful, thoughtful present and I'll treasure it always."

Anne could only nod in return, struck uncharacteristically mute by a wave of emotion. Tears clogged her throat, but tears of *joy*. Every day, she was grateful for whoever mixed up Marilla and Matthew's request for a foster boy, but none more than today. The universe had listened to countless nights of yearning and hopeful dreams, and had transformed them into a reality she'd scarcely let herself believe was real until now. For the first time, it felt like she had a real family. People who cared for her, would keep her safe and wanted to see her happy.

Finally, she had a *home*.

Her heart full, she rose from the couch and followed Marilla, and the scent of sweet cinnamon, into the kitchen. To where her family was waiting to have breakfast with her.

Chapter 23

Now

A nne shrugged off her coat as she followed Marilla, Rachel, and Matthew into the entryway of the Blythes' house. She'd never been, having avoided get-togethers here when they were teens, in an effort to not murder Gil in his own home. Mrs. Blythe bustled up a moment later, thanking them for coming, taking their coats, and unmistakably, giving Anne a discreet once-over.

Anne was doubly glad she'd worn her new dress, despite the bitter cold winter evening. It was a thick, soft, dark green wool dress with a draped cowl neck and tight, long sleeves, offset only by a pair of knee-high black, heeled boots and a strand of Marilla's mother's pearls. After accepting a glass of wine, she glanced around the room, sipping as she took in the festive decorations. It seemed everywhere her sight landed was draped in gold garland, festooned with large, gilt-edged bows, or draped with sparkling tinsel.

"I know what you're thinking," came a murmur in her ear.

Anne's lips curved as she looked down at her glass of wine and leaned just the slightest bit into the warmth of Gil's chest pressed against her back. "That your parents are very enthusiastic decorators?"

He laughed. "Something like that."

She turned then, smiling up at him. He looked so *good*. His curls were brushed back from his forehead, tamed for once, and he'd swapped out his usual ratty kicks for buffed leather lace-ups.

"No one should be able to make elbow patches look cool, but somehow you're managing," she murmured, fingering the navy leather on his dark gray blazer.

Gil's dimple popped out as he grinned down at her. "I can't compete with you—" Here he let out a silent whistle as he took her in, sweeping her with a gaze so intense, Anne could almost feel everywhere his eyes touched. There was no way she wasn't blushing, given how quickly her body flushed under his study. "But I do my best."

"Your best is very good."

"Thanks." His grin softened and he leaned forward to brush his lips over her cheek. "Happy New Year."

She fought the urge not to turn into the kiss, to push her mouth against his, and let her tongue dip in to taste him. But she wasn't ready to announce them to the world, or most of Avonlea, as it were. It was nice to keep it between the two of them for the time being.

Anne cleared her throat, lifting her glass to take a sip of wine, the liquid cooling her throat as it slid down, and turned back to face the room. She waved at Diana, standing over near the cheese table, as per usual, and flashed a smile across to Jane, who was chatting with Dr. Blythe.

"Do you feel like walking?"

"Sure." She set her glass on a nearby table and slipped her hand into the crook of Gil's arm, letting him maneuver them through the various rooms. He kept up a murmured, running commentary of all the gossip his mother had filled him in on the last few days, keeping Anne laughing as they walked.

"Ohhh," he said as they paused at the threshold of the sitting room, nodding his chin to where Marilla stood speaking with the local vet. "Do you want to hear some *prime* gossip? This is the good stuff."

"You sound like your mother."

"Bite your tongue."

Anne laughed, then looked up at him through her eyelashes, enjoying the way his eyes went dark and a little unfocused. "The good stuff, hmm? What's the price?"

"Open-ended favor. I'll decide later." His grin was wicked and sent a shiver down her spine. "So, I was talking to my dad last night, and did you know that he and Marilla used to date? Not just date—they almost got engaged, according to him."

Anne's eyebrows flew up in surprise, seduction forgotten. She looked across the room at Marilla again, assessing, trying to see her with the brash, jovial Dr. Blythe. She couldn't picture it.

"Really? I wonder what happened."

"He didn't get into the details, but they'd had some falling-out over something minor. It turned out to be the death knell for their relationship. One thing too many, I guess. He met my mom not long after their breakup and that was that."

"Huh." She watched as Rachel came up to Marilla, cheerfully greeting the vet, her hand settling on her partner's lower back. It was sweet, the way the two women unconsciously seemed to adjust their positions to lean into each other, as if they had their own force of gravity that kept them in close orbit. "I guess it worked out for the better for them both, didn't it?"

"I think so," Gil replied, his own hand drifting around to touch her hip, shifting her closer to him. Then one of their former classmates from high school came up to say hello, and Anne stepped away, just enough to feel the cool air rush in to the fill the spots where they'd been pressed together.

She'd missed the feel of him in bed next to her over the last week, her body already accustomed to waking up next to his most mornings. She missed the sex, obviously. But most of all, she missed the way she'd lie across the bed in the evening with her head on his stomach and read while he slumped against the pillows with his eyes closed, listening to an audiobook.

The rest of the night passed much the same, Gil's soft touches and flirtatious comments fleeting between catching up with old friends. Anne was delighted to reunite with Diana's aunt Josephine, who at eighty-seven and counting hadn't slowed down one bit. She gave Gil a solid smack in the shins with her cane and called him a sly one when she caught him playing with the ends of Anne's hair, then fondly ordered him away to refresh their drinks.

"Keep an eye on that one," she advised Anne, painted eyebrows wiggling in suggestion. "He's always been a handful."

Anne just barely managed to swallow her laughter. "Yes, Auntie."

The old woman's face crinkled into a smile. "Now tell me about this boy Diana's seeing. She refuses to talk to her mother, which is how I know she's serious about this one. I love my niece, but I can't deny she's scared away more than her fair share of Diana's boyfriends and girlfriends over the years."

Anne lost her battle with the giggles, and the two of them spent a very nice twenty minutes talking about men with sexy tattoos. When they parted, she might have known a bit more about Aunt Jo than she'd ever wanted to, but she'd also laughed hard enough to set her ribs to aching.

As it neared midnight, Anne began to wander the rooms, looking for Gil. They might not be ready to bring their relationship into the open, but it didn't feel right to be anywhere except by his side when the old year rolled over into the new. Grabbing her coat from the downstairs guest room, she made her way to the back patio, slipping out the door, somehow knowing she'd find him outside.

There he was, no overcoat, hands shoved into his jeans as he rocked on his heels, looking up at the sky.

Anne slid up behind him, threading her arms around his

waist to press her cheek against his shoulder blade. "What are you doing out here? It's *freezing*."

"I know, sorry." He covered her hands with his own, trapping them between the hard planes of his stomach and his palms. "I just needed a minute. It's hot in there, and I let Charlie talk me into taking a couple vodka shots. Should have known better. Bad choice."

Anne laughed into the scratchy wool of his blazer, feeling a little tipsy herself after several glasses of wine. She was glad Rachel had decided to be their designated driver for the evening, because she was definitely no longer up for the task.

Turning around, Gil opened his blazer so she could step in and soak up the heat of his body, his arms snugging her up against him. He rested his chin on the top of her head, her breath fluttering against his throat. His aftershave smelled so good; Anne couldn't resist flicking her tongue out to taste the soft skin there. He made a noise, shifting, hands sliding down to grip her hips.

"Are you really looking to start something? Out here? On a patio half covered in ice?"

She laughed up at him, then licked his Adam's apple, enjoying the small groan he let out.

"Maaaaybe."

"You pick now, with a houseful of people, and neither of us remotely sober, to tease me after a week of forced celibacy," he grumbled, but ducked down to catch her mouth in a kiss. She rose up to meet him, lips clinging to his, until she didn't feel the chill of the night air any longer.

The crescendoing volume of noise from the house had him drawing back to take a quick peek at his wristwatch. "One minute till midnight. Stay here or go in?"

There wasn't even a comparison of benefits. In there it was hot and noisy, and she couldn't touch Gil the way she wanted. Staying outside in the cold meant she didn't have to share him with anyone else, and she was feeling greedy tonight.

"Stay," Anne pressed, sliding her fingers into his hair and drawing his head down.

Five . . .

A smile curled his mouth as their lips brushed.

Four . . .

She moaned into the heat, the brush of his tongue against hers electrifying.

Three . . .

Their bodies bumped, molding to each other as the kiss deepened.

Two . . .

Gil lifted his lips from hers, brown eyes dark with promises.

One . . .

"Happy New Year, Anne," he breathed into her mouth, her head swimming as he filled her senses. She lifted her lips to his again, pulling him back into the kiss.

After all, she wanted to begin the new year as she meant to go on.

Chapter 24

Gil stretched, his muscles loose and relaxed, his mind comfortably empty of anything but the feel of Anne draped across him, her fingers tracing random patterns on his chest. The sweat from the sex they'd had earlier was cooling on his body now, making him feel sticky. They'd both need a shower soon, and he had to leave for his Friday night shift in a couple hours, but for now he was content to just lie there and let her touch him.

A rustling noise had him cracking one eye open. Already in her jeans, Anne picked her sweater up off the floor and shook it out, then pulled it over her head. As she drew her hair out from inside the collar, he propped himself onto one elbow.

"You going?"

"Don't you have to work?"

"Yeah, but not until five." He climbed out of bed, gathering a change of clothes. "Why don't you come with me? I'll snag you a stool at the end of the bar and keep you knee-deep in Irish coffee and cheesecake."

She looked at him in amusement, sitting down to zip into her knee-high boots. "You're trying to bribe me to sit through your six-hour shift with cheesecake?"

"And Irish coffee."

"Tempting, but no."

Dropping his clean clothes on the end of the bed, Gil snagged Anne by the wrist when she stood, pulling her to him. "We could come back here after and make Fred regret rooming with me."

An adorable flush made her freckles stand out. "I don't think so. All my schoolwork is at home, and I have at least three things I can finish in those six hours, sorry." Anne leaned in and kissed him, sweet but firm, and slipped out of his grasp. "But I'm free tomorrow night. I'll pack an overnight bag and we can make Fred question all his life choices then."

"I'm holding you to that," he grumbled, pulling her in for one last kiss before she broke away with a laugh and headed out.

Turning on the shower, Gil leaned against the wall and waited for it to heat up, his thoughts drifting. He wouldn't see her again tonight and resigned himself to an empty bed and restless sleep. Ducking under the hot spray, he dumped a handful of shampoo into his palm and scrubbed it through his hair. It wasn't until the scent of bright citrus reached his nose that he realized it was the bottle Anne had left behind last weekend. Squinting past the water dripping into his eyes, he saw she'd also left some conditioner and a razor.

And that got him thinking.

They now had a big bottle of lotion on the counter next to the sink, and the brand of creamer she used in the fridge. The area he and Fred kept their chips in now boasted three kinds of pretzels (because she needed a variety, apparently), and she had commandeered an entire drawer of his dresser for extra clothes. She spent an average of four nights a week at his place, and they had even settled into his side and her sides of the bed. Add it all up, and there was only one conclusion: Anne was already halfway moved in.

What would it take to get her to finish the job? Gil wondered.

Because that's where he was now. They were three months away from graduation, and maybe if he made it clear how serious he was about the two of them, then Anne would stay. He knew Priorly College was her first choice for employment. Dr. Lintford had been talking up his connections at the university. Gil rolled his eyes as he stepped out of the shower and wrapped a towel around his waist. He was looking forward to not working with the man anymore, who seemed unable to hold a conversation for five minutes without circling it back around to himself. Not to mention, he couldn't seem to let go of this idea that Gil should follow in his footsteps and apply for a university position. When they'd met last week for an individual progress check-in, Gil explained his post-graduation plans, and the lack of enthusiasm from Dr. Lintford was disappointing. Not entirely unexpected, since the man was a walking cliché of academic snobbery, but still kind of a letdown.

It made him more determined not to say anything to Anne

until everything was set in place, because that reaction coming from her would be gutting. One thing he'd always admired about her was that she had figured out a long time ago what she wanted, had drawn up a plan, and went about making it into reality with single-minded determination. He was in his last year of grad school and still trying to decide what to do with his life, for God's sake.

So as soon as he had a full business plan drawn up, Gil would tell her. Then she'd see what he was trying to accomplish, she'd understand how much he cared about it. That he was taking this seriously. It would be only a little while longer, just until he heard back from the bank about a loan, then he'd sit her down and show her everything.

If Anne's interview went well, then maybe Priorly would offer her the associate professorship position. It was a decent salary, and with his two jobs, they could afford something for just the two of them. They'd move in together, staying in Brooklyn, and he could work on getting his foundation off the ground.

Getting Anne to agree to move in with him depended on a lot of fluid factors, but as far as things went, it wasn't a half-bad plan.

Chapter 25

There was only one week left in the program at Herschel and Anne was torn between relieved exhaustion and sadness. She was going to miss the kids, especially Jenna, who'd grown in leaps and bounds as a writer over the spring. Anne had sat down with the girl and her mother last Tuesday, and while Mrs. Brown was still transferring Jenna to a local STEM high school in the fall, she reluctantly agreed to stop yelling at her daughter about writing, after she read the girl's stories. It was as good a compromise as Anne felt they were going to get, and she'd given the girl her email and told her to keep her updated.

During the students' next to last session that afternoon, they'd gone back to the beginning and written some micro fiction. The difference in how far they'd come in just a school year made Anne's chest ache with pride. The excitement she felt when holding solid, visible proof in her hand that she was *good* at teaching only confirmed she'd made the right choice to pursue it. Knowing she'd helped make a tangible difference in the way the kids viewed writing, reading, and everything that went with them felt like such an accomplishment.

She and Gil would be handing in their thesis papers in a few days, which they'd spent the last month working on separately. He wasn't thrilled about the many hours spent apart, she could tell, but Anne wasn't willing to risk a case of accidental plagiarism just because he was an out-loud thinker. More and more frequently, he'd asked her to stay when she came over; he'd made room in the closet *and* given her an additional drawer for her things as bribery. It was starting to feel like he was trying to ease Anne into moving in with him, but never actually asked if she would, and she wasn't sure how she felt about taking that next step. On one hand, it felt a bit precipitous to completely merge their lives like that.

On the other hand, she and Gil had known each other for over a decade. Yes, sex was a new addition to their relationship, and the lack of passive-aggressive competition between them made for a nice change. (Finding out he was a shameless bed hog, less so.) But he was still *Gil*. Maybe it wouldn't be so rash to consider living together.

Of course, this was all banking on him even being interested in something like that, and he hadn't said anything, so . . . maybe not. Phil was taking a job in Chicago when she graduated, but Anne and Diana had a comfortable arrangement and could just continue to share a place. It was fine.

What *wasn't* fine, however, was the way Dr. Lintford was currently looming over her chair.

He'd gotten up a few minutes after she'd sat down and planted his ass sideways on the edge of his desk, right in front of her, with one knee drawn up. Which put his crotch at almost eye level, and uncomfortably close to her face.

Letting him drone on, Anne stewed, anger building within her. The professor knew exactly what he was doing and had been doing all along. He'd asked her to come in for a private meeting, citing a need to talk about her individual thesis. But so far, he'd just talked in circles, not saying anything of substance. If he didn't stop inching his hips toward her, she was going to bludgeon him with one of the fancy glass orbs on his desk, like in a game of Clue.

Professor Lintford, murdered in his office, with a paperweight.

". . . we could have a nice dinner, and then afterward, you can show me your paper. Or whatever other talents you think I might be interested in." The professor's oily smile as he leaned over and touched her knee had her recoiling. He was making it very clear the talents he was hoping she would demonstrate involved taking her clothes off.

"*Don't touch me.* I have absolutely zero interest in showing you anything." Shoving her chair back with a loud noise, Anne stood, so full of fury that she was shaking. "And it's so far beyond inappropriate to invite me to your house for dinner and—" She waved her hands wildly, causing him to flinch away. "I hardly have the words for it."

The professor began to bluster, his neck flushed dark red as he moved back behind his desk again. "I've made the same offer to plenty of students, and I don't think I care for what you're insinuating. As much as you would like to think so, young lady, you are not special."

"I never said I was, but now I'm even less happy to be part of a group."

"Well, I'm sorry you don't understand how this works," Dr. Lintford snapped. "I'm a very busy man, and already over-worked, what with the *extra* grad students this year. Girls like you always expect preferential treatment, but if you can't ac-commodate my schedule when I offer you extra help, then I'm afraid I can't help you."

How exactly was he turning this around on her? And she never asked for extra *anything*.

Her fingers positively itched for a paperweight.

"I think I understand perfectly well what you were offering and how you expected me to accommodate you, and again, I'm not interested," she said, her hands shaking. She'd had a feeling he would try something like this, but it was another thing alto-gether to be in the situation. Enough was enough. "I can't believe anyone lets you teach here. Or maybe they just don't know how you are yet. Maybe they *should*." Grabbing her things, Anne was almost at the door when Dr. Lintford's words stopped her.

"How did your interview at Priorly go, Ms. Shirley?"

She turned back to find him seated again, his demeanor of icy control back in place.

"I would hate to think"—he paused, his dark eyes glittering with malice—"your unprofessional behavior might make its way back to the dean there. Who is a close, personal friend of mine. As a gesture of consideration, I will agree not to mention this little incident to her, and I suggest you do the same. Good positions at colleges in the city are so hard to find, after all. Word travels fast."

Nausea rose in her throat at the threat to sabotage her chances at employment in the academic world. She knew it wasn't an idle one; he was famous around campus for helping boost the students he mentored into prized jobs. But now she wondered just what he'd demanded as payment for those recommendations.

Unable to speak, utterly disgusted, Anne just threw him one last venomous look and wrenched the door open. She didn't stop until she was outside and halfway down the block, jerking to a halt, trying to calm her breathing. Mind racing, she collapsed onto a bench.

It was unthinkable to keep silent, just so she could be guaranteed an offer for her dream job. Not only would Anne's complicity put others at risk in the future, allowing him to continue to prey on his students, abusing his power, but *she* deserved better than this. To be blackmailed into ignoring his predatory behavior.

She'd worked so hard to get here and was so close to fulfilling the first step in the life she planned. This was an impossible situation!

Except it wasn't, when it came down to it. Scrubbing away tears she didn't realize had escaped the corners of her eyes, Anne stood, adjusting her backpack with trembling hands. She knew what she had to do.

Chapter 26

After ten days of silence, Anne started to think she was in the clear.

The day after she'd reported Dr. Lintford to the administration, filing an extensive complaint against him for sexual harassment, she'd received an email from Priorly requesting a second interview. Which was great news, it meant she'd been moved to the short list of candidates. Confident in her academic résumé, and how well the first interview had gone, she started to relax again.

She said nothing to Gil.

He'd only want to know why Anne hadn't shared this earlier, wouldn't understand why she had felt the need to deal with Dr. Lintford's behavior herself. What was done was done, and even if she did feel a pinch of guilt at excluding him, she couldn't change it now. Besides, there wasn't anything either of them could do until she received the result of the school's investigation into her claims.

She let herself just enjoy the rest of the week, putting the situation with the professor out of her mind.

Gil had made French toast with leftover burger buns Saturday morning, after she'd spent the night, because he'd forgotten to get bread. Watching him use a plate to smash the buns flat enough to fry made her wrinkle her nose in skepticism, but she ate them anyway. They weren't half bad . . . with enough syrup. She'd gone home with a full belly, slightly shaky legs, and a date on Wednesday.

She'd finally broken through her writer's block and finished her paper for Romantic Lit after lunch. The world would be agog at her genius. Well—maybe not. But *she* was happy with it.

Tap class wasn't packed, so she was able to move without feeling like she was going to kick another dancer in the ankle and was literally dripping with sweat by the time it was over.

And when she got home that evening, Perdita and Winnie were at the apartment, and they'd brought chili crabs so hot Anne's lips felt like they were going to fall off. Even the steamed buns couldn't save her. It was fantastic.

So, when she woke up to an email on Sunday from Priorly, canceling her second interview, it was a shock. There was no way this was a coincidence. Dr. Lintford has made good on his threat after all. It took ten minutes of steady breathing to swallow the urge to scream at the unfairness of it all.

Foolishly, she'd turned down an offer from NYU, the only other college in the city who'd had her back for a subsequent interview, on Friday. Her first meeting with the dean at Priorly, and the lack of follow-through on Dr. Lintford's part, had lulled her into a sense of false security; she'd been so confident in her prospects of securing the better-paid, more advanced professorship that she'd made a serious miscalculation.

Phil was at the hospital, doing her rounds, Diana was at work, and Anne didn't want to call home. Marilla and Matthew would only worry, unable to do anything to help from Avonlea. But Gil . . . Gil would be home. Suddenly she wanted nothing more than for him to put his arms around her, to breathe in the spicy scent of his cologne. Feeling numb, Anne took a cab all the way from Hell's Kitchen to Brooklyn, paying the outrageous fee without a blink when she arrived outside Gil's building.

Pressing the intercom at the front door, she waited impatiently. Finally, there was the crackle of his familiar voice, and the tears she'd been holding back clogged her throat. It took two tries before she could answer him, relieved when he immediately buzzed her in.

He was waiting for her at the top of the stairs, the outline of the welcoming, golden light spilling out from his apartment into the dim hallway.

"Hey, hey," he said softly, ushering her in, then wrapping her in his arms as soon as the door was shut. "What's going on?" He drew back, his concerned brown eyes searching hers. "It's not Marilla or Matthew, is it?"

"No. God, no," Anne managed. "Don't even put that out into the universe, I couldn't handle anything happening to them right now."

"I was scared for a minute, you showing up looking like this."

"Well, my life is falling apart, so I don't know how else I'm supposed to look."

Fred came to the doorway of the living room, stalling whatever reply Gil was about to say. "You okay?"

"No." She took a wobbly breath, drawing away from Gil.

The two men exchanged a look over her head, and irritation flared within her at the silent communication, before Gil said, "We're going to be in my room." But she let him slide an arm around her back, to guide her down the hall.

The other man nodded, his face set in a frown as he disappeared into the living room.

Once inside Gil's room, Anne crossed to the bed and sank down on the edge, ignoring its unmade state. He took the chair from his desk and turned it around, placing it in front of her and straddling the seat.

It took a moment for her to gather her thoughts, and he waited quietly, crossed arms lying on the top of the seatback.

"I made a mistake," she said finally. "There's something I should have told you, but I didn't. Now it's all such a mess."

Taking a deep breath, Anne met his gaze, and started talking. The entire story spilled out. Dr. Lintford's advances, the meetings she'd gone to alone, their confrontation, her subsequent report to the administration. The professor's threat and the loss of any chance at getting the job at Priorly.

Through it all, Gil sat silent, eyes on her face.

"And that's everything, I think," she finished up, spreading her hands. An odd mixture of relief and grief moved through her. When Gil didn't say anything, his gaze having dropped to the floor during her recalling of the last visit to Dr. Lintford's office, Anne felt a small flare of foreboding. She couldn't tell what he was thinking.

Finally, he spoke, his voice quiet. "So, this was happening all year and you felt like you couldn't share it with me?"

His choice of words threw her. "I was handling it."

"Yeah, you said." Standing, Gil lifted the chair with one hand, dropping it in front of the desk with a bang that startled her. "You were handling it, alone. Because . . . why? You didn't think I'd support you?"

"I—" she started, but he cut her off.

"Did you think I wouldn't *believe you*?"

"No," Anne protested. Frustration had her jumping up, not wanting to be sitting while he towered over her. He was making this about him, which was incredibly unfair. "It had nothing to do with you."

"Clearly." A muscle ticked in his jaw as he turned to face her, his brown eyes drained of their usual fondness, cold now with fury. "I thought . . . I don't know what I thought. I guess I thought we were a team. My mistake."

Oh, he wanted a fight, then. Fine. She clenched her fists, furious. "I can't believe you're turning this into a fight about our relationship."

Gil started to say something, then visibly reined himself in, taking a deep breath. Holding up one hand, he headed for the door. "Sorry. I need a minute. Just . . . I need a minute."

Thrown by his sudden departure, Anne just stood in the middle of the room for a moment, at a loss. Finally, she rejected the bed as too vulnerable a place to have the rest of their conversation (fight?) and decided to sit in the chair by his desk instead. Another few minutes passed, and she began to tap her fingers on the wood surface of the desk impatiently. She understood why he left the room instead of letting it turn into a yelling match, she did. Someone had to be the calmer one in this relationship, and that was never going to be her. But really, what was he doing, *napping*?

Reaching up to tighten her ponytail, she hit a pile of papers on the edge of the desk with her elbow. "Shit." Shooting a guilty look at the door, she bent to shuffle them back together into something that hopefully was close to the order they'd been in. The stack was as neat as it was going to be, and she went to place it back on the desk when the words on the top sheet jumped out at her.

—*your interest in Priorly College*
—*along with Dr. Lintford's strong recommendation*
—*pleased to offer you the associate professorship.*

The door opened and Anne looked up, the letter still clutched in her hand. "This . . . Priorly offered you the job?" His forehead wrinkled in confusion, then recognition dawned when he saw what she was holding, and he stepped forward. Anne shot up from the chair, stepping sideways when he reached out.

"Anne, it's not what it looks like," he said, voice low and calm in a way she found infuriatingly patronizing, as if he was trying to *soothe* her.

"You know," she ground out, tossing the letter back onto the desk, "that's what people usually say when it's *exactly* what it looks like. You didn't even tell me you were applying."

"I wasn't. I didn't. It really isn't the way it looks." His gaze was steady, brown eyes intent. "Look, I was going to call them, clear things up. I have a plan already, and I'll tell you about it in a minute, but it's not this. If you'd rather I just stay out of it, though, then I will. Let you handle it the way you seem to prefer—on your own."

The bite in his tone stung, even through her own confusion and fury.

"Wow. That's a little unfair, don't you think?"

"Maybe, but you're not being very reasonable about this."

"Excuse me for not understanding how you happen to get a job you supposedly didn't apply for? *And* with Dr. Lintford's recommendation?" Anne scoffed. "Explain that to me. Explain how that happens. Because I'm trying to understand it, Gil, and I just don't."

Striding over to the desk, he began to rifle through the stack of papers she'd knocked over, grumbling as he searched them. "What the hell happened to . . . the fuck? Oh, there it is. Look, I don't know what the job offer thing is about, but here. Read these. Please." None of the annoyance on his face had faded when he turned back to her and shoved a handful of pages into her hands.

"There. That's my plan. I really was hoping to tell you differently than this, but I guess we'll just do this instead." He leaned against the wall, crossing his arms over his chest. "Well, whatever, it's all there."

Anne held the papers for a moment, just looking at him. When he raised one eyebrow in challenge, she pressed her lips together and began to read. Her anger turned to confusion as she began to take in the information, flipping the pages back and forth, then rereading some of them. There were bank papers, grant and business applications, and what looked like some sort of mission statement. Looking up, she asked, baffled, "What is this?"

"I was waiting to tell you until everything came through." Gil sent her a smile, but his eyes remained serious as he gestured to the papers. "That one on top is a loan approval."

She lowered herself to sit on the edge of the bed while he explained how he'd fallen in love with the work with the kids they'd done at Herschel and outlined his plans for a not-for-profit organization. Part of Anne was in awe of all he'd gotten accomplished in between his job and school, that it was coming together just as he'd hoped.

But part of her was still simmering with anger. When he finally stopped talking, she glanced down at the pile in her lap, fingers tightening on the already wrinkled paper. "The loan was approved over a week ago."

"Well, we've both been busy, which is why I'm sharing this now. I'd actually planned on calling you this evening, asking you if we could grab dinner and talk about it. But then you showed up."

"Right."

"Anne, c'mon, don't—"

"And you don't have *any* idea why Priorly would offer you a coveted position on staff, out of the blue . . . ?"

"It's starting to piss me off that you think I'm lying about that." Gil narrowed his eyes. "I've already told you I don't know anything, and that's not going to change until I get a chance to talk to them."

"Fine, we'll put that one aside for the moment." That conversation was going nowhere. But there was a point she just couldn't let go. "I would like to know, though, how is not telling me about your plans for the not-for-profit, that you've apparently been working on for *months*, different from what you said I did?"

Anne pushed off the mattress and walked over to where Gil had straightened away from the wall. She slapped the papers against his chest, letting them fall to the floor when he didn't take them right away. He just stood and looked at her. "You were so pissed I didn't let you in, but here you are, keeping secrets too."

The *hypocrisy.*

"It's different because I only kept it quiet to surprise you with something good. Not because I thought you'd try to take over or something." Gil raked a hand through his hair, looking aggravated. "And don't think I didn't catch that part where you sidestepped telling me you know I'd never go behind your back and try to snake a job from under you."

It wasn't that she didn't hear the warning in his voice, but it didn't matter, in her mission to prove her point. "Just so I'm clear, though, the rules in this relationship are that you get to keep secrets, because they're fun, but I don't, even if they're deeply personal and *none of your business*?"

"Oh, yeah, sure, obviously that's how this works. For fuck's sake," Gil growled out, pacing to the window, then jerked around again to face her. "If you can't see the difference between those two things, I don't know what else to say. And I'm going to be honest, I think I deserve a little more than a girlfriend who doesn't trust me enough to tell me about something like being sexually harassed by our professor for an entire damn year."

She'd been so whipped up with righteous anger, it took a second for his words to register. Her stomach dropping, Anne took a step away from him, the backs of her knees hitting the bed. As furious as she was, she really hadn't even considered this possibility; the shock of it took her breath away.

"Are you breaking up with me?"

The silence hung heavy between them as they stared at each other.

"Anne, I want to be with you, but I can't see how a relationship with someone who only lets me into the easy parts of her life can work." He looked away; the set of his mouth unhappy. "You don't let me share the things that make this thing between us *real*."

"This is perfect. Just great. You're dumping me because I've committed the horrible crime of keeping the messier parts of my life to myself." Anne sucked in a breath, pushing past the pain in her chest. He didn't understand how impossible it was to let him that far in. *No one* had all the pieces of her, she couldn't even imagine giving that sort of power to anyone.

"That's not what I meant—"

"No." It felt like she was all jagged pieces, her edges sharp enough to cut. "I think I've heard enough."

And she walked out, not looking back even when he called her name.

Chapter 27

Graduation came and went. Anne spent the day with Marilla, Rachel, and Matthew, who'd come into the city overnight. She sat through hours of speeches under the hot sun, sweat trickling down her back, the polyester ceremonial gown sticking to her skin as she received her diploma, and then it was over. Diana and Phil nearly knocked her over with their exuberant congratulations.

She didn't look for Gil in the crowd.

The six of them went out for a celebratory lunch before the elder contingent of the group went back to Avonlea, loading up most of Anne's packed belongings into the bed of Matthew's truck to bring home with them. She would follow in a few days, after attending both Diana and Phil's graduations. Although she could have stayed and continued to work at the Lazy Lion, she desperately needed to clear her head and regroup. Moving back to her familiar and beloved Green Gables was the first step, and the only one she could focus on at the moment.

Her coworkers and the owner of the bookstore threw her a little going-away party the weekend before, which she hadn't expected. It was sweet, but only served to remind her she was at loose ends now.

Her thoughts kept drifting to Gil. She'd turned it repeatedly in her mind, wondering if she'd been in the wrong or he was. Or if it was both of them, or neither—just the natural conclusion of a relationship they never should have gotten into.

Sighing, Anne pushed away the bowl of popcorn she'd barely touched and lowered the volume on the TV as Diana came into the living room. She looked gorgeous, her newly cropped head showing off the long curve of her neck, curls bleached golden blond swirling tight against her scalp. It was a haircut Anne could never pull off in a thousand years, and this was a fact proven by a horrible accident with black hair dye in eighth grade, but Diana made it look elegant.

"Are you sure you don't want to come tonight? There's still time to get dressed," her friend said, fastening on silver earrings that dripped down in long strands to brush the tops of her shoulders.

"Nope. I've got a date with Timothée Chalamet." Anne drew her knees up and rested her chin on them.

"Oh God, you're going to depress yourself even more."

Laughing, Anne threw a piece of popcorn that Diana dodged. "He's cute, and I like movies that make me cry."

"Hmm." Diana looked unconvinced. "Are you sure you're okay with Fred coming here to get Phil and me? I could ask him to wait downstairs, he won't be offended."

"No, it's fine. I feel sort of bad I ran out of there the other morning and didn't even say goodbye," Anne added sheepishly.

Diana sat down on the couch next to her to slip on her heels and buckle the ankle straps. She glanced over at Anne, giving her a look. "You know he understood. He just feels bad how it all went down." Leaning over, she pressed her bright red lips to Anne's cheek, drawing back with a mischievous grin when she made a noise of protest and rubbed at the spot. "If I see Gil tonight, do you want me to kick his ass? Because I can, even in these shoes."

Dropping her hand, making a face at the red smeared across her fingertips, Anne shook her head. "There's really no point. Besides, I know you guys are friends, you don't need to get in the middle of it."

"Anne. Are you fucking kidding me?" Diana drew back, looking offended. "*You're* my best friend. You. I've always liked Gil, but if I had to choose, you're going to come out on top every damn time."

Phil walked into the living room then, glancing over at them as the intercom rang, and she went to buzz Fred in, then left the front door cracked. "How come no one told me we were doing group hugs?"

"I will always take hugs." Anne opened her arms.

Fred poked his head from around the door, looking wary. "Can I come in?"

"Only if you're bringing me hugs," she called from the couch, making him smile. He pushed the door the rest of the way open and made his way over. Grabbing her, he pulled Anne up and into a tight hug.

"I know I'm not the height of fashion like this goddess over here," he said, gesturing to Diana, who flashed him a saucy grin. "But I don't think you want to wear pajamas tonight."

"She's not going," Phil called from the kitchen.

"We tried," Diana added.

"What? Why?"

Anne sighed. "You know why."

"So, you're not gonna go to what's going to be an amazing party because Gil may or may not show up after work?"

"That's about the size of it, yes."

Fred leaned against the arm of the couch; his expression meditative. "You know he's miserable without you. Almost unbearable to live with."

"Fred." Diana's voice was sharp.

"Just trying to help." He stood, hands rising in placation. "C'mon, Anne, go get dressed."

"Nope." Just to be contrary, she plopped back down and threw the lap blanket over her legs. With an overly sweet smile, she made a shooing gesture. "Don't be late."

"Let's go." Diana practically pushed Fred out into the hallway, rolling her eyes at Anne behind his back as she left. Phil followed, blowing Anne a kiss before closing the door behind them, the apartment ringing with silence in their wake.

So *what* if Gil was miserable? He broke up with her. In the end, really, it was his own fault.

Anne flipped through her queue, looking for something that would hold her interest.

And if he cared so much, why hadn't he called? Or texted? He hadn't even come by to pick up the stuff he'd left here, his shirts and extra toothbrush. Surely, he missed his favorite Oakland Athletics baseball hat, he'd worn that thing until it was almost ready to fall apart.

But she'd heard nothing from him.

Clearly Fred was wrong.

Choosing a movie at random, Anne burrowed down in her blanket and turned up the volume.

Chapter 28

The party was in full swing by the time Gil got there, people spilling out onto the front lawn, every window in the house lit up. He hadn't really felt like coming, but Fred had threatened to physically drag him here if he didn't show on his own. While Gil might be several inches taller than his roommate, Fred had at least twenty pounds of muscle on him, so it wouldn't have been a very fair fight.

But as he walked toward the house through a crowd of people he didn't know, squeezing up the steps and in through the front door, Gil wished he'd taken the chance and just gone home after work. The double shift had drained him, when he was already tired from not sleeping well. He hadn't really had the energy to do much of anything since he and Anne broke up. Since *he'd* broken up with her.

God, what had he been thinking? He'd regretted the words even as they left his mouth, but there was no taking them back, not with the way she'd looked at him before she'd walked out the door.

After their graduation ceremony, he'd searched the crowd for her, but found Diana first. She'd warned him away with a glare, and he'd gone to find his parents instead, not wanting to ruin Anne's day. He'd thought about calling or texting her a thousand times since, but what would he say? Maybe he'd over-reacted, but that didn't mean he was wrong. Maybe she'd had a point, but that didn't make her right either.

Everything was a mess.

It killed him that he'd been working up to asking her to move in with him, and she hadn't even trusted him enough to tell him what was going on with Dr. Lintford.

That piece of trash. It had taken every ounce of Gil's self-control not to go looking for the professor after finally hearing Anne's story. The only thing holding him back was knowing the reason she didn't want to tell him to start with was because she thought he'd do exactly that. It might not matter to her any-more, that he was trying to respect her wishes, but it mattered to him.

After wandering what felt like the entire house, Gil finally found Fred in the backyard. Thunder rumbled in the dark sky overhead, a warm breeze ruffling his hair. Phil stood a few feet away talking to another woman, and gave him a small half wave when she saw him. But as soon as he walked up to where Fred and Diana stood, Diana looked at him and said, "You're an ass-hole," in a very loud and clear voice.

Ignoring the scattered laughter from others hanging out

nearby, he just sighed. So, they were going to do this now, right here.

"I know."

"If you know, then why are you still being one?" A raindrop fell on Diana's bare shoulder and she brushed it away impatiently.

"It's not that easy, D," Gil said, running a hand over his jaw, absently noting he really needed to shave.

"It is that easy," she retorted. "You just pick up the phone and call her."

"Guys, we should head in." Fred glanced overhead uneasily, as a few more raindrops fell onto the concrete patio.

"Do you even know why we broke up?"

"Of course I do, I'm her best friend." The "you dumbass" hung silently in the heavy air, as she marched into the house to get out of the growing splatter of rain. Gil followed, waiting until she'd found an unoccupied corner of the kitchen to speak again.

"Did you know already? What she was dealing with?"

"A little. She'd told me some of what was going on, but not how far he took it." For a second, her face looked troubled, then smoothed out again. "I get it, okay? It hurt that you think she didn't trust you enough to tell you what he was doing. But, Gil, *think*. Do you know what her life was like before she came to Avonlea?"

He looked at her in silence, his pulse suddenly loud in his ears.

"It wasn't like that, no one hurt her. Or actually, more that no one hurt her physically. But the people she was supposed to be able to trust let her down over and over. After a while, I think she just stopped leaning on people out of self-preservation. It took literal years before she stopped looking surprised when I came over when I said I would, and longer than that to get her to tell me anything about her past." Diana bit her lip, looking torn. "Look, I'm only telling *you* because I don't think you meant for it to go down like this. Which is also the one reason I'm talking to you at all, by the way."

"She's not the only one who's trying to not get hurt, you know."

Her dark brown eyes softened. "You love her, don't you? Like, actually love her."

"Only since we were twelve."

"God," she said, letting out a shocked laugh. He wished to hell he could laugh too. "I knew you had a crush on her when we were in high school, and she told me about that complete disaster of a hookup senior year, but . . . really?"

"Really." Gil leaned the back of his head against a kitchen cabinet and closed his eyes, tuning out the party. "I don't know how this became such a mess. And I don't know how to fix it."

"Give me your phone."

He cracked an eye to see her wiggling her fingers at him impatiently. "Why?"

"Just give me the damn phone."

He pulled it out of his pocket, tapped in the passcode, then handed it over. Diana scrolled for a moment, let out a little "aha" sound, her fingers flying over the keyboard. She waited a few minutes, hushing him when he tried to ask what she was doing, then looked smug when the phone buzzed with an incoming text. She typed in a reply, closed the app, and slapped the phone back into his waiting palm.

"Here's your opportunity to fix things."

Unlocking his phone with a wary feeling, Gil scrolled until he saw the texts. She'd sent Anne a message asking her to meet him at the coffee shop near her apartment that they'd had breakfast at on the weekends occasionally, in . . . he checked the time. Just over an hour.

Shit.

He shoved his phone back in his pocket, then hesitated. "Do you really think we can?"

"I really do. Because she loves you too. You just need to show her you're sticking, that she *can* trust you with her heart," Diana said, then gave him a little shove. "Now, go."

Gil flashed her a smile, the weight that had sat on his chest since Anne walked out of his apartment lifting a little. He gave Fred and Phil a hurried goodbye, waving over his shoulder at their yelled good wishes, and moved quickly through the crowd. He was out of breath by the time he got to the nearest subway, taking the stairs down two at a time to catch it before it left the station. The entire ride was spent staring out the window, willing the cars to move faster, as the time ticked down. As soon as they pulled into the stop closest to the coffee shop, Gil was at the doors, shouldering through when they opened just enough for him to squeeze out. He took the stairs at a run again, only to find the sky had truly opened up while he was underground.

Wishing he'd thought to bring a hoodie, Gil shoved the

dripping hair out of his eyes and jogged down the sidewalk. It seemed like he caught every Do Not Walk light, hovering impatient on the edge of the curb, sometimes only pausing for traffic to let up enough for him to get across without waiting for the green. He couldn't be late; she'd probably never give him another chance if he screwed this one up.

It was at the fourth light that Gil made a miscalculation.

The rain was lashing down now, stinging his eyes, and he swiped at the water ineffectually, cursing the line of umbrellas waiting at the crosswalk in front of him, blocking his view of the cars. Ducking around the far end of them, he glanced up the street, saw there was no oncoming traffic, and started out into the intersection.

There was a squeal, the sound of tires fishtailing on wet pavement, and twin beams of bright light burned through his vision. Something hit him hard, throwing him across the road like he was nothing, where he landed in a heap against the far curb.

Brilliant pain blossomed under his skin, spreading like fire, and something caught in his chest when he tried to breathe, making him cough. A metallic taste flooded his mouth.

People were yelling and someone was telling him not to move, the rain on his face stopping when a shaking umbrella was held above him.

The sound of a distant siren came closer, then cut off abruptly, and the scared faces hovering over him were replaced with two people in medic uniforms.

"Hey, buddy, can you hear me? I don't want you to move, okay?" A young black man with kind eyes leaned over him while his partner did something Gil couldn't see. He didn't think he could move if he tried. He couldn't think much at all, the edges of his vision sparking with black.

The medic continued to walk him through every step, asking Gil questions he couldn't answer. He was just barely hanging on to consciousness as it was. But there was something, something he needed to do . . . it was just out of reach, the thought slipping away as the medics moved him to a hard board and pain screamed through his right leg.

There was a flurry of movement at his cry of pain, quick voices, someone pressing a cloth to the side of his mouth, where the metallic liquid had dripped out of his lips again.

"All right, deep breaths, my guy," came the medic's voice again, from just behind Gil's head. "We're going to get you up on the stretcher and into the ambulance, and then we're headed to Uptown Regional, okay?"

Thankfully, he didn't seem to need a response, because then they were lifting the board, and Gil blacked out.

Chapter 29

Then

He wasn't allowed to climb the tree.

Well, to be honest, he'd never exactly been allowed to climb it. But he'd always *planned* to, one day. The day before, Gil heard his dad tell Mr. Hartley next door that the tree was "a menace and was going to have to come down." So, if Gil didn't climb it now, he might not get another chance. He'd never get a chance to reach the top and see if he could see all the way down to the bay. The thing was, Dad worried too much. He said since he was a doctor, he'd seen things that would make Gil's hair curl (which was weird, because Gil's hair already curled), and he said it *every time* Gil wanted to do something.

Gil never got to do anything.

That's why he was gonna climb this tree today.

The first part wasn't so hard. The branches were low and thick and had lots of knobby bits to put his feet on. As he climbed higher, he had to stretch for the next branch. Once his foot slipped on a patch of mossy bark, and Gil flung himself against the trunk, fingers digging into the wood, his heart pounding. The tree creaked, and leaned just a touch to the left, as if pushed by a sudden breeze. But the air was still and muggy, waiting for the summer storm hanging along the horizon to roll in that afternoon.

Maybe this wasn't the smartest idea he'd ever had.

But he was six now! He wasn't the baby his dad thought he was anymore. Anyway, he was halfway already. He was *going* to reach the top.

Taking a deep breath, Gil let go of the trunk, grabbing the branch overhead and sliding back out onto the limb he was balancing on, glad he'd taken his shoes off before starting up. The bark was rough on the arches of his feet, but he could grip the branch a whole lot easier with his toes than with the tips of his sneakers. It was a good thing he'd been practicing holding on to things with his toes by using a pencil to write stuff. It had only been a week and he already could almost get his name to look like an actual name now, not just wobbly scribbles.

Unfortunately, even his wonder monkey toes didn't save him when he hauled himself up onto the next limb and stuck his hand on the edge of a bird's nest. The mama bird flew at his face, screaming, his cheek stinging where she managed to peck him. Panicking, Gil flailed, and lost his grip on the branch.

He dropped back to the limb below, but he landed too hard, stumbling sideways to slam his shoulder against the trunk. The tree creaked again, this time louder, and there was a cracking noise, and then everything just *shifted*. Gil lost his balance as the tree listed to the left, as if it had gotten tired of standing in the same spot for the last twenty years, and now wanted to pick up and wander off somewhere else.

He made a valiant effort to steady himself despite the tree slowly falling over, but it was no good.

It felt like he hit every branch, every knot, *every* hard thing on the way down, pain slashing through his body as he tumbled through the branches. The landing slammed the breath from his chest, his head bouncing off a tree root painfully. His arm was on fire, the right one, and he couldn't move, still struggling to get air. Stomach roiling with nausea, Gil kicked what was left of the tree's trunk with the heel of his foot, trying to distract himself from the way the burning in his arm was starting to roll over him in waves. At least it had fallen one way and he had gone the other.

His last thought before the black dots in front of his eyes merged to form a thick blanket that dragged him under was how much he *hated* it when his dad was right.

Chapter 30

Anne checked her phone again, but only the time and date shone back at her in digital green. No messages, no missed calls, and it was nearly midnight. She'd sat in the coffee shop forty minutes past the time Gil asked her to meet him, but it was clear he wasn't coming.

So that was it, then.

Her movements slow and precise, she gathered up some crumpled napkins and the empty cup of coffee she'd been nursing and stood. Weaving between tables, she dropped them into the trash before pulling the hood of her sweatshirt over her hair and stepping out onto the sidewalk. Rain pelted her, instantly soaking her jeans and sneakers, making her duck her head to keep it out of her eyes.

Mind blank, Anne shoved her hands into the pockets of her hoodie and began the short walk back to the apartment, the slow rhythm of her breath loud in her ears.

It had been foolish to agree to meet him, she'd known it when she texted back *yes*. Maybe she still couldn't figure out what had happened for them to wind up here, but it was clear she needed to make a clean break. She'd spent more than a decade tangled up with Gilbert Blythe in one way or another, and it was enough—before her heart was so irreparably shattered that she couldn't put it back together.

Suddenly struck with a sharp longing to be back in her room at Green Gables, rain sliding down the window as she sat in the alcove seat and leaned against the pane, looking out over the fields as her breath fogged the glass, Anne picked up her pace. Her bags had been packed, boxed, and already shipped out, so there was nothing left to keep her here. If she got up at five, she could be in Avonlea by mid-morning. Her chest ached at the image of Marilla, the stern lines of her face softening as she opened her arms and enveloped Anne in one of those firm hugs that always signaled love and safety, and she knew she had to go. She *needed* to go.

She was going home.

Chapter 31

The bus ride home was interminable.

Nothing kept Anne's attention for long, not even the short stack of novels she'd crammed into her backpack. The near impossible had happened: no one had claimed the seat next to her, leaving her entirely to her own thoughts. Sluggish as they were. She'd had a hard time sleeping the night before, which she was blaming on the coffee, and absolutely not on her brain once again racing in circles over the events leading up to Gil's midnight abandonment of her at the cafe. So instead of diving into the historical romance she'd been unable to resist on her last day at work, Anne found herself listlessly watching the scenery rush by. At least it wasn't still raining.

She'd snuck into Diana's bed that morning to say goodbye, waking her incoherent best friend with a tight hug. They wouldn't see each other until Anne came back to the city in the fall. Diana would be much too busy with her new junior designer position at House of Giventi. *If* Anne came back, that was. It very much depended on whether she could find a teaching position.

Maybe she should broaden her search. The idea of moving too far from Green Gables, Matthew, and Marilla, however, was nearly unthinkable. Especially as they grew older. She'd only just found her family a decade earlier, how could she be expected to give them up, to move hundreds of miles away in pursuit of a career? But as much as she hated the thought, permanent university-level teaching positions were hard to come by, even in a city as large as New York.

The brakes hissing to a stop interrupted Anne's morose train of thought; she shouldered her backpack and shuffled off the bus along with the other half-awake commuters. Waiting as patiently as possible—which wasn't all that patiently, she was a fidgeter—for her rolling suitcase to be unloaded from the bowels of the steel beast, she glanced around. Squinting against the rays of early-morning sun peeking over the top of the squat bus depot, she almost missed Matthew, under the shade of a large oak. Giving a hasty thank-you to the driver, who unloaded her suitcase, Anne began yanking it behind her, across the parking lot, then cursed as one wheel caught on the curb and tipped the entire damn thing on its side.

Stopping, she closed her eyes and stood as still as possible, inhaling air through her nose in an effort to battle the urge to scream. When there was a slight tug at the handle, her eyes flew open, fingers tightening defensively on the plastic grip. Matthew's forehead crinkled in concern as he tried to gently tug the suitcase away from her again.

"All right there, Anne?"

The rage dissipated like ash on the wind, blown away by a swell of gladness, of rightness, of love. Of homecoming. Everything she'd been battling for the past few weeks, all the emotions she'd ruthlessly repressed, came roaring up like a geyser. Bursting into tears, she threw herself at Matthew, the older man dropping the suitcase back onto the pavement in a fumbling attempt to catch her before they both went down in a heap.

"Whoa, what's this?" He brought one hand up, the rough skin of his palm catching slightly on her ponytail as he petted her hair in a soothing manner. "What's going on?"

But Anne couldn't answer; every time she tried to stop crying, a fresh bout of tears would come rushing out. Murmuring things she couldn't quite catch, but made her feel cared for regardless, Matthew guided her to a bench set against the brick wall of the building, then went back to secure the suitcase. He settled next to her in silence, waiting until she was ready to talk, as he'd always done. Marilla would chive it out of her, with limited sympathy for tears and wailing, sorting things out in her mercilessly efficient way. But not Matthew. His patience was endless, even when she knew he had many other things he needed to be doing. He'd never once made her feel like she was anything but one of the most valued people in his life, something she didn't realize she couldn't do without until that moment.

Weeping outside a busy, public bus station was hardly her finest hour.

Finally drawing out from under Matthew's arm on a shuddering breath, Anne avoided his gaze as she rooted around in her backpack for a wad of tissues. Pulling them out, she busied herself with blowing her nose and wiping her eyes. Clenching the damp tissues in her hands, she sighed, feeling wrung out, and let her head rest against his shoulder.

"Sorry," she said, voice hoarse from the unexpected tears. Clearing her throat, Anne tried again. "Sorry, I really didn't plan on that happening. It's been a rough couple weeks."

Matthew placed one of his hands over the fists balled in her lap, patting them in a reassuring manner. "Rachel said you and Gilbert broke up."

"Rachel said, huh?"

"Ah, you know how Marilla is. Can't drag gossip out of her by hook or crook." The smile she caught a glimpse of out of the corner of her eye was crooked with amusement. "That's why she and Rachel make a good couple. That woman's never met a secret she didn't feel the immediate need to share. Kind of balances them right out."

The smile Anne dredged up felt wobbly, but she managed to pin it in place. "The breakup wasn't a secret, really. I know I didn't talk to you or Marilla much about what was going on between Gil and me. It wasn't that I wanted to keep it from either of you. It was just . . . I don't really have a good explanation. But I wasn't trying to hide anything from you."

"I know," he said. "Some things just feel more private. They're harder to share with everyone else, they *feel* like a secret, until, well, they're not. I'm guessing you and Gil didn't make it to the sharing point."

"No." Her laugh was abrupt and watery. "We did not. Maybe because, deep down, we both knew it would end like this. Our history is too complicated and fraught, it was ridiculous to think we could have any sort of lasting relationship."

Matthew sighed, then slapped his thighs with both hands and pushed into a standing position. "Well, Anne, God bless, and I love you, but if that isn't the biggest load of horseshit."

Her mouth dropped open, shocked at his near-unheard-of use of profanity. Indignation rising, she leapt from her seat to trail after Matthew as he started wheeling her suitcase toward the parking lot.

"Excuse me! It is not."

He snorted, not turning around.

"It isn't." She halted next to him as he dropped the gate of the truck, then hefted her suitcase into the bed. "I tried. I really did try, Matthew, I wanted it to work." She hauled herself into the cab, throwing her backpack at her feet as he turned the key in the ignition. "I *love* him."

Anne sucked in a lungful of air as her brain caught up to the words that had tumbled out of her mouth. She hadn't let herself admit it, but there it was. She'd gone and really, truly fallen in love with Gilbert Blythe, the one thing she should have known better than to do. And then she'd lost him. Or . . . they'd lost each other.

She hadn't thought loving someone could hurt so much.

The drive back to Green Gables was half over before either of them spoke again. Matthew glanced at her, his face somber. "I'm sorry I upset you."

"I'm sorry too," she said immediately. She hated fighting with him, and always regretted it as soon as it was over. "I shouldn't have snapped at you like that."

"You know what your relationship with Gilbert was like, best of anyone. I trust you on that." He was quiet for another minute, then ruffled his hair with one hand and sighed. "So, I'll only ask this—do you regret it? Being with him?"

"Yes." Anne paused, then pushed past the pain and anger to the truth. "No. I wish I did, then I could write this whole thing off as a slip in judgment. But I don't, because nearly all of my best memories this year were made with Gil."

"Ah," Matthew said softly. "That's something to think about, then, isn't it?"

"Maybe."

"I don't know the details of what happened, and I don't need to know. That's between the two of you." They turned off the highway at the exit for Avonlea. "But I will say this. I don't think I've seen you as happy for years as you were over winter break. I just hate to see you lose that."

He slowed down to bump over the wooden bridge just before the turnoff for the Barrys' driveway. "But if you need me to, I can use him as vine fertilizer. Either way, pumpkin, I just want you to be happy."

Anne laughed long and loud. "I love how both you and Diana immediately offered to make him disappear."

"I always did like that girl."

Her mood lightened, Anne was able to exit the truck and run up the steps to where Marilla and Rachel waited for hugs.

She didn't miss the unspoken looks the siblings exchanged but chose to ignore them to link arms with Rachel and let the other woman draw her into the house. Anne knew she'd have to sit down and have a variation of the same conversation with Marilla at some point, but she just couldn't do it right now. There were only so many times a girl could open an emotional vein in one day and not bleed out.

So instead, she spent the rest of the afternoon organizing her belongings in her old room, harassing the chickens (they missed her, she was *certain* of it), and wandering the vineyard to say hello to everyone. It didn't escape her that all of it was busy-work, something to keep her body occupied, but it helped.

The next morning, Marilla sat down at the kitchen table and told her that she, Rachel, and Matthew agreed that a change of scenery would do Anne good, so they were all going away for a little while. When Anne protested that Avonlea was a change of scenery, Marilla gave her a flat look and told her to go pack.

Anne paused in the doorway. "What about the winery?" She tried to think of a time when they'd all taken a vacation at the same time and knew there wasn't one.

Making an impatient *tsk*ing noise, Marilla wrung out the wet sponge and set it to dry on the dish rack. "Don't worry about that. Petra and Harry have it covered; they've been managing this place alongside Matthew nearly as long as you've lived here. *Now,* will you go pack before the oceans dry up and the sun burns itself out? Whatever is most comfortable."

Throwing her hands up in defeat and disconcerted by how quickly things were moving, Anne climbed the stairs to her childhood bedroom without another word. Rolling her clothes into tight, neat cylinders, she had her bag packed in no time, and brought it down to leave by the front door. Matthew's old, battered army duffel was already there, and she left her bag tucked up against it before heading back into the kitchen. In silence, Anne helped Marilla make dinner, then sat and ate her food quietly, letting the conversation ebb and flow around her.

Sleep didn't come easy. She woke every few hours, her heart beating fast, groggy mind confused. With a huff, she'd roll over, punch her pillow a few times, and drift back into a restless sleep.

They left at dawn, Anne climbing into the back seat of Rachel's old sedan next to Matthew, placing a small stack of novels and her laptop between them on the seat. She still hadn't been told where they were going but found herself strangely incurious. Content to let herself be directed, herded wherever it was they wanted her to go. It was nice to just slip on a pair of sunglasses and rest her head against the back of the seat, watching the sun rise through the trees as they drove away from Green Gables, flashes of brilliant gold between the dark green.

The miles passed, slipping away as they drove across bridges and along crowded highways, through thick forests and busy cities. Marilla stopped somewhere between Boston and Portsmouth for lunch, switching out driving duties with Rachel. Matthew fought a nap, his head lolling forward until his chin would touch his chest, then he'd jerk back up, until a few moments later he'd start to droop again. Anne hid her grin behind a book.

It wasn't until they approached the Canadian border that she began to feel the first stirrings of curiosity, but only handed over her license to the border patrol agent without comment.

In Moncton, Anne pulled on her cardigan when they got out to get a snack. Rachel declined to share a packet of squeaky cheese curds with her, a look of faint horror on her face. Cheese was cheese was cheese, and it was *all* good, in its own particular way, Anne thought with a half shrug as she climbed back into the car.

When they reached the Confederation Bridge, Anne put down her book. She'd never seen anything like it. It stretched off into the distance, out into the ocean, toward the Prince Edward Island shoreline. Massive concrete risers loomed out of the water, supporting the road above, and Anne felt a frisson of nerves when the car left solid ground behind. But her wariness was soon overtaken by wonder, the expanse of the dark blue ocean on either side fascinating in its ambition to chase the sky along the horizon. Only briefly taking her eyes off the view to slip her earbuds in and call up her favorite playlist, Anne spent the rest of the drive watching the puffy white clouds overhead throw shadows along the surface of the gently rolling waves.

Once they left the bridge behind, it wasn't long before they were driving through balsam firs and spruce trees, past patchwork farmland and open fields, then finally down a series of one-lane roads. Finally, Matthew took a left and bumped down a long driveway that curved around until a small grouping of cottages spread over emerald-green grass lots came into view. Anne got out of the car, relieved to be out of the cramped space, and made a beeline right for the glint of water she could see beyond the cheerful, blue-and-white house they'd parked in front of, right on the edge of a wide flat beach.

Beyond the brilliant red ripples of sand, the ocean gently lapped at the shore, and Anne felt something crack open inside her. She took what felt like her first breath in days, sharp and tangy with salt. It wasn't like home in any way, and yet, something called to her.

Anne spent the next couple of days walking the sands with Marilla, touring the local markets and shops with Rachel, and searching out the best fishing spots with Matthew. She left her cell phone turned off, sitting at the bottom of her suitcase, wanting to lose herself in the moment and detach from the wider world as long as possible. Her hours were filled with soft laughter, reading through the collection of books she'd brought with her, and gossip from home, and she quickly learned that the beautiful crimson sand she'd so admired got into *everything*. Including her hair, somehow. Marilla took to sitting behind Anne on the porch steps every morning and weaving her hair into two long, tight plaits; an old, half-forgotten habit of theirs from Anne's childhood, when her unruly hair was the bane of both women's existence.

No one asked about Gil, and each braid woven with Marilla's careworn, loving hands was like a balm for Anne's sore, battered soul.

After two and a half lovely, sun- and sand-filled days, Anne was reluctant to leave. She knew it was time, she couldn't hide away from reality forever. But the break had been exactly what she'd needed, and she would be forever grateful to her family for knowing that. She tried to maintain the relaxed, open feeling she'd achieved during their stay at the red sand beach over the drive home and through her first night back in her own bed. It wasn't sustainable, she was aware of that, but if she could just hold on to it a little longer . . .

Perhaps, Anne thought, if she tried hard enough, it might just be possible she could avoid thinking anything of gravity until at least the end of summer.

But nothing lasts forever, proven by the house phone ringing on the afternoon of her fifth day home at Green Gables. On Marilla's orders, Anne was cleaning the baseboards of the living room, her hair tucked up under a bandanna, her T-shirt already streaked with dust. She heard Rachel pick up, then a moment of silence, and then—

"Anne! Diana's on the phone!"

Not an unusual phrase in the Cuthbert household, but the way Rachel said it had Anne's heart thumping. There was a wobble of panic in the older woman's voice she did *not* like. Dropping the dust rag, she jumped up and ran to the kitchen, grabbing the receiver Rachel held out.

"D?"

"I've been leaving you messages on your phone for days. *What the hell*, Anne?"

"I didn't know. We went to P.E.I. and I just let my cell die; I needed to just . . . disconnect, you know?" Anne replied, biting her lip. When she'd gotten home, she'd dropped her phone in the drawer of her nightstand, just needing to separate herself from everything that wasn't Green Gables for a while. She knew

Diana and Phil had her home number, although it slipped her mind that Marilla staunchly refused to connect it to any sort of voicemail. "I'm sorry, I didn't think you might be trying to check in while I wasn't here. What's going on? You sound awful."

"Thanks so much." Despite her biting words, Diana's voice just sounded tired. "Where's Rachel?"

Anne blinked, dread curling in her stomach. She glanced over to where the older woman was lingering in the doorway. "She's still here."

"Okay. Good." Diana paused, then blew out a loud breath. "Yeah, there's no good way to say this. Gil's been in an accident. He's in the hospital."

"What." Her voice felt flat. Flat and empty. Blindly, she reached out for Rachel's hand. The other woman crossed the room in a rush, taking it, her face creased with worry. "What kind of an accident? How bad is it?"

"He was crossing the street and a fucking car turned a blind corner, going way too fast, and hit him. I mean, we've all been bumped during traffic clog-ups, but this was different. Broke his leg so badly he had to be rushed right into surgery, they put a metal rod and pins in." Her shudder was practically audible. "And there was some internal bleeding."

At Anne's noise of distress, Diana rushed on, "But he's okay! Or . . . he will be. Fred says the doctors are telling the Blythes that Gil should make a total recovery. Eventually. They're going to take him home when he gets released tomorrow."

"Here? To Avonlea?"

"Yeah, because he's in a wheelchair and needs help with, you know, getting dressed, bathing, getting in and out of bed. That sort of thing. Plus, he's going to have an ass-ton of rehab before he can get back to walking without a cane or anything, much less take up running again. Mrs. Blythe apparently got real loud about him not going back to the apartment, especially because Fred works so much."

Rachel led Anne over to a chair at the kitchen table and pushed her into it, as she whispered, "I'm going to get Marilla. Be right back, just sit tight."

Anne nodded absently as she listened to Diana fill her in on what else Fred had passed on, mostly about how Mrs. Blythe had second-guessed the doctors' every move, until Dr. Blythe threatened to lock her in the bathroom. Apparently, it had provided the laugh they all needed, so no one had a breakdown instead.

A thought occurred to Anne suddenly, and she interrupted Diana midsentence, panic fluttering in her throat again. "Wait. When did this happen? You said you've been trying to call me for two days."

"Sunday night. Remember that crazy thunderstorm? That's why the driver didn't see Gil, the rain was so bad. Why he didn't just take a cab, I don't know." Her friend hesitated, then asked, "So I'm guessing he didn't show that night? I had really hoped the reason I hadn't heard from you, before we heard about Gil, was that you two had worked it out and were off somewhere making up for lost time. But then I couldn't get ahold of you, and he was in the hospital, and I didn't know *what* to think."

"No," Anne said, faintly. "I thought he just bailed."

It felt like someone had just punched her in the stomach, knocking out all her air. He'd only been out in the storm because of her. And there she'd been, stewing in that coffee shop, thinking he'd not even cared enough to text her that he wasn't coming after all.

"Oh, honey, no." She almost couldn't stand the soft sympathy in Diana's voice.

They sat in silence for a moment, then her friend continued, "Fred came back to our place Sunday night, and he'd brought his stuff, so he didn't even go home until closing the shop on Monday night. When he woke up Tuesday morning, he had something like six missed calls from the Blythes. A nurse couldn't even notify them until Monday afternoon, when Gil's phone dried out. It had landed in a puddle; it was sheer luck the medic saw it before they left for the hospital."

She sighed. "The whole thing was a shit show."

Marilla came through the door then, Rachel on her heels, taking in the way Anne was half curled over the phone, one arm tight around her middle, and swooped over to pry the receiver out of her hand. As Rachel crouched down next to her, rubbing her back in soothing circles, Anne distantly heard Marilla asking Diana sharp questions.

"All right. Thank you for letting us know," the older woman finally said, her voice as steady as always. "I'll have Anne call you back when she's feeling better. Yes, I will let her know to charge her phone. Love you too."

With care, Marilla replaced the receiver, ignoring the way the long, kinked-up cord had twisted into a tangled knot. Anne had spent many hours as a teenager lying on the floor of the kitchen in a spot of sun ("Like a damn cat," Marilla would always say), talking on that phone. She'd prop her legs up on the wall, cord stretching between her toes, then looping down to wrap around her forearm in coils. Once, she'd asked Matthew why they even still had a landline, when practically everyone else just had cell phones; he'd only shrugged and said it was in case a hurricane knocked out the towers. Whatever the reason, she'd loved talking on the clunky, olive-drab monstrosity. Loved the feel of the smooth rubber-coated cord between her toes, the way the receiver would warm to her body heat after the first few minutes, and the way she could wrap her entire body up in the extra-long cord, then spin out like a ballerina.

But now, it was like a foreign thing she couldn't puzzle out, something to focus on instead of looking at Marilla's face. She was afraid. Afraid that she'd see something terrible there. That maybe Diana had been downplaying Gil's injuries, horrible though they already were, but she'd left it to Marilla to break the really bad news. So, Anne couldn't look at her, because she might see the truth, and she wouldn't be able to bear it.

Because it turned out, her love for Gil wasn't in the past tense, after all.

If she thought it was painful before, when he broke her heart, it was nothing, *nothing*, to this agony.

"Anne. Anne, look at me. *Anne*."

Startled at the forceful tone, Anne jerked her eyes to meet Marilla's. The older woman's gaze was calm, which helped ease the tightness of Anne's chest. Surely Marilla wouldn't be so cool and collected if she was about to give Anne the news of Gil's impending death.

"Rachel, would you mind putting water on?" When the other woman nodded and rose to go fill the teakettle, Marilla crossed the room to sit at the table. There was no sound for the next few minutes, other than the noise of the tap running, then the *click* and *whoosh* of the gas burner. When Rachel came back over and sat down again, Marilla gave her partner a slight but warm smile, then turned to Anne.

"I'll be calling Patricia in a little bit, to see what we can do to help. She's already got her hands full with John, though I hear he's on the mend now, so at least there's that." And that was Avonlea to the core. Tiny towns had both a good and a bad side. Sure, everyone was up in everyone else's business. But they also tried to pitch in when there was an emergency. Anne had no doubt the news of Gil's accident was burning through the houses along the bay's edge at that very moment.

"But right now, what's more important to me is what we can do to help *you*." Marilla dipped her head to catch Anne's eye. "Matthew told me what happened at the bus depot—no, don't get mad, you had him worried. I've been waiting for you to come to me, or to Rachel, but you haven't. Now there's this, and frankly? I have absolutely no idea what to do next because I don't even know what's going on. I know it's more than you've told us."

"I'm sorry." Anne rubbed her fingertips against the denim of her shorts, feeling restless and jittery. She was distracted, her mind circling back around to an image of Gil, pale and still, lying in a hospital bed. "I'm not hiding things from you all. Or I don't mean to, anyway. God, I've gotten really bad at communicating, for someone who just graduated with a master's in education, haven't I?"

Rachel got up as the kettle's whistle interrupted them, then brought her a steaming mug. Anne carefully added milk and sugar, giving the task much more concentration than it warranted, as she thought of what she wanted to tell the older women, and how. The few brief romantic relationships she'd had when still living in Avonlea weren't particularly fraught with drama and tension, hadn't been the source of much conversation in the house. Anne took a sip from her mug, then another, and finally set it down.

"So, it turns out that I love Gilbert Blythe."

There was a moment of silence as they all looked at each other. Then Marilla made an impatient noise and waved her on.

"Yes, obviously. And? What happened?"

"*Yes, obviously*? How is that your answer? I just realized I loved him a few days ago!"

The two women exchanged amused glances.

"Fine. Whatever." Anne threw her hands up, exasperation finally piercing the fog clouding her mind. "The short of it is, we were together for just over half a year, and I thought things were good, really good; enough to fall in love with him, apparently."

They all sat in silence for a minute, while she lifted her tea to her lips again with hands that were slightly shaking. When she was feeling more under control, she continued, "I've had some trouble with one of my professors, and I lost my chance at the job I really, really wanted, and then when I told Gil, he made everything about *him*. We fought. We broke up. It was awful."

"Let's take this one thing at a time," Rachel spoke up, finally, folding her hands in front of her on the table and leaning in. "Tell us about this professor."

Anne sighed. She didn't want to go into this yet again; it was exhausting.

"Dr. Lintford. I think I told you over break that he's my advisor, and Gil's as well; he paired us to work on our thesis project together. Gil didn't know, and I never had any intention of telling because I was *handling it on my own*, but Lintford kept doing these little things all year that made me so uncomfortable."

The way Marilla's lips folded into a tight line and Rachel's shoulders went back, she knew the older women understood exactly what Anne meant.

"Whenever Gil wasn't there, he'd find ways to touch me, to say things that were *just* on this side of inappropriate." Anne gave a little half shrug. "Nothing I could really call him on, you know?"

"Unfortunately," Marilla said, grimly.

"Then one day, he tried to get me to meet with him at night, just me, at his house. He made it really clear what he wanted in exchange for some extra 'help' with my thesis." She shuddered at the memory of the way he'd looked at her. "I was just *done*, right then and there, completely done trying to pretend he wasn't doing what he was doing, and finally ripped into him."

Rachel looked fierce as she gave a sharp nod. "Good."

"He didn't take it well. Not at all. First, he tried to act like I was overreacting, making it into something it wasn't. Then he flat-out threatened to spread around that I was difficult to work with, that I was trying to make trouble for him when all he'd done was attempt to help me." She clenched her fists in her lap. "It scared me that he had the power to actually do it, but I reported him anyway."

God, that had been terrifying. She'd been so sure no one would believe her, and while she still wouldn't know the outcome of the investigation into her complaint for another few weeks, the horrified look on the assistant dean's face gave her hope Professor Lintford was about to finally experience the consequences of his actions. "I just couldn't stand the idea that next year, he'll be doing that to another student."

Marilla let out a hum of agreement, then her eyes narrowed as she studied Anne thoughtfully. "How did this lead into you and Gil breaking up? You both looked so happy at New Year's. Neither of you said anything, but it was fairly obvious there was something going on between the two of you. At least, to those of us who know you well."

"I think," Anne said, slowly, "that we've been dancing around each other our whole lives. I see that now. He's always been there, in the periphery—except the years we separated for college, obviously. Even then, there were too many times I'd think of him when the most random thing would occur. He was never completely gone from my mind."

"But something changed when he came back east."

"Yes." Anne rubbed the tip of one finger over a scratch on the worn table surface. "I don't think he felt the same as I do, though. It seemed pretty easy for him to walk away, in the end."

Marilla rubbed her forehead, looking like a headache was brewing. "Before I say this, know I'm on your side, no matter what, and that will never change. But—that boy has been madly in love with you since seventh grade."

Anne opened her mouth, taken aback. The denial on her lips died as she darted a glance at Rachel, only to find the other woman nodding in agreement.

"I find it hard to believe that he finally managed to get you to fall in love with him back and threw it away just because you had a fight," Marilla continued.

"It wasn't just some fight." Anne flattened her palm on the table, stilling the movement of her fingers. "He took the situation with our professor and turned it into being about *me* not trusting him. Not letting him in. But I don't want to rely on other people to fix things for me. I can't."

"Do you think he has a point?"

Jerking her head up, Anne stared at Rachel. Her first, knee-jerk reaction was to deny it. To feel offended. But she forced herself to take a tiny step back instead, and there was some truth to it that she didn't like. Because it made her feel small and mean.

"I don't know," she faltered, then buried her face in her hands. "Probably. Not about all of it. I did try to be open with him, in a lot of ways. I honestly didn't think about telling Gil about Dr. Lintford in the beginning. It never occurred to me that that's not something you keep from someone you love, when you're part of a couple. It's . . . hard for me to trust like that."

"I know it is. I still recall the moment you let yourself believe Matthew and I wouldn't send you back if you weren't upbeat and positive all the time," Marilla said with a sigh. "About a year after you came to live with us, we had that fight because I thought you'd borrowed my sun hat and lost it. Do you remember? The one with all the fabric flowers."

"How could I forget? It was so cute."

"She loved that hat," Marilla confided to Rachel, with a small smile.

"I really did." Anne nibbled her bottom lip. "You thought I took it and lost it somewhere in the woods and was lying about it so I wouldn't get in trouble. I think there was a Sunday school ice cream social at church or something on the line?"

"Yes, and you almost didn't get to go, but it turned out Bailey was the culprit all along."

Marilla had been so angry to realize the Labrador had snatched the hat off the hall table and destroyed it. They'd found bits and pieces of fabric flowers for weeks, all over the house.

"What do you remember about the single night that you were grounded, before we found the remains of my hat?" Marilla asked, watching Anne closely.

She thought back, unsure what the older woman was trying to pull out of her. "Just being completely devastated. Ugly-crying into my pillow because you didn't believe me, angry because I got punished for something I didn't do." Anne gave a little laugh. "Smugly vindicated when Bailey pooped out a mangled cotton violet the next morning."

"That was the first time you showed us anger. We'd been told when we decided you should stay that you had quite the temper, but neither Matthew nor I had seen any evidence of it. You seemed like such a cheerful child," Marilla mused. "But that day, you raged. Oh, you were so angry! And then running upstairs, slamming your door, throwing yourself onto your bed and crying up a storm—it was everything I'd been afraid of happening when a little girl showed up instead of the boy we'd requested. But by then, I wouldn't have sent you back for anything."

Anne drew in a shuddering breath, again wondering at how lucky she'd been to be placed with the Cuthberts.

"And it occurred to me that your temper tantrum was a *good* thing. That you trusted us enough to show us your ugly parts without fear we'd turn away from you. You finally let us in." Marilla leaned back in her chair, not looking away from Anne. "You've only let in a handful of people like that, since. Diana. Jane. Philippa too, I think. But being open with a partner, in a romantic relationship, is a different sort of vulnerability. And I think that's what you were struggling with."

"He was meeting me to talk, you know. To try to work some things out," Anne said, her insides twisting. "The night he got hit by the car. He was only out in that storm because of me."

"Stop that right now. You are not to blame for his accident."

"It feels like it."

"Well, someone up there thinks you should have a second

chance to figure things out with Gil. If you want to, that is." Marilla sighed and leaned over, wrapping her arms around Anne, only huffing a little when Rachel got up and squeezed them both into a hug. "It sounds like you have a lot of thinking to do."

"Yeah," whispered Anne, letting them hold her, placing her hands over their crossed arms. *This* was why she'd come home. To be with her family. "I think I do."

Chapter 32

Then

Anne Shirley was a weird child.

Everyone said it and she didn't deny it. Maybe it *was* weird at twelve years old to still imagine herself the lost princess of a faraway country or believe there were elves hiding in the forest. To make up stories about a hidden martian colony on the moon and cover the mirrors in her bedroom every night because the possibility of ghosts on the other side watching her while she slept was kind of creepy. Although . . . she wasn't opposed to ghosts as a general concept, if they came with a romantic and tragic backstory. And okay, maybe it was weird to refuse to give up secret imaginary friends that traveled from foster home to foster home with her. But sometimes they were the only ones she had, and they kept the loneliness at night away, so she couldn't understand why adults got so worked up over it.

Really, truly, Anne didn't really mind being weird. She'd rather be weird than boring, anyway, like her last foster parent, Mrs. Hammond, whose imagination didn't extend beyond imagining Anne doing the dishes and babysitting her three sets of twins. Three! Boy, was she glad to be out of there and on her way to a new home, even if it was a kind of farm or something. Maybe they'd have chickens. Or a crotchety old horse that only she could get close to and would eat apples out of her hand and let her brush its beautiful, flowing mane. They'd become great friends and Anne would visit her every afternoon; she imagined a horse would be a very sympathetic listener to her stories. She rested her cheek against the cool glass of her social worker's car window as they drove across Long Island to her next home, and envisioned a majestic creature with a shiny coat and a white star on her forehead. Just like in that old book she'd read, *Black Beauty*.

So no one could blame her for being disappointed when they turned down a long blacktop driveway lined with wooden fences, thick twists of vines and wide green leaves covering them, instead of open fields and a prancing, dark horse. They slowly drove past a long, low building with glittering glass windows, a sign that read GREEN GABLES WINERY on it, and a large parking lot, of all things. The lone car in the lot was an old, faded blue pickup truck, baking in the summer sun as if someone had parked it there decades ago and forgotten to move it. She caught a glimpse of several more trucks and what looked like a tractor around the back of the building as they rode past it.

Well, she comforted herself, a tractor surely meant a farm.

And the possibility of chickens and a horse. No point in giving up hope yet.

When they rolled to a stop, she resolutely fixed a cheerful look on her face, her best first impression smile, and followed Mrs. Spencer, the most recent caseworker in a long line of them Anne had had in the last seven years, out of the car. A woman with gray hair scraped back into a tight bun, her plaid shirt rolled to the elbows to reveal wiry arms and strong, work-roughened hands, had stepped out onto the porch when they pulled up. Her face didn't look like the kind that smiled often, with blue eyes that held more of a glint than a twinkle, but the set of her mouth wasn't unkind. Anne knew how to read unkind; she'd learned that early on, and it helped make her less nervous to see the lack of it in this stranger who she was supposed to live with now.

That settled, she took a moment to study her new home as the two women exchanged greetings. The house was old, definitely built back when women wore long dresses and people rode everywhere in carriages. It stood two stories tall with a dark green, shingled roof and white wooden siding, a long porch that wrapped around the sides, and boxes filled with crowds of colorful flowers fastened underneath each window. And a tower! A round tower attached to one side of the house, with a pointy, cone roof and three tall windows that looked like something a princess would lean out of to let down yards of hair so her lover could climb up to rescue her.

Anne knew what a lover was; she'd stolen Mrs. Hammond's romance novels before she got sent back to the group home and read them cover to cover. Skipping the gross parts, obviously. Macy, one of the older girls there, had laughed at her and said one day she'd appreciate those bits, but Anne had her doubts.

This tower, however, looked like the perfect place for an epic romance. Something with a prince or dragonslayer, or maybe a grumpy, handsome duke who was desperately in love with her. She wondered if it was a bedroom, and if it was, if she could beg her new foster parent to allow her to sleep there for however long she was allowed to stay. Even a few months would give her enough imagination fuel for years of daydreaming.

Marilla Cuthbert, she'd been told, was a single woman in her fifties who lived with her brother and had (*graciously*, Mrs. Spencer had reminded her several times on the drive over) decided to foster for the first time. Mrs. Spencer couldn't understand why she'd do it, considering Ms. Cuthbert's age, and that she'd specifically requested an older child, who were never in as much demand as the babies.

Babies were cuter and didn't come with as many authority issues.

But she had, and Anne was supposed to be grateful and behave, and not make Ms. Cuthbert regret all the choices so far in her life that had led her to taking in an orphan with a suitcase filled with more books than clothes and a history of talking too much. She wasn't sure how to do that, exactly, since she didn't have a great track record so far. Looking at the stern expression on the older woman's face as she turned to her, a critical light in her eyes as she looked Anne over, then a shake of her head as if the girl had already come up short, the odds she'd be back at the group home within a month climbed several notches.

"I specifically asked for a boy," Ms. Cuthbert said crisply, as she turned back to Mrs. Spencer. "There's been a mix-up."

Anne closed her eyes. She'd known it was too good to be true.

"I have the paperwork here, Ms. Cuthbert, it clearly says a girl."

"Well, the paperwork is wrong. I've no interest in dealing with a preteen girl's drama and moods."

"Oh, I'm not moody and dramatic *at all*," Anne burst out, opening her eyes again to meet the older woman's gaze, hoping to change her mind. She was lying through her teeth, but it was worth a shot. "You'll hardly even know I'm here."

Ms. Cuthbert pursed her lips, tapping the papers the case-worker had given her against her thigh. "I don't know what I'd do with a girl."

Her voice was reluctant, but not as firm as before. Anne felt a surge of hope, biting her lip to hold back her eagerness.

"I can help with chores. Feed chickens or milk a cow or clean toilets. I've got a lot of practice cleaning bathrooms, mopping floors, and doing laundry."

"We don't have chickens or cows." Well, poop. There went that portion of the dream. But there was still the possibility of the princess room to fight for. Marilla went on, "And everyone here pulls their own weight, chores are a given. But I asked for a boy and this is not what I signed up for, regardless."

Mrs. Spencer shifted next to Anne, her posture awkward. "I understand the dilemma, I do, but there's a process to be followed and paperwork to fill out if you are refusing a foster child. I can start that first thing tomorrow morning, but would it be possible for her to stay just the night? I really don't have anywhere else to put her for now."

Anne concentrated on keeping her breathing even, eyes fixed on the way the thick line of trees at the far edge of the fields swayed, and beyond that, the glint of sun off what might be the bay. But she couldn't push back the tears that slipped out, spilling down her cheeks, as the pain of rejection filled her yet again.

"Oh, for the love of— Is she crying?" There was a frustrated, gusty sigh from the front porch. "Fine. She can stay the night, I'm not a monster to turn a child away without a bed. But I can't promise anything beyond that."

Anne whipped around, eyes wide, swiping away the tears. "Oh, can I sleep in the tower, Ms. Cuthbert? It is a bedroom? Can I keep the window open to smell the flowers and evening breeze? Please?"

Ms. Cuthbert looked taken aback by her rapid-fire questions, but rallied. "It is a bedroom. Not the one I'd planned on converting, but there's no harm in you sleeping there for one night. And I'd rather you call me Marilla, if you're staying."

One night in the princess room, then back to the group home that always smelled faintly of pee and Lysol. Anne could fit a lot into one afternoon and night, if she could convince Ms. Cuthbert—Marilla—to let her wander the fields and maybe even the woods. If she was lucky, there would be a path somewhere to the bay she was positive was close by. She could hear the faint lapping of waves from the front yard. She'd never lived anywhere near the water; it would have been nice to fall asleep to the sound of it every night.

But if nothing else, she'd have the memory of sleeping in a magical tower and that was something.

Resolved to make the best of what little time she had, she dragged her suitcase out of the trunk and climbed the porch stairs. Mrs. Spencer said her relieved goodbyes, promising to return in the morning, got into her car, and drove off.

"I don't know what we'll do until the morning, but we might as well start with dinner and go from there." Marilla broke the shared silence after a long moment, her voice gruff. "I don't suppose you know how to make mashed potatoes."

"Yes, ma'am, I can." Now *this* was something she could do. Cooking was a chore she'd gotten stuck with a lot at Mrs. Hammond's and it turned out she was pretty good at it. Anne picked up her suitcase, comforted by the thought of a good dinner and a princess room in her near future. "I make the best mashed potatoes in the state of New York. You won't ever look at them the same after you've had mine."

"Well then," said Marilla, a ghost of reluctant amusement turning her lips up. "Get on in there and show me your magic."

That night, after a dinner made only slightly awkward by Marilla's stilted attempts at conversation and her brother Matthew's shy silence, Anne hauled her suitcase upstairs to the princess room. She walked in, wide-eyed, her mouth falling open as she took in the perfection of the rounded tower bedroom. Aged floors gleamed golden in the setting sun that filled the room from three tall windows bowing outward. Just beyond the glass, the enormous oak tapped gently against the house, summer breeze rustling the green leaves, as if in happy welcome. The room itself was sparse, only furnished with a chest of drawers, a single bed covered with a simple blue quilt, and a small bedside table. Dropping her bag just within the doorway, she rushed over to the window seat, leaning forward to practically press her nose against the glass. The view was everything she could have hoped for and more.

"If you were mine," she whispered, hardly louder than a breath, pressing her fingers to where a slender tree branch brushed the window, "I would call you Gloriana, after the beautiful queen."

"What's that?" Marilla sounded impatient.

Dropping her hand to her lap, Anne turned back with a wide smile. "Oh, I just meant to say you can see the harbor from here. Not much—just enough. It's like a painting, with the fields and trees and dark blue water. I don't know how you get *anything* done, I would just sit here all day, daydreaming about mermaids and tree dryads."

Raising her eyebrows, the older woman picked up Anne's suitcase from where she'd abandoned it and laid it on the bed. She walked over to the window, peering out with a furrowed brow, as if she didn't see anything remarkable. Maybe she didn't, if she'd lived here every day of her life, as the framed row of yellowed photos of the house marching up the stairwell, filled with people dressed in old-fashioned clothes Anne assumed were now-deceased Cuthberts, seemed to say. She'd told the siblings at dinner this was her third placement in as many years and she was really disappointed to have to leave in the morning. Not that she was trying to guilt them into letting her stay or anything. Well, not *much*. But with every hour she spent in the house, she fell a little more in love.

It was going to be horribly heartbreaking to have to leave again. In the romance novel she had hidden at the bottom of her suitcase, the village girl had to leave the duke's castle when he found out she wasn't *really* a stable boy, and Anne could sympathize with the deep, dark despair she must have felt.

But that was for tomorrow. Tonight, she wanted to cram as much exploration in as possible.

"Can I go outside for a little bit?" The heavy bunches of grapes hung from straight wooden frames that marched in rows all the way to the woods, she wanted to see if they smelled as nice as they looked. Did grapes smell? She couldn't remember. Apples did, and peaches, so maybe grapes did too.

"No, it'll be dark soon and you don't know your way around the property." Marilla glanced at her watch. "The last thing Matthew and I need right now is to wander the vineyard all night looking for a lost little girl."

"Oh." Anne slumped against the window, disappointed her plan to find all the secret spots on the grounds brought to a halt.

Marilla's lips pursed for a moment, then she shrugged. "If you have time before Mrs. Spencer arrives in the morning, you can go out then."

"Thank you, thank you a million times! I'd like to visit the vineyard, if that's okay? Also the woods, although I won't go in,

I promise, and you have a nice large yard out back. I think I saw blueberry bushes? Something with berries, I don't know, I'm not a berry expert, but I think I can at least recognize a blueberry if I get close enough. I love blueberries. Raspberries too. Cherries. Grapes are always delicious, of course, no offense! Do you eat any of the grapes you grow here?"

"All right, child, calm down." Marilla crossed the room, pausing in the doorway to the hall. "You have so much energy, I get tired just listening to you."

"You're not the first foster parent to tell me that," Anne said absently, already planning her route out for the next morning.

A small twist of amusement quirked up one side of the older woman's mouth, making her look so much more approachable, in Anne's mind. "To answer your question, yes, those are blueberries. Although the season is just about done, there might not be much left. And no, we don't eat our grapes. I guess we could, but we don't."

After Marilla left, Anne pulled on the old sweats and T-shirt she usually wore to sleep and climbed into bed. She left the curtains open for two reasons: one, the evening light through the trees was enthralling, and two, the sun should shine right on her in the morning to wake her up. She didn't have a cell phone (Who was going to pay for one? Definitely not the state.), but there was an old alarm clock on the nightstand that looked like it'd been there since 1975. Just in case the sunlight didn't work, she'd set the clock for six-thirty A.M. Hopefully that would do the trick. That way she could be up early and have plenty of time for an adventure before going back to her boring life where nothing interesting ever happened, unless she counted surprise bedroom inspections.

And those were *not* the fun kind of excitement.

The next morning, the sun did its job and gently nudged her awake five minutes before the alarm went off. Anne rolled out of bed, threw on shorts and a T-shirt, ignoring her open suitcase as a problem for later, and ran down the stairs. She tried to be as quiet as possible, just in case the Cuthberts were still sleeping, but she shouldn't have worried about it. The siblings were both in the kitchen, sipping cups of coffee and eating plates of eggs and toast. Anne's stomach growled, because she was "a bottomless pit," a feat she'd been told was impressive for a child as scrawny as she was. Marilla rose as soon as she paused in the doorway, going to the stove and scooping eggs onto a plate.

She stuck two pieces of wheat bread in the toaster. "What do you like, jelly or butter?"

"Oh, I was going to just go out, actually," Anne said, glancing over her shoulder, torn between starting her adventure and filling her stomach. The nice smell of toast began to fill the air, and she wavered only a moment more before stepping fully into the kitchen and sitting down across from Matthew. "I guess I could eat first. Jelly, please."

"I wouldn't want to force it on you."

"That's okay, I don't mind!"

"If you're sure," Marilla said, humor in her voice as she set a plate piled with scrambled eggs and toast in front of Anne. A moment later she placed a large glass of milk and a pot of what looked like homemade strawberry jam next to her as well.

Anne's mouth watered, tart and sharp, at both the sight and smell of it all, like she hadn't just stuffed herself with mashed potatoes and pork chops the night before. After thanking Marilla, she fell silent, working her way through the laden plate as the two adults went back to their conversation. She shoveled in eggs, trying to remember not to chew with her mouth open, and eavesdropped.

". . . So then I said—" Marilla suddenly broke off and looked over at Anne, who immediately dropped her eyes and concentrated on eating in as innocent a manner as possible. The older woman lowered her voice even more; Anne had never before been grateful for her oversized ears, but today she was. "I told her that this was their mistake and they better fix it. Then she said the system is overcrowded, there's nowhere to place the girl yet, and asked if we could possibly keep her another few weeks. Imagine!"

There *was* hope after all. Maybe.

"I gave you my opinion last night after the social worker called back." Matthew never looked up from his newspaper, cup of coffee in hand.

"Yes, thank you so much for your support," Marilla replied, her voice back to a normal volume as she threw up her hands in exasperation. "Fine. I'll call and tell her Anne can stay for a few more weeks." Anne's heart was nearly jumping out of her chest with joy, but she managed to keep it together when Marilla turned to her and asked, "I assume that's all right with you?"

"Yes, ma'am. Marilla. And Matthew too, of course. Yes, I'd

like to stay *very much*, thank you." The toast crumbled in her tight grip, crumbs scattering across the plate. She would have two whole weeks of summer, if she was lucky, to explore Green Gables! What to do first? The long list of exciting options tumbled around in her brain, but after a few seconds, she drew a deep breath and reined them in. She had two weeks to work her way through them. No need to rush at all.

"That's settled then." Marilla pulled a cell phone out of her back pocket and walked out of the room, punching in numbers as she went.

Anne sat in silence a moment longer, staring at her toast but not seeing it. Then a rustle across the table reminded her that Matthew still sat there. She smiled wide as the older man peered at her over the top of his paper. He'd hardly said more than two words to her since she arrived the day before, but he had kind eyes and a quiet voice, and she appreciated both.

"So what do you do?"

He lowered the newspaper slowly. "Do when?"

"*Do*, do. What do you do all day? Do you make wine? Do people still squish it with their feet, like in that old *I Love Lucy* episode? I love that show, sometimes if the family I'm staying with gets cable with reruns, I can catch it."

"I don't make wine all the time. Sometimes I do," he said, folding the newspaper and placing it on the table. "But sometimes I check the vines and talk to my field manager, or visit the man who makes all our barrels. There are days I just stay in the office in the tasting room building, doing paperwork and working on our bookkeeping with the accounts manager. Once in a while I travel to other vineyards to talk shop or learn new ways to make wine."

"The paperwork doesn't sound like fun, but the rest of it's kind of . . . cool." Anne forgot about her plan to find her way down to the beach and propped her chin on one palm. "Which part are you doing today?"

"I'm headed out to the fields this morning, checking to make sure no rot or bugs have gotten into the crops."

"Can I come?"

"And walk the rows with me?" Matthew looked surprised.

"Sure." She stood up, grabbing both his coffee cup and her empty plate, dropping them in the sink on her way toward the door. "You can teach me about grapes, I don't know *one fact* about them except they're delicious. I like knowing a little about a lot of things, it makes everything so much more interesting, don't you think?"

Matthew rose and followed her to the door, pulling his ball cap on. "Never thought about it that way, but I guess it does."

Anne grinned up at him as she skipped down the stairs, and wondered how long she should wait before asking him to show her how to get down to the beach. Maybe there were shells, pretty ones she could clean off and tuck into her suitcase to take with her. She could pull them out from time to time and remember that, for a little while at least, she'd lived in a princess room by the sea.

Chapter 33

Now

The call from Priorly came a few days later.

Before leaving the city, Anne had written out a long email to the dean there, detailing her experiences with Dr. Lintford, including reporting him for sexual harassment, and the subsequent investigation by Redmond's administration. She couldn't help but think he'd had more than a little influence in their decision to so abruptly cut her from the list of candidates. Some people would say that was presumptuous, but Anne felt vindicated when the dean called her herself, to speak with her further on both her thesis project and review her application for the associate professorship.

"Is this a follow-up interview?" Anne asked, about halfway through the call, sitting down on her desk chair with a thump.

"Not that I'm complaining, but I thought the position had been offered to someone else."

As it turned out, the job *was* open again, because Gil had turned it down just yesterday.

"Now so much of the confusion we've had surrounding the post is clear," the dean said, wryly. "I can't say much, legally, but Mr. Blythe specifically asked that you be informed he was bowing out. I do hope your experience hasn't soured you on Priorly, because I truly think you'd be an excellent addition to our staff."

Anne accepted on the spot, because *of course* she did. It was exactly what she'd worked so long for, and she finally had it in her grasp. She set up an appointment to meet the dean in person again the following week, and then another with the staffing department to fill out the proper employment forms.

It wasn't on paper yet, but it was official—Anne was a college instructor.

When she got off the phone, she immediately tracked everyone down and told them her news. They celebrated with lobster rolls, dripping with butter, and tangy coleslaw from a local seafood shack for lunch. Afterward, she texted Diana and Jane, then took a book down to the shore. Climbing onto her reading rock, a large flat boulder at the edge of the water, she attempted to concentrate, but found herself just staring at the pages instead of taking anything in.

Anne was home, she was with family, she had the job of her dreams now . . . but everything felt off. Because she couldn't share it with Gil.

Abandoning the book, she tucked her legs up and rested her

chin on top of her knees, staring out over the bay. The wind tugged at her hair, and she remembered the feel of his fingers in the long tresses. The look on his face as they'd lie in bed, talking about anything and everything while he'd comb out the tangles with his fingers, brushing the hair off her forehead gently. She missed that with an ache that felt like it was going to tear her in two, and suddenly Anne knew she couldn't give them up without a fight. Maybe it was too late. Maybe he wouldn't want her anymore, or it was terrible timing. But she had to at least try.

Picking her book up, Anne went back up to the house to ask Matthew if she could borrow the car.

Chapter 34

It was a beautiful day. The light filtering through the branches of the huge trees was so bright, it almost hurt Gil's eyes, but the shade at the edge of the patio kept him cool enough he didn't feel the need to sit inside the air-conditioned house. Which was good, because he'd only been home a few days and was already wanting to wheel off into the woods and never return.

He could live off acorns, and sometimes oysters from the beach, and never again have anyone ask him four times in a row if he needed a nap.

His mom was great, ready to help whenever he needed it, but as it turned out, she was a bit of a hoverer now. It was like something in her had fundamentally changed over the past year, and now that his dad was cancer-free, she didn't quite know what to do with herself.

If he was being honest, though, what got to Gil the most was the loss of autonomy. His parents' house wasn't even remotely set up for a wheelchair user, and he couldn't get around by himself for more than a few minutes without losing his breath. Apparently even a small tear in the lungs was enough to lay him up for the next couple months.

Not to mention the steel rod in his leg.

On second thought, let's not mention that at all, because then his mother might ask him if he wanted a nap, and he might have to admit that a nap sounded pretty good. And right now, just out of rebellion, he was anti-nap. It had been hard enough not to snap at her when she tried to put sunscreen on for him, gently taking the bottle from her instead, and promising he wouldn't forget. And he wouldn't, because a sunburn was exactly what he didn't need right now.

It was possible he was a little cranky and actually *did* need a nap. Fuck.

Tipping his head back, Gil closed his eyes.

What would Anne be doing right now? He knew she was home, like him, not even six miles away. It could have been an ocean between them, the distance felt so untraversable. Diana had texted the night before, to let him know she'd finally gotten ahold of Anne and told her about Gil's accident. He'd tried not to but couldn't help checking his phone every couple hours since he woke up. Each time he was met with text messages from what seemed like everyone he'd ever met, but none from Anne; he promised himself he'd stop looking.

Which was a lie, because he always looked one more time.

"I hope you put on sunscreen, sitting out here like this."

Blinking against the light, Gil looked toward the source of

the familiar voice, the same one he'd just been thinking of, and wondered if the pain pills were finally kicking in to make him hallucinate Anne standing at the edge of the patio. She looked good in ragged shorts and an old Avonlea Prep T-shirt, her normally pale skin turned a light golden color by the summer sun since he'd last seen her.

"Gil?" She moved closer, her eyes clouding with concern when he didn't answer.

"Over there," he said, gesturing belatedly toward the sunscreen he'd tossed onto a nearby table, still processing her showing up just when he'd been thinking about her. She glanced over, then went and picked it up, turning back to look at him.

"Do you need a hand with this?"

His eyebrows went up. All these things unsettled between them, and Anne was offering to help him put sunscreen on? When he didn't say anything, her face fell, and she started to put the bottle back down.

"Maybe this wasn't a good idea."

To his horror, her mouth started to tremble, and tears welled in her eyes.

"Wait," Gil blurted out, panic streaking through him when she turned toward the house, scrubbing at the damp skin on her face with the back of her wrist. "Yes, you can help me. Put on the suntan lotion. If that's something you really want to do.

"Thanks," he added, starting to feel like a fool, but desperate to get her to stop crying. Fighting was something he could handle. Her beautiful gray eyes wet with tears killed him. That it was *his* fault Anne was crying was horrifying.

After a delicate sniff, she picked up the bottle again, making her way across the patio to where he sat half in the shade. Neither of them spoke as she tapped out a small puddle of lotion into her hand, handing him the bottle to hold. After rubbing her palms together, she moved to stand between his legs, and carefully smoothed the lotion over his cheeks. Neither of them commented on the drying tear tracks still visible on her face. Using her fingertips, Anne traced the lines of his cheekbones, smudged the silky liquid over his brow, and stroked it along the angle of his jaw.

It would have been more convenient to blame his punctured lung on his difficulty breathing, but that would have been a lie.

He held himself very still in an effort not to set his hands on her hips and pull her close, running his lips over her collarbone until she climbed into his lap. When she smoothed the sunscreen down the sides of his neck, lingering at the base of his throat, he couldn't stop himself from leaning into her touch for a moment.

"Gil?"

It wasn't until Anne spoke, her voice wary, and still so close, that he realized he'd closed his eyes at some point. He'd be embarrassed about it, except he was feeling looser and more relaxed than he'd been since his accident.

"Thanks," he said, again, as she stepped back and capped the bottle.

With a jerky nod, as if she hadn't basically seduced him by putting suntan lotion on his damn face, Anne pulled up a chair and sat down. She gave him a small smile that faded all too soon, the uncertainty coming back. "I feel awful that I wasn't there after your accident, because I was so busy being mad at you for ditching me. Except you didn't, and I would have known that if I'd just talked to Diana or Fred sometime over the last week."

"It's fine."

"It's really not," she disagreed, lacing her fingers together tightly in her lap, still glistening with sunscreen. "I spent the ride over here trying to figure out what I want to say. Because it's a lot, and I need to get it right. And I'm really afraid I might be saying it too late to make a difference."

In his mind's eye, he saw the terrible look on her face when she thought he was rejecting her earlier, and knew he had to say something honest. If he wanted this, wanted *her*, then he was going to have to go all in. Maybe she loved him, maybe she wasn't there yet. How she felt wasn't going to change what he did, and there was something freeing in that realization.

"Anne, I've wanted you since before I knew what it was to want someone," Gil said, leaning forward to catch her gaze with his own. "Even when the only time you ever looked at me was when we were fighting, all I could see was you. So, when you ask me if it's too late, believe me when I tell you that's not possible."

Her breath left her in a rush. "I really thought you might tell me to go."

The thing about Anne was this: Gil had loved her for so long, he thought he knew all of her expressions. The ones she wore when she was surprised, or angry, or had just won the regional spelling bee. There was nothing left for him to discover in her tired frown or the way she chewed the inside of her cheek when she was nervous. He knew what her face did when she looked at her first boyfriend or her best friend, or her family.

But this half smile, immeasurably soft and just a bit shaky, wasn't anything he'd seen before, and it fascinated him. He wanted to study it for hours.

If she left now, if Gil let her go *again*, he'd have to chase after her, broken leg or not. How many more second chances would the universe give him? It wasn't worth finding out.

"I want you to stay."

Chapter 35

Anne knew Gil was waiting for her to say the things she'd come to say.

It would be easier to form words if her heart wasn't lodged in her throat, however.

"I think . . ." She looked away. "I think it all got tangled up in my head, because it's never been easy with us, right? For years before you went away, we fought. Sometimes it was awful, but sometimes, sometimes it was actually kind of nice. No, not *nice*, but it was okay. Because you were funny, and occasionally sweet, and *definitely* awkward, and you made me like you just a little bit. Even when I didn't want to. I really, really didn't want to like you."

Gil's smile was slow, his eyes warming. "I'm sorry I made fun of your hair."

"You *have* tried to apologize for that one before, but I'll go

ahead and finally accept this time." The relief at the affection for
her that he gave so freely, even now, was so immense, it almost
made her dizzy. "I'm sorry I assumed you were the kind of boy
who would use sex to best his archenemy—"

"Archenemy?" The look of glee on his face at the word made it
hard not to stick her tongue out at him. God, he really did bring
out the twelve-year-old in her sometimes.

"—and ruined a perfectly nice moonlit kiss on the beach," she
finished.

"*Nice*," he scoffed. "I've been thinking about that kiss on and
off for six years. It was amazing, try to deny it."

"It was *very* nice?" Anne bit her lip to hide a grin, knowing
she wasn't successful. This was just like him to take what could
have been a painful discussion and somehow manage to blunt
all the edges, so they didn't cut themselves on them. "Fine, I'll
admit I might have thought about it once or twice."

"I'm sorry I let you believe I didn't care that you thought I'd
use you like that, because my ego got in the way." Gil sobered.
"And I'm sorry that you ever thought you couldn't tell me things,
or lean on me, or that I would try to step in and take over. I'm
not sure how I can prove to you that I won't."

"I'm sorry that you were right, and I *was* withholding my
trust, not because you deserved it, but based solely on the actions of other people in my past. You've been pretty great, actually. I hate that I almost messed that up."

"*We* almost messed that up." He paused, then that devilish
glint in his eye was back. "Wait. You're sorry I was right?"

"No! The other thing.

"Although," Anne said, with consideration. "Yes, a little bit of that, as well."

"Anne, I love you. You know that, right?"

She did know, because even if he hadn't said it right now, his face was doing this thing that left her no doubt that she was everything to him. It knocked the breath out of her. The idea of his love was exhilarating and terrifying at the same time. It was like a trust fall; letting herself believe she could let go and he'd catch her—but even if he didn't, he'd stick around to help pick up the pieces. It made her feel like she could say things to him that she couldn't say to anyone else.

In that moment, taking his face in her hands and pressing her lips against his mouth was easy as anything.

"I used to give my heart away so eagerly as a child, desperate for love, to people who couldn't be trusted with it," she confessed, brushing her thumbs over his cheekbones, loving the feel of his smooth, warm skin. "It took me longer than it should have to learn how easy it was to be crushed when you flay yourself wide open for others again and again. A lesson a child should never have to learn, but once I caught on, I absorbed it too well, I think."

"You've always been a fast learner," Gil said lightly, one hand coming up to encircle her wrist with long fingers, drawing her closer. He turned his head and pressed his mouth against the delicate skin of her inner arm before releasing her.

"Spectacularly unhelpful in this case."

"Can we just agree that this"—he gestured to them both—

"won't work if we don't say what we're thinking? We aren't the same people we were when we met in eighth grade, or who we were when we last saw each other at the age of eighteen. I thought I knew who you were, because I spent so much time looking at you, and trying to figure out how to get you to look back at me. But it occurs to me that I missed a lot. I just want a chance to know you, Anne."

Then he dimpled at her. "And if I start being a stubborn jackass again, you have permission to smack me over the head with whatever's handy."

"Don't think I won't take you up on that offer." She'd meant for it to come out joking, but the breathy sound of her voice ruined it, because Gil was holding her hand in one of his now, stroking his fingers along the creases of the life lines on her palm. The soft touch gave her a shivery feeling, one she felt from the top of her head to toes that curled in delight at the sensation. She'd never get tired of the way he touched her.

"So before this all went to shit," he started, breaking the silence, gaze still on his fingers moving up and down the outsides of her fingers, "I'd been thinking of asking you to move in with me."

Anne's heart leapt. He'd used the past tense; it didn't mean he was still interested in them taking that next step now. But the idea of talking late into the night, curled around each other, then waking in the morning still at his side, made her yearn for it.

"Oh, really?"

"Really." The corners of his eyes crinkled when he raised

his head and met her gaze. Their fingers laced together, palms warm where they pressed against each other. "So, what do you say? Think you can deal with me chewing on all the pens in the house and leaving my shoes in a messy pile by the front door?"

"Isn't that love?" Anne laughed, something inside breaking free as she scooted to the edge of her seat and threw her arms around his neck in a tight squeeze. "Sticking around even if your partner keeps putting the roll of toilet paper backward?"

"I would *never*. What kind of monster do you think I am?"

Drawing back just far enough to see his face, she searched his eyes. "You know I love you too, right? I love you so much, sometimes it hurts. But in the best way. The kind where you think you'll crack open with it, because how can one person contain that much love and not die from it."

"If I didn't know you since we were twelve, I'd be alarmed by the amount of drama in that sentiment," Gil murmured, releasing her hand so he could cradle her face between his palms. With infinite care, he pressed small kisses along her cheeks, her forehead, over the freckles across her nose.

"Ex*cuse* me—"

Anything more she would have said was lost as he urged her forward, making a hungry sound when her lips opened to let him in. Her hands came up to clutch at his biceps as she leaned in farther, careful not to bump his cast with her knees. One of Gil's hands slid into her hair, holding her to him, his breath hitching as she gasped. Heat flared, making her limbs tremble with restlessness, wanting to move against him, but knowing *that* was going to have to wait for a while yet. He needed to heal before anything very . . . athletic.

A tragedy.

The sound of a throat clearing had them pulling apart, although Gil wouldn't let her go far, his arm staying around her waist. The sight of Fred leaning against the open door to the house, ankles crossed, crunching on a chip from the bag in his hand, had a flush racing up to her face. Well, that was a mood killer.

"Sorry to interrupt," he said cheerfully, not looking particularly sorry. "Pattie wants to know if Anne's staying for dinner."

"When did you get here? I thought you weren't coming down until tomorrow." Gil sounded grouchy. "Does she know you've started calling her Pattie?"

Fred looked at him like he was nuts. "*Obviously* I don't do it when she's within hearing distance."

"Because you don't have a death wish?"

"Because I don't have a death wish," Fred confirmed, and Anne fought a giggle, picturing Mrs. Blythe's face if someone dared to give her what she'd surely consider an undignified nickname. "So, Anne. Staying, yes or no?"

Standing, Anne brushed off the back of her shorts, then touched one handle of Gil's chair with a questioning look. The warmth on his face dissolved into a wide grin and he nodded. With a nudge, she started pushing him toward the house, feeling lighter than she had in weeks.

"Yes. I'm staying."

Acknowledgments

Firstly, thank you to my editor Tessa Woodward at Harper-Collins, for putting out a call on Twitter for a modern Anne of Green Gables novel, and believing in me and my vision. I can't imagine having written this book for anyone less invested, anyone who didn't love Avonlea and its residents as much as I do. Thank you to my other editor Elle Keck as well, for answering my millions of questions and being there for me every step of the way. Much appreciation to Jen Udden, Suzie Townsend, and everyone at New Leaf Literary for all the hard work and advocating they do on my behalf. A shout-out to Ali Trotta, Carin Thumm, Reese Ryan, Nicole Tersigni, Alex de Campi, Suleikha Synder, Cat Sebastian, and Elsa Sjunneson for being the best support system a girl could ask for. Thank you to Zoulfa Katouh, for reminding me how hot boys in flat caps are! Thank you to Melissa Blue for being both a good friend and thorough sensitivity reader. Any mistakes I've made with Diana in this book are one hundred percent mine; Melissa is an amazing editor and reader. A huge thanks to my best friend, Cortney

Wofford, for listening to me complain, making me laugh, and being my pandemic buddy! You've kept me sane over the last six months (the last six years, really). I owe more than a thank-you to my parents, however, for their unending support and for always pushing me to believe in myself and my writing. We've been through some rough times together, and I wouldn't be the person I am today without your unconditional love. Lastly, I have to give thanks to my husband and kids. Nate and Brady, I appreciate you both putting up with my long hours in front of the computer and cranky face during deadline. I love you beyond words, and no, I'm not buying you to anything to show that gratitude and love. (Okay, maybe some ice cream is in order.) Shawn, thank you for forever supporting my dreams and endeavors, and providing me with the time and space to realize them. I feel pretty damn lucky we found each other, all those years ago. Love you with all that I am, babe.

BRINA STARLER writes and reads romance novels and romantic fiction; really, anything with kissing will do. She loves to bake, garden, and tweet for posterity about the bizarre things her kids say, and is working her way through a truly frightening backlog of fan fiction. Brina lives in North Carolina with her husband, two boys, and a pup who bears a strong resemblance to Falkor the Luck Dragon. She has finally resigned herself to a future of asking tall people to get stuff off the top shelf.

Reading Group Guide

1. What made your book club choose *Anne of Manhattan* to read? If it was because of its connection to *Anne of Green Gables*, had everyone in the club read the original book?

2. What were some of the differences between *Anne of Manhattan* and *Anne of Green Gables* that you liked? What were some you disliked? Why?

3. Couples often have problems from miscommunication and personal issues. Did you feel the main conflict between Anne and Gil was realistic? Why did you feel this way?

4. With the #MeToo era upon us, do you feel Anne's situation with Dr. Lintford was a common one? Do you think she handled his behavior appropriately?

5. There were some jumps back and forth between Anne and Gil's past and the present. Did the flashbacks add context

and depth of emotion to the story for you? What was your favorite scene from Anne's or Gil's younger years?

6. If you've read *Anne of Green Gables*, how did you feel the author did keeping to the feel of the original book while updating it for current times? Did changing some of the characters' ethnicities and sexualities add an element of realism to the modernized version or did you feel they were unnecessary alterations to the characters? What changes did you like or dislike?

7. Do you think the author did a good job of capturing the voices of Anne, Gil, and the other Green Gables characters? Did they feel like the characters in the original book? If so, what are some of the similarities you discovered?

8. What were you expecting or hoping for before reading *Anne of Manhattan*? Were your expectations fulfilled? If so, in what way?

9. What were the major themes in the book? Have any of them ever applied to your own life? Did the author develop these themes to your satisfaction? Do you feel each situation in the book connected to these themes were brought to a fulfilling conclusion by the end of the story?

10. One of the major locations in the original Anne of Green Gables series was Green Gables itself. Did you feel the au-

thor did a good job of including that setting in *Anne of Manhattan*, considering so much of it was set in New York City? Which of the Green Gables scenes did you like best, and why? How did you feel about Green Gables being moved from Prince Edward Island to Long Island?

11. Overall, did you enjoy reading *Anne of Manhattan*? Was there anything else good or bad about the book that you'd like to discuss? Would you recommend it to a friend? Did reading this novel make you more likely to try the author's other books?